monsoon

NAZI GORENG

Marco Ferrarese [is a writer] and freelance [journalist who has toured] internationally in Europe and the United States, hitchhiked from Singapore to Milano, taught English in China, hung out with Kurt Cobain's alleged murderer, sold pizza in Chicago's Puerto Rican neighborhood and lived in a van for three months as he drove across Australia. He might or might not have a direct lineage with the homonymous Venetian explorer Marco Polo, but what's certain is that he currently calls Asia home, and he's resolute in bringing danger back into literature. Follow him at *www.monkeyrockworld.com*.

Praise for *Nazi Goreng*

'amazingly written' CLIVE, Malaysia

'The book has a tight structure, personable characters and a real ease of prose – yet, what is most apparent about Ferrarese's writing is his ability to draw the reader into the world inhabited by his characters.' LOUDER THAN WAR, United Kingdom

'*Nazi Goreng* is a grim but haunting debut novel by a maverick author who's very understandably described in the blurb as being set on "bringing danger back into literature" … a welcome addition to the literature on the region. Maybe it took a foreigner living in the country to shine a flashlight on the racial tensions, police corruption and adolescent fascist sympathies that characterize some areas of Malaysian life.' TAIPEI TIMES, Taiwan

'In exposing Malaysia's dark side through the light of literature, Ferrarese has bravely travelled to a place where few, if any, authors have gone before, in a promising and harrowing debut that marks him as a writer to keep both eyes on.' THE NATION, Thailand

'I will give *Nazi Goreng* two thumbs up for its fun entertainment, audacity to tackle taboo subjects, realism and relentless pace. Grab it while you can.' PENANG MONTHLY, Malaysia

NAZI GORENG

Young • Malay • Fanatic • Skinheads

MARCO FERRARESE

monsoon

monsoonbooks

Published in 2014
by Monsoon Books Pte Ltd
71 Ayer Rajah Crescent #01-01
Mediapolis Phase Ø, Singapore 139951
www.monsoonbooks.com.sg

Second edition. First published in 2013.

ISBN (paperback): 978-981-4423-35-9
ISBN (ebook): 978-981-4423-36-3

Copyright©Marco Ferrarese, 2013
The moral right of the author has been asserted.

All rights reserved. No part of this publication may be reproduced, stored in a retrieval system, or transmitted, in any form or by any means without the prior written permission of the publisher, nor be otherwise circulated in any form of binding or cover other than that in which it is published and without a similar condition being imposed on the subsequent purchaser.

Cover design by Cover Kitchen.

National Library Board, Singapore Cataloguing-in-Publication Data
Ferrarese, Marco.
Nazi goreng : young Malay fanatic skinheads / Marco Ferrarese. – First edition. – Singapore : Monsoon Books Pte Ltd, 2013.
pages cm
ISBN : 978-981-4423-35-9 (paperback)

1. Malays (Asian people) – Fiction. 2. Muslim youth – Malaysia – Fiction. 3. Ethnic conflict – Malaysia – Fiction. 4. Social problems – Malaysia – Fiction. 5. Malaysia – Fiction. I. Title.

PR9120.9
828.994503 -- dc23   OCN855123543

Printed in Singapore
16 15 14   2 3 4 5

If you're gonna ride, baby,
Ride the wild horse.
We can't drink no more,
But we'll try.
You can't find us, baby,
In the basement.
And we'll slug you in your fucking head.

Kyuss 'Gloria Lewis'

KEDAH DARUL AMAN

1

'When was the last time you actually kissed the floor like that?'

They were sitting behind a dumpster, guzzling beer from plastic bottles, their small sin wrapped and hidden in paper bags. They were looking at the mosque's terrace, only a few hundred metres away, where a man was kneeling on the ground, kissing the carpeted floor with the front of his rounded cap. He was facing Mecca. The man remained motionless.

'I've heard that in Melaka they don't pray like that.'

'Have you ever been there?'

'No.'

'So shut up, Asrul. How can you say that if you've never left this town?'

Alor Star was a backwater rivertown filled with mosques. It was one of those godforsaken equatorial places that made it into travelguides only because it was a state capital and because travel writers were forced to write something respectful about it.

Asrul, however, had no respect for it. None at all. And this despite the fact he had been born and raised in the town, had attended school in the shade of its black, bulgy domes.

'I said, when was the last time you prayed?'

Asrul realised he had not been listening.

'Well ... this morning, of course.'

'Really? Oh my gosh, Asrul, you are such a good boy.'

A long silence stood electric between them. They watched as the heat of another Malaysian afternoon unnaturally bent shapes at their edges, melting them into the palm tree-lined horizon. The man raised his head from the floor and contemplated the space in front of him for a few very long seconds. Then he returned himself to an upright position, lifted himself to his feet and moved swiftly across the carpeted terrace until he had reached the edge. Asrul observed as the man reached for his sandals and put them back on, without bending over again, and finally moved out of sight.

Alor Star was filled to the brim with people like this man. True believers. Asrul's family was like that – they'd rather be found dead than not attending the prayer hours at the mosque. Consequently, he, Asrul, had also developed a great amount of respect for his God. His faith was not something he could shake off to please his unholy friends, Asrul decided. He felt in touch with the soft carpeted floors of the mosque. He felt at ease inside a mosque's domed womb. He felt contented even in the tiny prayer rooms tucked away quietly in busy bus stations, shopping malls or highway rest stops. Whenever the time was right, when the muezzin issued his high-pitched call for prayer, Asrul needed to put his head down. And when he put his head to the ground, the hatred he reserved for his boring small town's world poured out of him, down into the carpet's knots. It was as if his head were the mouth of a strange kind of uncorked bottle, releasing the contents of his polluted soul.

'You see, Asrul, I do not understand you. It seems like you want to have your feet in two different kinds of shoes. What if one day, as you are bent down like that, someone was to come and kick you in the ass?'

'What!'

Asrul tried to reach for Malik's throat, but his friend was much faster and stronger, and looped his hand quickly around Asrul, taking him by the neck. Asrul spilled his beer on the ground, wishing instead he could soak the mosque's floor with his own mental hatred and allow the pain to flow from him.

'Do not move. Listen to me, you idiot. Just do as I say.' Malik tightened his hold, choking Asrul. Asrul tried to get out, but he couldn't. 'Be a good boy and listen,' repeated Malik. 'You see those people there, right? In and out of the bloody mosque every single day, too many times a day. They do nothing real for the cause. Do you really want to be like that for the rest of your life?'

He loosened his grip, slapping Asrul on the back of his head. Asrul fell to his knees. His beer had already emptied itself completely into the ground.

'Well, let me continue the sermon: you don't. You stupid little stubborn fuck, you would be totally lost without me. You know that, right?'

Asrul was on the grass, sitting on his haunches. The silent seconds that followed fell as heavy as bricks on Asrul's head.

'Great, don't even bother answering me. I have a plan, dear confused believer, which can help you find what you really believe in. And it starts by getting out of here!'

'Why?' Asrul asked, though he knew the answer to his own question.

'Man, there is nothing great to be had here besides nasi kandar. And some praying as a side dish. This town is dead. You get me, right? *Dead.*'

Asrul didn't reply.

'I have big plans, my dear Adik …'

Asrul watched Malik as he brushed dust off his pants and shirt.

'… we have big things to do, Asrul! We are getting out of here, man!'

Malik stood against the sun like a shaven king, the light striking his back and falling away, outlining his form in a halo of gold.

'And where are we going?'

Malik opened his arms as to embrace the sky.

'We are going to Kuala Lumpur, Adik!'

Asrul received these words still squatting down in the low grass, grabbing the tips of his shiny army boots, looking up at Malik like a chimp with no hair. Asrul looked over to the mosque again and saw that another man was kneeling there, pouring out his soul's juice into the carpets.

'Why aren't we going to Penang?'

'Why should we go there?'

'Because they have the sea, and it's cheaper to live there. The bus ticket's cheaper too, and it's closer to home. What if we have some problems?'

Malik stared at him for a long time, his face blank, without emotion. Asrul knew his friend was thinking.

'Well, man, OK,' Malik said finally. 'It doesn't really matter to me. You may be right – Penang first, then we'll rip KL a new asshole later. We will be richer and tougher by the time we get to KL!'

'Rich?'

Malik offered his hand to him and waited until Asrul, reluctantly, took it. He pulled him up and the two friends stood next to each other again.

'If you beat me again, I will kill you. I promise.'

'You silly praying boy … Let's see if you can even hit someone, let alone kill. So far, you've been nothing but a disappointment.'

Asrul turned away. He saw the man at the mosque raise his head from the floor and contemplate the space in front of him for a few very long seconds. Then he returned himself to an upright position, lifted himself up and moved swiftly across the carpeted terrace until he had reached the edge.

Again. And again. And forever again, as it must be.

Malik was right. And, deep inside, Asrul had always known too, that there was no way out of this relentless cycle.

2

PUNK ROCK had been the cure to all his sins. A crude and loud cure. Since his childhood, Asrul had been good at hitching lifts at the back of swanky four-stroke motorbikes down to the garages where bands played. It was quite easy for Asrul to dodge the police as he was Malay, and they didn't bother to disturb their own kind too much. But had he been Chinese, or Indian, riding away on one of those bikes would not have been so easy. The cops could be very harsh with bikers, as they knew that the most common place to hide drugs was under the saddle.

Watching fellow Malays bang their heads and shake their hair in long black whirlpools was the most inspiring, refreshing and exciting thing he could do in Alor Star. Punk and heavy metal had been thriving in Malaysia then – dozens of bands would come together and put on underground shows in rehearsal rooms or garages, fuelling sonic revolutions. Inside closed walls, hundreds of kids lived in their own version of a foreign paradise made of loud guitars, screaming their guts out with a 'say-what-you-want' attitude. They were not really free, but Asrul and the others felt like they were. Asrul would find himself headbanging the music away only to realise that three bands had come and gone off stage, even before he had stopped to take a breath. That was the most liberating sensation he had ever felt.

Sometimes he would get in a car with the older kids and drive down to Sungai Petani to catch more shows. That was how he'd learned to drink; being out of town meant being far away from any possible parental control. The shows were all about screaming loudspeakers, explicit lyrics and a blur of drunken fun.

And then, Kuasa Melayu had come down on him, had clasped him in its claws like a raptor attacking from the sky. Malay Power, the supremacy of the brown race. It had just come along so strongly, had become necessary for his survival, for his climbing up the ladder of the societal jungle. After that night, it had felt right to hate everyone else who polluted his nation with their fairer or darker skin. Asrul had realised that he belonged to the only group with any real right to be there, to own Malaysia. They were Bumiputera and proud of it. Who needed Indians and Chinese, anyway?

He would always remember the smell of that night in vivid detail; it brought with it a pungent stench of encrusted sewage channels where rats swam in dark waters like big, furry ships. He'd blamed the music and the booze for making him feel as vulnerable as a mangy dog, but he knew he should blame himself for being such a pussy.

He had just stepped out of the garage, his head still buzzing from the reverberation of chaotic sounds vomited from flimsy loudspeakers, and had approached the street corner from where the riverside path that he always used as a shortcut on his way home branched off. On that night, he'd known that something was out of place. It was as if even the palm trees had cast a different play of shadows under the lamp posts' electric glow. Something had surely felt out of place, but he'd kept marching on, treading his fat basketball sneakers along the dusty gravel road. He had been so convinced that this was the perfect setting for the appearance of an Orang Bunyan that he completely ground to a halt when he saw the first man step out of the woodwork, stopping just ahead of him, blocking his path. According to the legend, the Orang Bunyan had a fairy-like appearance, looked courteous and smelled like trees. This figure, however, was tall and terrifying, had a huge beer gut and smelled like cheap Orangutan whisky. He was as terrifying as an Indian night spent sharpening razorblades in a dark alley. A few seconds later, four other giants came out of the forest, swaying slowly, their grinning smiles flashing like the beams of a lighthouse in the otherwise pitch-black darkness.

'Hey, hey, hey! Look at what we got here ...' The thunderous voice of the first big, black man broke the night's soundscape.

He looked mean, and he smelled of strong cologne mixed with stomach-wrenching fumes of alcohol. The other four figures stood back, occupying the space behind the big man, like a group of spiders spinning a cobweb for their prey.

Asrul watched as the man drew a big knife from his back pocket. The blade shone in the darkness as if it had its own gut-ripping life.

'You wanna give me all your money or slash-slash, you get me ...' He twisted his wrist, cutting circles of darkness with flashes of his long blade.

Asrul was terrified. The booze had loosened his senses, and his legs started shivering, uncontrollably. He started jerking around a bit, looking for a way out of the situation. Onwards, the path would lead towards certain mugging, or worse, a slashing. Backwards, there were only the empty city streets, where nobody would come out to help at night.

'I have no money,' he finally said.

'Sure, everybody says that ... Now, pay up or cry.'

'Please, I really have nothing. I'm a student,' Asrul cried out, sandwiched between five angry thugs on one side and the dark street corner on the other.

'You don't understand, kid. You see this? It's a knife. It cuts. It makes you bleed. You don't want to cry from another mouth-hole we cut into your face, do you? I'm sure you understand ... Throw what money you have onto the ground.'

Asrul didn't have much choice. His heart was racing with fear. He reached for his pockets, turned them inside out, making a few coins and a couple of one-ringgit notes fall down in the dust. One of the Indians inspected the floor by waving about his flashlight in quick light circles. The pack suddenly became stiffer. The big man in front caressed the knife with his fingers, and then ran it along the front of his pants, slowly and carefully, cleaning both sides of the blade.

'Are you sure that's all you got?'

'Yes, yes, I swear ...' Asrul didn't realise that he was crying. After all, he was only a teenager, he told himself, a poor thing caught in the mouth of a strange madness that might have ended on the wrong side of the blade.

'Well boy, I think we'll have to make sure that you aren't fucking with us. This is not much, for sure.'

The man stepped back, rhythmically followed by the unholy four, still stapled behind him in the same triangular array, like a deck of bowling pins at Deep Black Hell's bowling alley. The last thing Asrul felt was a hard slap, the back of one strong hand hitting his jaw and making his neck twist, his teeth opening to let out his horrified pain.

The rest was just glorious mangling, and he couldn't recall most of it. But before he'd finally slept it off, it had felt like a bunch of horses had decided to play basketball on his ass.

3

HE WAS SCARED. After two days at the hospital, he was damn scared. To even put one foot in front of the other and walk. Everything on the street looked dangerous, sounded like it was roaring at him, seemed to want to eat him alive, as if it were all psychotic lions made out of Chinese paper. Every other face looked threatening, even the Chinese man who sewed clothes discreetly at the back of that one-room cellar-like shop. He might have been sent in to spy on Asrul's moves, to kill him whenever he found the chance. And what about the pretty girl who lived next door: do not be fooled by her wide smile and peachy, soft cheeks. She is dangerous. She is half Chinese. An inbred horror, a freaking ghoul with a half-Chinese face. Under that attractive mug, she hides sharp fangs. She will rip your heart out, and eat your guts directly from the hole she's gnawed.

And, of course, the Indians. They were everywhere, and they were mean. He was still so scared that he could feel his knees jerk when he saw one of them walk past him on the street. His body still ached from the thrashing they had given him, still had the blue imprints of their clawed hooves all over his chest and legs.

They had almost killed him for seven ringgit. For just two bloody American dollars and twenty cents. One doesn't kill a boy for such a lousy amount of cash. No, one does not. Indians are just scary fucking trash, Asrul decided, and they deserved to die. He wanted to kill them all if he could, with the same knife they had pointed at his face, and skewer them side by side, make coconut jam out of their saggy bones. Asrul swore to God that he would become strong, would then kill all of those motherfuckers.

His thoughts were hissing, steaming hot, pumping into his head and inflating it like an air balloon. Asrul had never been so scared of walking, talking, of just living a normal life. After the accident, he kept glancing at the long, dark line running across his left forearm, a souvenir from that night, something he would have to carry for a lifetime. A souvenir he did not want, nor need. He spent his days sitting at the same mamak stall, slurping one teh tarik after the other, drowning himself in a chain of sweetness to nurse his wounded soul. He realised that he needed something new to believe in. Music was not enough anymore, to help numb what he felt, a feeling as if his skull was bouncing against the dirt road.

He was distracted from his thoughts, one day, when a shape entered suddenly into the upper corner of his vision. The man stood by Asrul's table, like a neatly dressed waiter hanging about for a customer's order. He was Malay, with a perfectly shaven head, and was wearing big sunglasses. He had on a striking t-shirt with some army boots printed on it and a pair of long, perfectly fitting green army pants. Asrul observed that he wore the same kind of boots pictured on his shirt.

'It's Skrewdriver, Boots and Braces – a White-power band from England. Quite cool,' he said. Asrul gave him an uninterested look and waited for his next move.

'May I sit down here?'

'There are plenty of empty tables in this place. Why do you want to sit here with me?'

The young man pulled a chair back anyway and sat himself in front of Asrul. He pulled down his sunglasses to his nose, revealing deep, strong, black eyes set in a face of fiery features. Asrul couldn't help but think the man was cool and powerful.

'My name is Malik, and I know about your accident. I want to ask you a couple of things.'

He extended an open palm across the table, stopping just over Asrul's unfinished tea, then retracted his arm and touched the left side of his chest, just above the heart.

'Assalam Aleikum.'

Asrul noticed a muscular line crawling from the guy's open hand and running back over his broad shoulders, adding to his magnetic and forceful appearance.

Asrul touched his own chest to return the salute; he did it without the same conviction, but he felt obliged to repay the courtesy. Besides, he already felt connected to this strange man and his great halo of strength.

'I'm sorry for what happened to you, Asrul. And don't ask me how I know your name – we all know it, because to us, you are a hero. You survived them. And this shit has to stop.'

Asrul felt a stirring inside. The wild feelings trapped inside the small sea of his chest were gasping for air, desperate to be let out.

'Would you be able to recognise them?' Malik went on, scanning Asrul's movements with his deep, penetrative gaze.

'I don't know. It was very dark.'

'That's a pity. Because if you could, I thought we might pay those guys a visit ...'

Asrul felt his bowels roll inside him, as if some strange entity was mixing them up with a long wooden stick. This guy had a knack of saying things in the most inciting way.

'What for? Who are you, Mister Malik? Are you a cop?'

Malik relaxed against the metal chair and put an open palm to rest on the table.

'No, of course I'm not.' He gazed down and then quickly upwards, piercing Asrul's face with a serious stare. 'You may call me an avenger. Or an aid worker. A social harvester. I am just like you, and I hate the scum who kicked your ass as much as you do.'

He finished the sentence by shoving the sunglasses back on his face, closing off the black magnetic powers of his eyes to the outside world.

'Our usual meeting spot is just down the road from the practice space. You like music, don't you? I've seen you down there a few times, headbanging like crazy. You have some good energy, man. Put it to good use. Just come down and see me whenever you feel ready.'

Malik got up and tossed a crumpled piece of paper across the table. 'My address and number are on there. Call me anytime.'

The paper floated across the table's smooth surface and landed exactly in front of Asrul. Asrul took a quick look at it, and when he looked up again, Malik was gone, as quickly as he had come. Asrul found himself alone, lost in the noise of clanking glasses and frying pans and sizzling brown rice and Maggi noodles. He looked at the paper again and memorised the address before sliding it into his pocket.

* * *

'Look at them.'

The steamy silence of the night was interrupted only by the intrusive sound of excited crickets.

'Can you believe this? They're eating each other out. Here, in the park.'

Malik furrowed his eyebrows into a black, pronounced line, trying to get a better vision in the dark. He moved a branch aside and stepped deeper into the bush, like a tiger looking for prey.

'They cannot come here, to our territory, and do this. Look at that! Go to the frigging motel for that!'

Asrul stood behind Malik, caught between two other boys, smelling the acrid stench of their sweat-soaked t-shirts and with the stifling, hot smells of the hot night.

'Are you sure this is a good idea, Malik?' he blurted out, moving closer to his friend.

Malik flashed him a severe look. There was no time left for talking. Asrul found himself thrown out into the shadows of the park, his friend's hand pushing him on the nape of the neck. The two other skinheads followed, moving their feet in unison as if they were a death squad prepared to strike.

Asrul couldn't remember how long he'd been a part of their group, but he could remember vividly the day he joined them. He had followed Malik's directions to his place and had found himself outside one of those traditional little Malay houses made out of wooden planks stapled together with beautiful but decaying woodwork. Malik had been sitting bare-chested on the porch, puffing on a cigarette and blowing smoke slowly into the air. Some other boys sat around him, occupying the ample space of a wooden veranda, which creaked with the enthusiasm of supporting the prime exponents of God's chosen race. Asrul could smell the familiar rustic aromas of steaming Malay curries coming from inside the house, seeping through the walls.

A woman whom Asrul assumed to be Malik's mother – a big, silent woman, her head wrapped in a tudong – could be seen through the open door, manoeuvring long spoons inside pots as if she were steering the wheel of the house. Asrul had felt immediately connected to the place.

On that day, Malik hadn't talked too much. Sitting on the porch, he'd looked like a different person, rocking back and forth on that old squeaky chair. But despite his silence, Asrul had immediately understood that Malik was the alpha male, the leader of this pack of tame young wolves.

'This is the way to be. This is our land, we are entitled to it, and we have been put here by God himself. The others are all threatening scum. You have to understand – this is our land. And you can help protect it. If God wanted you to be beaten, it was to show you the path. Remember, Asrul, all paths leading to greatness must go through murder, violence and power.'

He had been beaten up and put in the hospital by the same kind of scum Malik seemed not to tolerate; Asrul would therefore have to join Malik. Malik's words kept toying with his mind thereafter. Those words were the only verbal tattoos Asrul had needed, enough to get him started.

Asrul realised soon enough that Malik had an incredible gift. He could make someone believe he really was important. He could attract passive people, induce them to do exactly what he wanted, yet make it seem as if it was out of their own will. The man had great power and also the ability to transform it into a catalyst to fuel other people's actions. Asrul felt a strange buzz shaking him from the very tip of his toes to the top of his head each time Malik's magnetic eyes looked into his own. Were it not so unmanly to admit it, Asrul might agree that he almost liked that kind of attention.

They approached the bench slowly, from behind, curved into the shape of silent prowlers. When they were close enough to smell the girl's warm perfume, they hid in the shadows for a few moments, but which felt so long to Asrul.

They continued to watch the couple sitting before them, Chinese teenagers clutched in each other's arms, sucking the tongues out of each other's mouths. This might have been ordinary stuff in some faraway Western country, but not here in Malaysia. In this country, religion dictated that such things be performed behind closed doors. The two were really getting busy, Asrul saw. The guy was trying to reach for the girl's breasts by extending his right hand under her shirt. When Malik rose from behind the bench and slapped the boy on the head, the girl jumped off the bench and cried out loud as if she'd just seen a Nazi ghost.

'What the f–' Almond Eyes grabbed the top of his own head and massaged it. His anger suddenly vanished for he must have realised that four horsemen of the ethnic apocalypse were standing around him. Suddenly, his face crumpled like a piece of dirty napkin.

'Mister, watch your language in front of a lady,' Malik said, carefully spacing out every word as if he was spitting silver bullets. 'What do you think you are doing here?'

'None of your business,' the Chinese guy tried to sound brave as he put himself between Malik and the girl in a clumsy attempt to retaliate.

Was he really doing this, Asrul wondered, attacking a couple of Chinese lovers, in the park, at night? Was this really Malik, the man who had just pounced on the thin Chinese guy, had dragged him down to the ground and was now punching him in the face?

It all felt so damn weird; everything seemed to move so slowly. He could feel his toes getting numb inside the army boots' hard shell. He wished he had worn sandals; these boots were not meant to be worn in Malaysia's heat. He wished Malik had worn sandals too, when he saw his boots kicking into the Chinese guy's sides, making him jerk like a wind-up toy. It felt painful to watch this.

The Chinese girl was standing there speechless, shaking in the dark. Asrul could see that she was trying to become smaller, to be absorbed by the surrounding darkness. But when the other two boys circled around the bench and grabbed her from behind, she started screaming, so loudly that a window lit up in a not-so-distant house.

'Go! Go! Somebody's coming, they'll see us!'

Malik quickly released the Chinese guy, who fell back into the grass, motionless, breathing heavily. Soon Asrul and the others were all running along the dirt road. Until they disappeared behind the corner wall, he could hear the girl's screams, the voice painting the night in dark blue, scary colours. Malik's nape looked even darker and firmer as he ran ahead of the pack, his sweat shining in the low moonlight. Asrul knew they had done something wrong, horribly wrong. But deep inside, in the tight place between his ribcage and thumping heart, adrenaline had planted the seeds of pride and revenge. And Asrul felt an odd sense of victory.

PULAU PINANG

4

MALIK LOOKED very disturbed.

'Are you joking or what, Asrul? What is *this*?'

'Well, *this* is an apartment.'

They were standing outside the door of a corner unit on the eighteenth floor of a high-density building that contained at least a thousand other apartments. More than half of the building's population belonged to the usual places where immigrant workers came from to invade Malaysia. Men in Burmese longjis strolled down the corridor, scraping their flip-flops against the floor with every step. The open door of another unit revealed a group of women squatting on the floor, busy scooping food out of a gigantic rice cooker; a few of them were combing their hair under the helpful breeze of a wall fan that spun at the back of the apartment, muttering amongst themselves in what sounded like Indonesian. Asrul observed that Malik was shivering a little.

'Abang, what's wrong? This is our new place ... I found it for quite cheap. I've arranged everything already!'

'Asrul, I can see you don't get my point at all. You don't want to understand what I mean.'

'Well ...'

'This is like sleeping with the enemy, Asrul. This is like being surrounded by AK-47s in a fucking war, you idiot.'

'Why do you always want to call me names, Malik? I don't like it.'

'Well, fair enough. But I'm not going to stay here.'

Asrul felt hot and tired. He had been moving boxes up and down the elevator, between the huge parking lot and the new apartment, for the past day and a half. Malik had not helped; he'd been somewhere else. Malik had claimed he was busy 'running some business' on the other part of the island. He just didn't care, Asrul knew.

Asrul unlocked the outer security gate of the apartment, hung the open padlock on one of its steel bars and pushed open the door behind it. Before him was a nice, albeit smallish, livingroom, waiting to be filled with their Kuasa Melayu energy. As Malik stepped closer to peek inside, Asrul pushed him in. He then stepped in and closed the door behind him.

'What the hell!'

'Malik,' Asrul began. It was the first time Asrul had dared to confront his friend. 'Seriously, what do you think we can get for 300 ringgit a month, Abang? You want a swimming pool and twenty-four-hour security? Shit, I've been running around like a dog for the past two weeks looking at all sorts of apartments, and this is the best thing I found for what you want to pay. Where have you been all this while, eh? Why didn't you come and tell me you didn't like this place sooner? You want it cheap? Well, you get the immigrants thrown in — they like it cheap too!'

Asrul stopped talking and observed his friend, waiting for the expected outburst of verbal rage. However, Malik's lips stayed tightly pressed together, almost making a dent in his face. Malik neither moved nor spoke for a long moment. It seemed like the reaction of his smaller, chickenshit Nazi friend had shocked him. This was the first time Asrul had dared to talk to him like that, and deep inside his chest, Asrul felt kind of proud for doing that. Nevertheless, Malik was still the one in charge. The boss.

'Don't talk to me like that, Asrul. I already told you, that I had some business stuff to take care of …'

'What kind of business?'

'Business. Good stuff. I'm contacting some people for a job, for the both of us. I'll tell you all about it soon …'

'Malik, listen to me. I'm tired. And you're acting like a douchebag. Just chill. Relax, bro, we are finally in Penang!' Asrul moved backwards and opened his arms wide, a skinhead Christ on an invisible cross. 'Look at the view out the window; we have the sea just out there!' He realised that his braces had pulled his jeans up a bit too much and was making him look quite bodoh; he set down his hand on his belt as nonchalantly as he could and pulled it down.

Asrul observed Malik as he moved around, pacing the tiny room with sad relief – his friend checked out the bathroom and the two rooms. At last, he got closer to the windows, opened one and took a look outside. Asrul knew that at this point his friend would change his mind. The apartment may not have been the best one around, but the view it gave them was fantastic. From that height, the whole city opened to the left; one could count up to the last twenty storeys of KOMTAR, its facade rising up like the island's stiff erection. On the right side, the edge of a concrete development slowly left space to a beading of low-rising fishermens' houses on stilts – wooden boats rocked over the gentle waves, and motorbikes zipped around tiny alleys like electric guinea pigs let loose in a miniature maze. Anyone, even the fiercest Nazi skinhead, would have enjoyed this view. From up there, the way the sea rapidly engulfed the contours of the island before retracing away would give anyone the satisfaction of a king, of dominating the cityscape as it were his own ancient realm.

'How long have you signed for?'

'Six months.'

'Hell, we'll have to deal with the Bangladeshis out there for that long? Aiyoh!' Asrul almost burst out laughing as he saw Malik press his big hands against his shaven head and lean backwards mocking a dramatic faint and fall.

'C'mon, we're broke now. It'll be better later, I hope. We always knew it wouldn't be too easy, right? Or what did you expect? I couldn't ask for money from my parents, you know. That would suck, lah ...'

In this precise moment, Asrul understood Malik's scornful behaviour. It must indeed be quite difficult for Malik, a man with a clear ethnic plan, to tolerate this. Asrul suddenly started thinking of the great men Malik admired, such as Napoleon and Adolf Hitler. Surely they also had to cope with such situations in order to grow into the badass motherfuckers history remembers them as. It could not have been otherwise, Asrul was very damn sure of this. He knew he had to do something to ease the stress off his leader's shoulders.

'Well, bro, just relax. I'm going to buy some nasi kandar at the restaurant downstairs now, and then we'll settle this, alright?'

Malik nodded without looking at him. Asrul left his friend standing in front of the window, his sharp gaze fixed on the waves twenty metres below, floating all the way to Butterworth and back. Giving Malik a last glance before he closed the door behind him, Asrul was convinced his friend was trying to capsize those old rattlers of ferries with his enigmatic mind powers.

* * *

Asrul rushed down the corridor that connected his floor to the lift landing. When one lived on the eighteenth floor of a crowded apartment block, one had to be quick in order to get the lift on time and get down to the ground floor. He went past several open doors, other worlds withheld by the prison-like bars of dark security gates. There was not much Malayness behind those bars – his gaze grazed the sleepy eyes of a Bangladeshi man, slouched on a dirty mattress supported by a flimsy metallic bed-board. Three others occupied the tiny living space, Asrul saw, eating rice and fish with their hands from coloured plastic dishes. They chased him away with their hostile eyes, flashing him an expression that could only mean they wanted him to mind his own business. He walked past another open door and saw a man in a longji lying inside, lost in the horizontal magnetism of a small TV set. The remote control was almost dropping from his skeletal, dark hand.

Asrul didn't want to trouble himself by thinking about whether or not he'd made a bad choice. The apartment was good enough and it was close to the heart of Georgetown. He'd just about convinced himself that the place was perfect when he rushed round the corner and landed in front of the elevator, almost running her down in his stupidity stampede. He ground to a halt, barely inches from her face, and found himself going limp as her hot breath hit him, right between his nose and upper lip, in a wet invisible kiss.

'I'm sorry!' Asrul stepped back, growing rigid and assuming a soldier-like position.

From back there, he could see her in her completeness: she was petite, had a smooth porcelain face set against the dark and rigorous outlines of a blue tudong and a pair of maroon lips stretched back in a courteous smile. The veil died abruptly over a dark t-shirt. She had on a pair of jeans, which completed her sporty but careful outfit. Her feet were wrapped inside a pair of low-heeled wooden sandals, her toenails painted black. She was the closest Asrul would ever find to a Venusian goddess this side of the Pacific Rim.

The sword of Cupid had already flown across the poorly lit lift landing and impaled Asrul, ripping him open. Asrul could almost feel his guts splatter against the dirt-encrusted wall behind his back.

'Not at all. It's nothing,' she chirped.

Before Asrul could speak, a distinct bell sounded and was followed by the opening of the elevator's sliding doors. Asrul saw that the elevator's tiny confined space had been reserved for the two of them, for them alone. His brain was already projecting weird fantasies onto his heart, before the latter could even summon the courage to make the first move. Asrul realised he was hooked, completely. And she was still smiling at him, the spicy goddess from another world.

'Don't want to get in?' She walked inside, her wooden heels clattering against the metal of the elevator. Asrul didn't wait to be asked again and got inside quickly, his blood steaming in his ears as the doors closed behind their backs, holding them within the walls of its metallic mouth.

Small beads of sweat collected on his back and neck, and then rolled off, like he had a pair of wipers sitting just below his shaven Nazi hairline. She was in front of him, her fingers fiddling with the lower side of her tudong, boring her mesmerising eyes into him, using them to lure him into conversation. However, he was feeling insecure and stupid – all of a sudden he regretted all the hours he had spent headbanging at the studio room, for music had distracted him, had given him no time to learn how to approach a woman, to charm her with conversation. The quick descent of the elevator was like the falling of sand in an hourglass; he had left himself with a mere thirty-seven seconds before they would reach the ground floor. That is, if she would get down there. She was now looking up at the lights fixed to the top of the metal cage they stood in. He knew he had to either risk it or be remembered as a douchebag for the rest of his life. The line on his forgotten gravestone would boldly recollect this moment: 'Here lies a Douche'.

'Hey ... so, are you going shopping?'

She removed all of her attention from the lights above her and cast a wilful gaze into his face. The walls behind her seemed to stretch far into the distance, as if his eye sockets had been fixed with a pair of fish-eye lenses and she was focussed at the centre of it.

'Yes, I have to run some errands. I'm going to Gama, in Georgetown.'

All these details left him stunned. She butterflied her long eyelashes, made longer by a light coat of mascara. He felt as if the distance between them was getting shorter, as short as the inexorable descent to the ground floor.

'I'm not familiar with that place, sorry. I'm new here, just arrived.'

'I know! You and that other big guy. The scary couple,' she giggled, getting closer.

Asrul felt the soft touch of her breast against his side as she bounced excitedly on her feet. Each pause in her speech was punctuated by a bounce.

'You guys just came in today, right?'

'Yes,' he almost blushed.

'Well, my name is Siti Ara Manustia. I'm from Sumatra, Indonesia ...' She stopped talking and froze her face into a nice, heart-melting smile that spread across the whole width of Asrul's fisheye sockets.

'Just call me Siti; it's easier. It is nice to live here, you'll see. It's a very central place, close to Georgetown, good for getting to anywhere you need to.' She seemed to have a point, Asrul thought.

'Ah, OK ...' was the only thing he managed to say.

'Are you OK?' she moved closer and then bumped into his side again, this time letting him have a feel of her hip. He shuddered. He almost lost control. He felt like he was about to piss in his pants, let it fall directly from his bladder and down his right leg, slip into his army boots, make a hot pool of insecurity below his heel and soil himself in his own dumbness.

'Yes, yes. I've just arrived, and I don't really know about the places you're talking about. But they're probably fun ...'

'Well, not fun exactly. It's just a supermarket,' she smiled. 'One day, soon, I'll take you there. To show you, OK? But not today. I really have to run. What's your number?'

'Great, thanks. You're very friendly. My number's 0178575954.' He watched her press down on the keys of her phone as he spoke the numbers.

'OK, here goes. Giving you a miscall ...'

Asrul's cell phone buzzed a couple of times, vibrating silently inside his pocket. Then, the elevator reached the ground floor with a soft thump and the doors slid open again. He saw that dozens of faces painted in so many different skin tones were waiting impatiently to claim their hard-earned place inside the elevator, which had been, until only a moment ago, Asrul's own small private paradise.

'Perfect, see you around, Asrul,' With the same, sweet smile plastered across her face, she disappeared, squeezing her way out between an Indian woman carrying a big shopping bag across her back and a Chinese boy lost inside the world that lay buzzing beneath his iPhone's display. Asrul stood there for a while, the other dwellers pushing and pulling him out of that ethereal space as they moved into the elevator, filling it up with their sordid reality.

When the door closed and he was left standing outside, alone, he finally realised that Siti was gone. And that he had forgotten his wallet on the table, in his apartment, eighteen floors above where he now stood. While he queued up again to reserve his own hard-earned place in the elevator, he saved her missed call under a carefully typed and hi-capped SITI. And with that, he had already made his day.

5

A GROUP OF FOUR BOYS was standing in front of the park bench. Malik sat at its centre. He was screening the boys, one by one, to confirm his decision. Asrul was walking up and down the park's entrance, surveying the scene, to check if anyone was coming through.

'You all know this is bloody serious. We have come from the north for this – it is a sign, understand?'

The boys nodded, silently. They were all Malay. Perhaps a bit confused, but they were indeed Malay, of the solid type, Asrul observed.

'This island is special, guys. Unfortunately, it's also a magnet for working-class scum of all kinds: Bangladeshi, Burmese, Indonesian, Vietnamese ... You know what I mean, right?'

Besides firmly nodding, the boys did not do much else.

'... and the Chinese, my gosh. They took over this island so long ago they're the most solid bunch to overcome. They have their hands everywhere, you see, confining us poor Malays to live outside of Georgetown in the countryside. Do you like living like this, kampong style?'

This time, Asrul saw, the heads shook horizontally.

'Great. I knew you would understand. You may be some of the chosen few, my friends. You have been appointed directly from the hand of God to help me go through with my mission, to help free our land from the massive import of scum that Immigration freely allows to get by.'

'Yes,' cried one, grinning slightly.

A bunch of girls appeared at a close distance, carrying shopping bags filled with vegetables and chatting amiably, their hair diligently tied to the back of their heads, their feet poking out of worn-out flip flops. As they got closer, their chatter became distinctly louder and foreign; the fact was rendered more evident by the thick thanaka stains applied to their cheeks, making them look like they had smeared their faces with liquid gold. Their bodies were slim and firm, their hips shaking under the effort of balancing their shopping bags, their short pants showing off bronzed thighs, the legs left exposed until under their buttocks, where the pants shut their skin away from public view.

Malik frowned, and cupped his big hands over his eyes. Asrul observed that his friend had left enough space between his fingers so as to peek at the girls, at their shaking hips.

'You see what I mean, my brothers? This is too much to handle for good Muslims like us. I cannot take it anymore; this foreign trash has no respect for our culture. They think they can just show their flesh off, like meat lumps at the butcher's stall. I cannot deal with this any longer.'

'Yes, but ...' a voice emerged from the bunch.

'But what, brother?'

'They are very sexy, good to watch, lah!' the guy smiled profusely, looking around for the compliance of the others.

Asrul had a sudden impulse to hit the guy right in his mouth, but before he could act on it, Malik stood up as fast as lightning, moved to the guy and punched him straight in his lower gut. The guy crumbled down on his knees, as if his legs were made of jelly, and he spat out breath and saliva, completely taken by surprise.

'OK then! You can fuck off back to mama or go to hell with one of those dirty hags. Go, and try to figure out what she's saying as you try to get into her panties. Shame on you! What would your father think of you, you idiot? You disgust me. You are a disgrace to your own race. Fuck off.'

Asrul saw that Malik was really mad. His eyes were wide open, his neck reddened in fury.

When the guy regained his balance and got back on his feet, he tried to apologise. Malik looked him right in the eye and ordered him to leave, pointing his thumb back over his shoulder.

'You are out of our league, you slob. There is no place for you here. Piss off and go with those prostitutes. That's a good place for a traitor and a cunt like you.'

Asrul watched the funny guy leave the pack and walk back down the road, his hand pressed against his stomach. Asrul certainly didn't want to trade places with that loser. Malik was right: those immigrant girls were sluts. They were not as gracious, morigerous and angelic as his Siti was. He turned back to Malik, and continued listening.

'Now we are five only, counting me and you. And I am really pissed, so tonight it's out to lunch. I need to show you what this is all about, that this is no fucking joke. I'm not clowning around.'

To Asrul, this was both good and bad news.

* * *

The moon was a glowing sickle, shedding its unhealthy light over the shaking trees. A few cars were zooming along the empty roads, heading to warm homes, beds, lovers' embraces, crying kids. They didn't know that a bunch of shaved werewolves was out on the prowl, hiding themselves in the night's dim light.

'Let's just hang around here and wait. They will be arriving soon.'

Malik had presented Asrul and the others with a simple, concise plan: a couple of days earlier Malik had gone down to the food court in Penang Road and had seen them working there. Two immigrant workers: Bangladeshis. They worked at the Chinese seafood stall, cooking fish. Asrul agreed with Malik: how could Malaysians want to pay to have their food contaminated by those dirty South Asian hands? Asrul couldn't understand this at all. Malik explained that he'd asked around about the two and had quickly found out where they lived; they were squatting with five other people in an apartment complex just behind Gurney Drive, on Jalan Kelawei. Asrul stood next to Malik as the whole pack waited for them, fangs ready under sealed lips. The food court had already closed by now. They knew the men would be coming their way sooner or later, walking together from the other side of the road.

'Sshhh! Here they come. Hide!'

The two men were carrying plastic bags, possibly filled with groceries, and were chatting the night away, smiling at each other, happy. They looked naive, with their perfectly shaven chins and their neatly cut hair. Asrul observed them spitefully from the darkness of his hideout. They looked like they really wanted to fit in and climb up Malaysian society's ladder, to be part of the same people who ate the food they made, to win their recognition. Asrul had a very different opinion of them: these Bangladeshis were only good for disembowelling fish all night long, seven days a week. The menial work of slaves – nothing more, nothing less.

'Oh, she was so pretty, Amid! She was tall, and with those long legs, oh my ...'

Asrul overheard one of the two saying this to the other. He felt a reflux of disgust rising up his oesophagus, transforming into an acid taste at the back of his mouth. These dirty-minded immigrants, always craving any millimetre of exposed skin they could find. Too dumb to realise that none of the women customers were interested in them, or in coming any closer to these men and the troughs filled with ice and shiny fish they had on offer.

'Really? I didn't have a chance to see her. Always working, working, working!'

'Trust me, you certainly cannot see this stuff in Dhaka, my friend. These women are so sexy, especially the Chinese ones. They don't even realise that by dressing up like that, in those short things, they are making all the men go crazy.'

'I am sure they know!'

Disgusting, dirty, sex-crazed parasites. Asrul saw them laughing together, their teeth reflected under the glow of a lamp post. They kept smiling and talking loudly to each other about curvaceous, soft-skinned Chinese women until they had turned into the shortcut and found themselves in the dim light of a backdoor alley. A high wall stood raised on one side, while a ditch filled with water lay on the other. The little bridge that connected the road with the back entrance of their condominium was about fifteen metres away.

The pack emerged swiftly from the darkness, detaching itself from the wall. Asrul and two other boys stood behind Malik, who guided them like the tip of a deadly spear directly towards the two Bangladeshis. At first, the men did not realise that the group had come for them; one of the Bangladeshis almost collided with Malik's chest. He moved to the side just before he hit Malik.

'I'm sorry,' he said, then continued on his way back home.

'Hey, where do you think you're going?'

These words were like the dropping of acid on the night's paper sky – you could clearly see it burn the surface, destroying it as it spread in fast circles. The colours of the night changed. The men's naïve smiles turned into sealed lips and muttered short, fearful words.

Asrul saw that there was no easy escape for the two men. On their left, a smelly mix of dark liquids gurgled at the bottom of a half-metre shallow sewage channel, while on their right, a wall closed them in. Asrul and two other shaven thugs clad in army boots approached from the front, and Malik and the last wolf barred their escape. The alley was now completely impassable for the Bangladeshis.

'Sorry, Mister, is there any problem?'

The one Asrul had heard being addressed as 'Amid' muttered this, his legs shaking. In that situation, Asrul felt like shaking was the best thing the man could do. Either that or trying to reach up for the sickle moon and decapitating himself. Offering his head to the fiery wolves as a ritual of self-sacrifice would have been appropriate to satiate them. Malik had told Asrul that these immigrants were quite used to all kinds of aggression. Some Indian drug smuggler would have already menaced them at knife point, demanding the money they had in their pockets. Something similar had happened in Kuala Lumpur a couple of months earlier; a Bangladeshi had almost gotten stabbed to death. Asrul had heard the story over drinks from a complacent Malik: the immigrant had gotten into a taxi, but the driver had swerved into a secluded alley, getting away from the main traffic lines, and had pulled out a crowbar from under his seat. All of a sudden, a bunch of Indian men had closed in around the vehicle, threatening the man into handing them all his money. The poor fucker had been planning to fly back home, to see his family after almost three years of working in Malaysia, and apparently had most of his savings stashed under his belt, inside his underwear. He made the mistake of resisting his attackers; their knife had been faster than him. Twenty-five stitches. A real bloody mess, but it had saved his ass and his money, as the Indian thugs hadn't expected the wound to end up so bad. The man's guts had sloshed out. The aggressors had run away, leaving the poor bastard in the dust, when a car had pulled into the alley. The driver had not wanted to put the Bangladeshi in his car as he had been bleeding badly and would have made a mess of the backseat; but the driver had managed to call an ambulance and saved the man's life. Malik had called this a 'pitiful mistake'.

Remembering this story only made Asrul angrier; it reminded him of his own past experience with Indian blades. He felt the shivers, the panic, once again. But he quickly shook them off, for this time he was among the winners. And he was ready to enjoy every minute of it. His catharsis was about to be unleashed upon these two immigrants. Tonight, he would not be the one to finish his story languishing on starched white hospital linens, watching life pass by through the transparent bag of an intravenous drip. Tonight, he had switched sides, he was on the safe end of the blade.

* * *

'Sir, what is the problem? We have no money with us now.'

'I don't want your dirty money, you piece of foreign trash. But we do have a problem. Yes, a big problem. You. What do you think you're doing here?'

'Nothing at all, sir, we just want to go home …'

'Do you think that we don't need jobs too, eh? Aren't there enough of you Bangladeshis here already, always buzzing around, everywhere?'

'Sir …'

'You are everywhere but in your own goddamn country! Piss off!'

Jerking forward, the thug pushed Amid straight in the chest. The small man, not expecting such force, fell back and rattled against the concrete. He didn't dare to move, but kept his eyes wide open, waiting for the next blow. His friend, Rajendra, tried to look around for a way to escape, but the skinheads were closing in from all sides. Soon Amid felt their hands all over him, pinning him down, hitting his back and head in spiteful strokes. Rajendra was lying on his back a few feet away, pushed down to the ground, receiving a similar beating.

The hits rained down on them from all sides. Amid and Rajendra tried to protect their heads inside the cocoon of their tiny arms, but it was like trying to protect an eggshell from the brunt of a thousand hammer falls. As his ribs took the beating, creaking and squeaking, Amid thought of his faraway land. The way it became suddenly dark there at six o'clock in the evening every day, the way the horizon ate up the sun in a mouthful, without spilling its blood all over the misty clouds and the tall coconut trees. Amid thought he was about to die. He curled up and assumed a foetal position. Suddenly the Nazi thugs stopped.

'What are you doing here, ah?'

Amid kept his eyes closed. He couldn't understand what was going on – first, the unexpected beating, and now, this pause. Suddenly, he felt the darkness dissipating in a flash as a light beam passed over his tightly stretched eyelids. He couldn't help but open his eyes a bit, to scan the scene before him.

Far up the alley, a dark figure was holding a torch, the light revealing only the contours of his moving obscurity. The man was a bit fat, Amid saw, his belly shuddering each time he took a step forward.

'I said, what are you doing here? What is this mess, ah?'

As the man drew nearer, Amid could discern he was a cop. His heart was racing like a rabid horse running wild to the end of a high cliff; however, he had no choice but to wait, to see how the events would unfold.

'Good evening, sir,' said one of the thugs, the apparent leader of the gang. 'We are just cleaning up a bit here.'

'Cleaning up what? Show me your ID, quickly …'

The leader-thug quickly extracted his wallet from his pant's rear pocket and handed a flashy card to the officer. The man looked at it for a long moment, under the beam of the torchlight's blazing eye. At first, his face looked kind of puzzled. Then he finally handed back the plastic to its owner.

'Bumiputera? OK. I thought you were Indians … Couldn't see you well in this darkness,' he cracked up into amused laughter. The leader-thug was looking at him in the eye, smiling as well.

'See, Encik, as I said we are doing a bit of cleaning here. You have said it yourself, that we are all Bumiputeras. And we are seriously worried for the future of our nation …'

'Is that so?'

'Yes, officer. These two here, they are Bangladeshi scum. As you might notice, we are not doing anything against the law.'

The thug's voice was like that of a God, or of an equally threatening force. Amid was impressed: the leader-thug had such an earnest way of talking that even Amid was almost convinced that it was right for him to lay here like this, face down in a dirty alley, and get beaten up. Amid would have never been able to pull off such a thing; this was probably the reason why he always felt compelled to cross the road whenever he saw any kind of officer stationed before him

'Ah, I see ...' the policeman looked excited now.

Upon sensing the officer's anticipation, Amid began to feel terrified. Twitching particles of fear began to attack him, rising up from his toes. And when they had completely devoured him, they transferred themselves to Rajendra, transmitting through Amid's long stare into his friend's eyes. Amid saw Rajendra instantly succumb to the same paralysing, eye-widening disease and turn into a soft stone against the hard ground.

'Very well. You see, generally I do not come here very often,' the officer continued. 'Those Indians, they gather in packs and rob people, and the Balai Polis always sends me here to check, all by myself. When I saw you guys down here, I thought I had to call for support. In fact, there are a couple of cars on the move as we speak. You better flee before they get here and start asking you all stupid questions.'

Upon hearing this, Amid saw that the leader-thug looked pleased and yet disturbed at the same time, his face severe but his eyes flashing like intermittent yet bright light-bulbs.

'But actually, Encik, we are about to complete a mission.'

'Listen, brother, I say you have to go. It's much better. They will be here in minutes and I cannot hold them back or say this was a mistake.'

'So what about these two?'

'Don't worry. I said the police are coming.'

Amid was scared. He had been taken into custody once. He remembered clearly how they had locked him up in a very small room with about fifty other immigrants who had no papers.

Amid, however, had carried with him his bloody papers. But the police had still left him to rot in there for a full week. His Chinese employer had come into the station every day, carrying along all sorts of documents, contracts, even his own work permit, but he had not been able to do much apart from raise some mocking eyebrows. The cops had fed them nothing more than a piece of roti canai every day. They had to shit and pee in a crusty bucket, which became so smelly after a couple days it was impossible for them to stand or sit over that tiny hellhole without desperately wanting to vomit. One time, they even took him out and abused him – they kicked him hard in the ribs, almost breaking his chest. He was happy he wasn't a woman; he could not imagine what those pigs would have done to him if he were. When they had finally put him on parole, he had to be hospitalised for a week. The mental scars, those were still raw though, and burning.

As the skinheads gathered together into a tight pack and left the alley, the policeman approached Amid and his now immobile friend. He looked down at them. Amid could see only part of his face from where he lay on the alley, the policeman's chubby belly restricting the view to the full span of his smile. He walked around them a couple times, slowly. He was a shark savouring the moments before a feed. Then, he stopped grinning and his fangs turned again into a smile.

'The choice is yours. The cops are coming and you might be able to escape if I fall down or you attack me. But how much are you going to pay me?' He took out his gun and pointed it straight into Amid's face, then retraced a couple of steps. Amid froze, his blood going cold all at once, sweat beading his forehead.

'How much, my dear people?'

Rajendra broke out of the petrifaction spell, pulled his wallet from under his left armpit and started counting the night's pay, watching the cop's smile grow wider and wider. In that precise moment, Amid thought again of Bangladesh and how the sun gets eaten up there in a mouthful by the horizon, leaving the clouds without any blood to sip on. He realised he would have preferred to starve to death in his godforsaken village.

6

To: 0178575954
From: SITI
'How r u? Have time for a drink? Call me :-)'

SHE WAS SITTING in front of him, across the plastic table, sucking slowly from a pink straw. The ice cubes in her kopi ice surfaced more and more as the brown drink emptied into her pouting lips. Asrul was mesmerised – he had never been so close to a girl he liked. So close that he could almost reach out and touch her. She had a fantastic, almost terrifying, way of eating him out with her eyes, while she calmly sipped her drink. He felt like he was being devoured by a curiosity cannibal.

'Are you from Penang?'

'No, I come from the north, from Kedah. Do you know the place?'

'Mmmm, maybe. Big place?'

'Not really. Alor Star.'

'Like KL?'

'No, hell no. Smaller ...'

She poked the straw at the ice cubes with firm movements, like she wanted to stab some invisible crab lurking between the plastic table top and the bottom of her cup. She opened her mouth for a moment, and Asrul saw her tongue stroking the lower row of her beautiful, white teeth.

Realising that she was at the centre of Asrul's attention, Siti smiled, and drew back a bit. The mamak behind her was pulling tea with fast, jerky movements – to Asrul's eyes, golden-brown lines blazed past Siti's figure, painting her in their wet streaks.

Under her neatly positioned tudong, she had on a nice blue t-shirt that exposed her arms. Asrul looked at her brown skin, blending into the patio's shade. He was almost convinced that Siti's body had soaked up the dense colour of her drink. Although people were walking up and down the noisy road at their side, the only thing that held his attention was the colour of the unveiled parts of Siti's body. He looked around for a second, to distract himself, and to show her that he was not so obsessed with her, after all. He did not want to lose this catch too early.

'So, tell me about yourself. You're from Indonesia, eh? How is it?'

Siti leaned her head forward and shook her left hand emphatically, to say no with all her strength.

'Indonesia is not good, Asrul. Too many people, not much work. It's hard …'

'Really?'

'Yes, I'm from Sumatra. You know the place, right?'

'Yes, sure,' he lied. He had only a vague idea of where that place was.

'I come from Aceh, from a small kampong. I had the chance to come here. To work, you know. There is an agency here, looking for housemaids.'

'Ah, so you do cleaning work, right?'

'Yes. It's not the best job in the world, but it's better than having none. I work for this Chinese family, in Tanjung Tokong.'

'And you live so far, in Georgetown?'

'Not really,' she laughed. Asrul simply couldn't resist staring at her white teeth and her big, dark eyes placed against her soft, brown skin, everything framed so perfectly within her black tudong.

'What are you looking at?'

'Who? Me?' Asrul blushed, retracting, sinking deep into his plastic chair. Siti laughed loudly, covering her mouth. He was hooked and she knew it. Damn kampong boy, Asrul cursed himself.

'Sorry …' she grinned and then continued, 'I only have to stay with them a couple nights a week, usually on weekdays. I cook for them, wash dishes and clean the house. I also take care of their children. Sometimes I have to be there at night, when they come home late; I have to get the children ready for bed and for school the next day. But most times the grandmother is there too, so I can just go home.'

'And do they treat you fine?'

'Yes, they're quite good. The pay is OK, and I get some time for myself too. It's not one of those families that lock you up in the house and treat you like a slave. You see, I can be with you now, and then go back to work later, around six this evening. It's perfect.'

'Ah, OK. Well, sorry that I asked about this, but sometimes I read about bad things happening to Indonesian maids. In the newspaper,' Asrul confided, a bit shy. 'I've read that some local families beat and torture them. Is it true?'

'Yes, unfortunately. It happened to a few of my friends. They've left Malaysia already; they couldn't take it anymore. You see, the Indonesian government is also very concerned. They try to monitor the situation, but … well, I'm lucky. And my family in Aceh is happy that I can send them some money,' she said, shifting about in her seat.

'And you, Asrul? What do you do here in Penang?'

'Well …' he wondered how he should answer her question. He could tell her the truth: 'I moved here to find better opportunities to beat the crap out of immigrant workers. Workers like you, for example.' That would sound fantastic, wouldn't it?

'Well … I just moved down here with my friend, Malik …'

'Sure, the big guy. He looks scary, eh?' Siti said softly.

'Nah, he's a good man. A bit rough in manners, but he knows how to pull it together. And yes, I guess I'm just new and looking for a good job.'

Siti stared at him for a long while; she was trying to reach inside his brain with those piercing, sensuous eyes, to find whatever Asrul was trying to hide. Then she suddenly changed expression, releasing her face into a warm smile.

'You're funny, Abang. I'm sure you'll find a good job soon. You're always lucky here, you Malays …'

'What do you mean?' Asrul's tone came out a bit defensive

59

though he didn't intend for it to happen. The last thing he wanted was to be schooled about his Bumiputera rights by this immigrant girl. She was as pretty as an angel, but he did not wish to indulge in such conversation with her. Besides, he had already listened to enough racial barbs from Malik and the rest of his gang.

Siti perceived she was getting into unpleasant territory and withdrew. The mood was slowly disintegrating, becoming like the swampy contents of the plastic cup, a brown mess of kopi remains and the thick water of what was once ice.

'I'm sorry. I just meant that it's generally no problem for Malays to get a job here, right?'

'Yes, right,' Asrul said bluntly. 'And no need to be sorry.' He smiled. He wanted to change the topic.

'Do you like cendol?'

'What is it?'

'Aiyooooooh! Never tried cendol? OK, follow me.'

He got up. He had decided to take control, to risk it. After all, other people were afraid of his pack of skinhead werewolves. And this was just a woman, right?

Asrul walked around the table and grabbed Siti's hand. Her beautiful lips fell open, and her eyes widened, flashing surprise like two emotional traffic lights.

'Follow me. I'll take you to the esplanade. We'll try some of that delicious cendol, and then …'

'And then, it's off to work,' said Siti, smiling. She left her hand pressed against Asrul's palm.

Before he could say anything, they were already walking down Penang Road, hand in hand.

* * *

As he put the key into the lock, twisted it and opened the metallic security gate, Malik was already facing him.

'About time. Come in.'

'I was –'

'There is no need to justify yourself, Asrul. I know perfectly well that while I was here, working my ass off for us and our gang, you were busy hanging out with that girl.'

'But, Malik–'

'Is she so special, Adik?'

'Well, I like her …'

'Never mind. I said, come in.'

Asrul entered the apartment. He could feel Malik's eyes following him, almost as if he were a barcode passing under the scanner at a supermarket counter. He threw his jacket on the couch, sat on the floor under the fan's titillating circle of fresh air and started untying his boots. He didn't like to wear them in this extreme heat; they made his feet burn all day long.

'Anything else you want to tell me, Malik?'

'Yes. And no, it's not about that special friend of yours, who has come from some ungodly place to lure you away from your real job, Asrul.'

Malik shut the front door, and then started walking in circles around Asrul. When Malik was present, Asrul always felt like he had to be better behaved and had to listen carefully to what the man had to say. Asrul didn't loathe him, for sure. Malik was a friend. A rude, direct, bossy friend. But he had been loyal and honest with Asrul since the day they met at the mamak stall in Alor Star. It was Asrul's desire for revenge that had drawn him to Malik and his group; Malik hadn't forced him.

'Asrul, I'm not interested in what you want to do with your cock – I want to be extremely clear about that. It's not my business, and we all need to get our rocks off sometimes, me included. But I'm just trying to tell you that something good happened today, my friend. And this, I mean, this girl, I'm afraid she will just screw up my plan, my dear Asrul. You are fifty percent of this plan, and I need you as a brother in this, all the way through.'

Asrul was surprised. He stopped halfway as he was manoeuvring his right foot out of the boot.

'So, tell me! What is it? What happened today?'

Malik moved to the back of the room, opened the window and took a glance at the spectacle of blurry lights that lay outside. It was getting dark; the sun was making way for bloody clouds reversing a scary, almost theatrical light on the ferry boats. They were shuttling slowly on still waters, seventeen storeys below them. Malik seemed to be enjoying the smell of rotten sea that only a real city-island sunset could give.

Then, he slowly sat on the couch, finding the most comfortable position. He looked Asrul right in the eye and gave him his usual spiteful expression, the one that could make him either the greatest leader or the most repugnant asshole in this world.

'When you were out trying to get your fingers wet in pussy juice, dear Asrul, I finally got us a *real* job. Well, unless you decide to screw everything up by saying something wrong ...'

'Tell me more.'

'Tonight we are off to Sungai Dua. You know the place?'

'Mmm ... Yes and no. Is it where the university is?'

'Yes.'

'What business do we have over there, Abang?'

Malik stopped talking and calmly brought his hands together, opening the palms and connecting each finger on one hand with its twin on the other.

'We are going to meet an important man, Asrul. His name is Mister Porthaksh.'

'Who? Doesn't sound Malay to me.'

'In fact, he's not, my friend. He is Persian.'

'What? Like the cats?'

Malik laughed loudly.

'You stupid asshole, I knew you would say that. He's a Persian *man* from Iran, Asrul.'

Asrul looked stunned. 'An Iranian?'

'Yes, Asrul. He's a real gentleman. I've been trying to get a hold of him for quite a while, and now, finally, I have done so. You remember when you got pissed because I was not here when you moved all this stuff in? Remember the business I told you about then? He is in the big business, my brother.'

'Big business of what?'

'Let's call it candies, for the moment.'

'Candies? Are you kidding me or what, Malik? What are we going to do with this man? Tell me.'

Malik was still watching Asrul from behind the tips of his joined fingers. He looked like he was praying to some sort of higher entity, a spirit that had possessed him. He was calm, dead serious; his face did not move at all.

'Asrul, just trust me. I've been working on this deal every day since we landed in this dump. And by the way, when we get the job, we move out.'

'Why?'

'Because this place sucks. I cannot stand the stench of foreign junk food any more; I have to smell it every time I step out from the elevator and walk to our door. All these Burmese and Indonesians and Vietnamese. I can't stand them, man. This is against my pure will. It is like, I am the devil, and you are forcing me to suck holy water from Holy Mary's tits. And forgive me, such an un-Islamic expression. As you can see, this place is cramping my style, fuck it.'

'But, Malik, Siti lives here ...'

'Don't mention that girl, Asrul. I don't care. I am Kuasa Melayu, and God willing, I will follow my instinct. And you are part of this – my gang – you're the best one, Asrul, my second in command. But I can see that you are losing it, more and more. I'm worried about you, Asrul.'

The two sat there, contemplating the nothingness, the rusty fan hovering above, cutting the hot air as a lawnmower might clumps of grass. Asrul didn't want to talk; he kept looking at Malik's face, without lowering his gaze. He wanted to show him that he, too, could resist.

'OK, Malik. Maybe I've been thinking of myself too much lately. I'm sorry about that. But she's a good Muslim girl, and I would like you to acknowledge that. Indonesians are part Melayu, you know this, right? Her skin is brown too, as brown as mine and yours. She can be as Bumiputera as me and you both rolled together into a fucking sandwich.'

Malik disjoined his fingertips. His prayer was finished, and the spirit that had possessed him seemed to have quickly dissolved into thin air.

'OK, Asrul, spare me your lessons. Do as you want, but be careful. Melayu or not, she is not pure Malay. And God willing, she will be OK for you. But I tell you this for the last time, Adik – do not mix pleasure with business. Now we're taking the next step. This is not just about bashing immigrant heads anymore. This is about money. A lot of money, Asrul.'

'You still haven't told me a word about this job, Malik. Speak up.'

'Mister Porthaksh will tell you much more than I can. I'm not really sure about a lot of things as well. I just know the job entails a lot of cash. Wads of cash, straight into our pockets. You can already forget those days we spent in Alor Star, drinking beer out of paper bags behind the dumpster, looking at the mosque. Now, we're entering a new league; we are winners!' He seemed highly pleased, Asrul saw.

'Now get ready. Don't wear a band t-shirt tonight. This man wouldn't understand, I'm afraid. Let's try to make a smart impression.'

'Alright.'

'Asrul, remember this always – we are smart, me and you. And we watch each other's backs, alright?' Malik got up and moved closer to Asrul, who was still sitting on the floor by his boots. Asrul looked up into Malik's eyes, he knew he could never have his mind penetrate the tough and controlled layer of his friend's thoughts. This was why Malik scared him at times.

'OK,' Asrul finally agreed. The men shook hands.

'And whatever Mister Porthaksh says, it's fine with us, and you have to accept it. We are going to do some delivery service for him, Asrul.'

'Delivery service? Of candies? Shit, that is a terrible job.'

'Do not fear, Adik. Malik knows best. These candies are worth a bloody fortune, dear Asrul.'

7

THEY ENTERED THE ELEVATOR, pushing past a bunch of residents. Asrul saw the web of deeply rooted buds of beard running all over their necks and faces; the men were unmistakably Middle Eastern, he decided. No matter how hard they shaved, they always looked like they had been tattooed with hair. Asrul realised they were returning from the swimming pool as they were shrouded in large, clean towels. They smelled of cologne and perfume even after having been soaked in chlorine. This was another amazing thing about all the Middle Eastern people Asrul had met thus far: they always looked and smelled neat. Syrians and Iranians, they were the neatest of them all. And their women, the way they slung their headscarves high above the top of the head, showing thick clusters of dyed hair sprouting out in wild and sexy growths; those women looked amazing. Malaysia was full of them, pullulating with them. And this part of Penang was their haven. Malik told him that most people liked to call the outer part of Sungai Dua: 'Little Tehran'. The huge, thirty-storey apartment blocks there had been built to become the concrete beehives of this imported species of Shi'a honey bees, producing nectar just for themselves, not sharing with anyone else.

Asrul couldn't afford to buy even one of those towels; he would have had to shell out a big cut of the salary he used to make serving tables at the mamak shop, back in Alor Star. Four ringgit an hour does not get one very far. Asrul was sure that these clean-shaven, perfume-scented bees did not know the weight and value of manual work. Observing the big golden rings that dotted their fingers, Asrul confirmed that these bees belonged to the best of their species. Even back home, in their own country, these hands had not experienced much else but cash, cream and manicures. No hard work for them. The other kinds of bees, the ones who did all the hard work, were unfortunately not imported to Malaysia along with big scholarships – they were tied to their homeland by the plight of labour, by the dream of joining the ranks of these more fortunate insects.

The elevator thumped to a stop at the fourteenth floor, shattering Asrul's thoughts in a cloud of mental sawdust. Asrul turned to look at Malik, standing next to him, cornered against the elevator's command panel. Asrul could sense anxiety in his still posture, saw his nails trying to bite furiously inside his palms. He knew that Malik being tensed generally never brought very good results. Asrul felt that this was his chance to prove himself valuable. He tried to regroup all his inner balance and strength as he stepped out of the elevator, leaving the perfumed honey bees to fly up to their leisurely destinations. He wanted to envy them, but he found that he was actually glad to be who he was.

'Let's cruise.' Malik went first, striding down the corridor. Some apartment doors had been left open, families secure behind thick outer doors and heavy padlocks. Asrul noticed a few kids running around a livingroom. They looked happy, rich and foreign. Nothing like the children who grew up in wooden houses, sleeping under a corrugated iron roof's constant, exhausting drill during the monsoon season, their house's heat barely cut by a shaky, rattling fan.

This world was the exact opposite: a space of air-conditioned comfort, populated by men in shorts who exposed fat bellies and a body covered in hair so thick they looked like gorillas. The women sat lazily on expensive leather couches, munching chips and watching something silly on TV, not noticing the crumbs that dropped onto the lower parts of their dark coloured tudongs. Asrul thought he wasn't in Malaysia anymore, but in some other, decadent dimension that had been built by smart engineers to keep this endangered Shi'a species at bay, to give them a beehive of luxury comforts, to make them forget their ayatollahs back home. Steel and plastic provided to them for the sake of an easy, mind numbing comfort. Their lives must feel like eating lotus directly from the core, Asrul imagined, getting inebriated quickly, getting blind and falling down into cement oblivion.

'Here we are: Number 26,' said Malik. 'Keep your cool and do not fuck it up, Asrul.'

He pressed the buzzer, fast and impatiently, and then stood back, waiting. The air around them was thick with anticipation. Asrul could feel it creeping down his neck, caressing his spine, and then going down swiftly in between his ass cheeks; he had to contract his sphincter to avoid it from getting inside him. That was extremely haram, and he could not let it happen right here and now.

The door opened softly as a small man in his thirties peeked cautiously outside. He looked like his face had been carved out of brown wood, his dark hairline in neat, stark contrast to his forehead.

'Are you Mister Malik?'

'Yes. Are we on time?'

'Perfect timing. No problem and welcome, Mister Malik.'

The man opened the door and came outside to unlock the security gate; Asrul noticed that he was a bit chubby at his waistline. As he continued to study the man, he had the vague impression that the bulging shape at the man's right might be the grip of a gun hidden under his loose shirt. Asrul shivered, he had never seen a firearm before, besides in the movies. He started to realise that Malik might have gotten him involved in something pretty serious.

He stepped cautiously into the house, trying to keep the man at a relatively good distance. As he took his shoes off and left them near the security gate, he scanned the apartment before him. It was sparkling clean and furnished in a simple, albeit precise, fashion. It had the typical 'L' shape of any Malaysian mid-to-upper-class condo: an entrance leading to a large livingroom with a huge French window facing the sea, an open kitchen to the side, and the bedrooms situated to the left or to the right, depending on where the 'L' decided to finish. His attention was immediately drawn to a huge carpet extending its reddish, deep colours all over the livingroom floor, enclosed by two leather couches on two sides. Piles of books were neatly positioned on a coffee table that lay between the two couches. Large framed pictures of foreign skylines hung on the walls, giving the place a carefully constructed cosmopolitan feel. Asrul especially liked the dim light that came from the two lamps situated at the opposite corners of the livingroom; they gave the place a cosy, warm atmosphere. The man asked them to take a seat and paced to the other side of the house where a small corridor led to the bedrooms, now hidden in darkness.

Malik sat down first and indicated to his right, where he expected Asrul to park his ass immediately.

'Sit down, Asrul,' he ordered coldly.

The pair sat there quietly, and the man soon returned into view. Behind the first man came Mister Porthaksh, then the first man suddenly swerved sideways and disappeared into the kitchen.

The Persian looked like he might have been in his mid-forties. He wore a purple silk shirt, comfortably unbuttoned just below the neck. A shade of dark, potent hair was rising from Mister Porthaksh's chest, giving him a very manly appearance. His face was thin and dominated by a big, secure nose and a pair of penetrating eyes rendered a bit inscrutable by age. Soft bags of skin blended into his perfectly shaven cheeks, the trace of a visible beard greying out under the dim lights. His hair was perfectly combed back, leaving space for his broad forehead, which balanced well with his big chest and sturdy shoulders. Asrul could estimate the man's weight by looking at his shape; this man could be the human counterpart of a small bull.

Mister Porthaksh came closer and they could see his face more clearly as the shadows were erased by the lamp's rays, forced to retract into his pores like mad vampires escaping the sun's light.

'Mister Malik, I am very pleased to meet you.' The two shook hands, Mister Porthaksh showing a clear firmness in his wrist. It was the first time Asrul saw Malik in a less powerful position, and secretly enjoyed being witness to this evident switching of roles.

'I guess this is the friend you told me about …'

'Yes, Mister Porthaksh. This is Asrul,' said Malik, still connected to the man by their handshake.

Mister Porthaksh released his hold of Malik's hand and retraced his steps without turning, knowing exactly where lay the space he wanted to occupy on the couch behind him. He sat without taking his eyes off the two of them. As he deposited his figure against the couch's black leather backdrop, his shirt looked even brighter, conferring him a strong and important appearance. The other man arrived moments later, carrying plates of pistachios, other nuts and neatly packaged chocolate bars. He placed them down carefully on the low coffee table and came back a second time to set glasses of water next to the plates, as if in preparation of a ritual conducted for great things to come.

'May I offer you some coffee or tea?' said Mister Porthaksh in a lavish voice.

'Coffee, thanks,' said Asrul, with the clear desire of marking the territory with his voice. He must have thought that his vocal piss might help sanction his stature among the other men, especially in a room where the air was getting thicker with overwhelming anticipation. His friend still did not seem very sure of what he was getting himself into, Asrul noticed.

The other man shuttled away. Mister Porthaksh slung his

shoulders comfortably against the cushions and extended his left arm over the edge, crossing his legs at the same time.

'So, Mister Malik, I would like to get straight to the heart of this matter as I am a very direct man. You see, you might find many Iranians trying to make a fool out of you with nice, poetic words and swift manners. Nevertheless, I feel this is not the time and place to be so formal; so, first of all, excuse me if I proceed directly to what I wish to speak about. Besides, I guess your time is as precious as mine.'

'Indeed, no problem at all. We are here to talk business, so please do get straight to it, Mister Porthaksh.'

'Perfect.'

The other man returned to the room, balancing two steaming glasses filled to the brim with hot, brownish water, and placed them on the table in front of Asrul and Malik.

'You see, Mister Malik, I will not hide the fact that when we spoke the last time, I sensed you could be a worthy addition to my organisation. I have been having some serious problems lately. Believe me, many families back in Iran have been suffering a lot because of this situation.'

He signalled to the other man quickly, bending his fingers to touch the palm, twice. The man disappeared again into one of the bedrooms and emerged a few moments later with a small stack of newspaper clippings.

'Take a look at these, Mister Malik. And please, Mister Asrul, you can have a read too.'

Asrul grabbed one of the first newspapers in the stack and took it close to his eyes to be able to read in the dim light.

Immediately, Mister Porthaksh snapped his fingers, and the other Iranian reached for the lamp and injected the room with a more potent light.

The headlines read very clearly now: they all portrayed a similar message, only differentiated by their geographical locations within Malaysia. Iranian men had been detained for drug smuggling. Iranian men had been executed for trying to smuggle crystal methamphetamine into Thailand. Three of the smugglers were women. No mercy for the Iranian smugglers. The death sentence was given to them, to the corruptors of Malaysian youth.

Mister Porthaksh had a grave expression on his face: as if a spirit had come to him with a staple gun and had pinned a grim mask on top of his face, shrouding him out of reality. He sighed heavily, uncrossed his legs, and leaned on the opposite side of the couch. The other Iranian brought him a cigarette, which Mister Porthaksh inserted slowly into the side of his mouth and lit up, puffing his first lavish cloud of smoke into the air.

'Can you understand, Mister Malik? Mister Asrul, do you follow me? My heart is full of grief. Those kids ... they are all dead or rotting in prison, waiting day after day to be executed. We tried everything. We even talked to the authorities, but there is nothing we can do.' He puffed out another heavy breath of smoke. He really seemed to be consternated.

Malik put the newspaper clippings back down. A mugshot of a veiled Iranian girl, who looked like she was in her late twenties, stared at them from the yellowish paper.

'My dear gentleman, I need resolute action,' Mister Porthaksh continued.

'What do you mean?' asked Asrul. 'You're showing us some newspapers, nothing much else. I assume these guys knew what they were doing by trying to smuggle syabu into our country.'

Malik immediately stared at Asrul with stern contentment.

Mister Porthaksh did not seem very impressed.

'This is exactly my point, Mister Asrul. Malaysian authorities have become smarter. They catch my guys by the handful. They know that Iranians taking international flights or driving cars across the border are trouble. I am in a very awkward position, Mister Asrul,' he pushed the cigarette's roach into a black, shiny ashtray buried in between the cushions and killed it. 'People in Thailand and Malaysia like syabu a lot, Mister Malik. I don't understand why, for it is such a terrible drug. In Iran, we like to smoke taryak. Many people love it, and I may understand why. It is relaxing. But this syabu, Mister Asrul, this is pure brain butchery!'

'What is taryak?'

'I see. You don't know,' Porthaksh looked happily surprised. 'Well, let's say it is raw opium. People smoke it for a good, relaxing time. We use taryak to make morphine and heroin. You see, this stuff has always sold very well with the Americans.'

Malik was still, listening quietly. He picked up another newspaper and stared intensely at the picture of two Middle Eastern men being ushered through a corridor by the Malaysian police.

'But here in Southeast Asia,' continued Porthaksh, 'people seem to prefer the jerky stuff. I don't know... Perhaps they like to take it before they go clubbing. I am just speaking from a purely business perspective, Mister Asrul: we get a profit of about 4,000 US dollars to manufacture and sell a kilogram of syabu in Iran. Do you know for how much I can sell the same stuff here in Malaysia and Thailand?'

'Not really' said Asrul, glancing at Malik who looked equally clueless.

'Well, about 80,000 dollars.'

'What?' the two young men rocked back in their seats. Porthaksh laughed loudly.

'Now you understand, Mister Malik, Mister Asrul. We all have families to feed and take care of, don't we? You may understand that there is a very big profit for you to be made if you would like to take on this job.'

Malik looked at Porthaksh with a soft smile. 'Indeed, we're very interested, Mister Porthaksh.' Then he looked at Asrul and put a hand on the latter's knee. He gripped it, firmly.

'I am sure you understand, my dear Asrul, that this gentleman has no time to waste. And neither do I, actually. This is the best thing to happen to the both of us since the day we were born. And if you think otherwise, I will be the first one to knock some sense into your thick head, Adik.'

Asrul was not feeling what could be best described as fear – it was more a strange kind of excitement, seeding deeply in his lower stomach, destroying his internal strength in spiralling circles. He felt like he needed to release himself. This time, however, the soft touch of a mosque's floor would not suffice, like it usually did. Asrul felt the weight of the situation push down from the bottom of his throat, all the way to his bowels; the only way he could eliminate the pressure on his entrails was by taking a massive dump, to let his shit and his fear, mixed together, drop into any toilet he could find. This was the feeling of a new, never-before-experienced sin. He did not dare to say anything, but only gulped noisily, his Adam's apple rocking up and down like a horse with rabies.

'So, my dear friends,' Porthaksh continued swiftly, 'the terms are quite clear – for every shipment, you get fifteen percent. Excuse me, but this is not negotiable because it is already a lot to start with. But I still want to be generous, as this job is risky. You know, if they catch you, there is definitely a jail term for you. Years of jail. But not the death penalty; I do not think so. You are Bumiputera, and there is always some kind of privilege given to your kind around here, unlike my poor boys …' He sighed and lit up another cigarette, sucking fire from it as if it were his source of ultimate strength.

'You cannot imagine how many mothers I had to personally visit, to share my grievance and condolences with. You clearly do not know how the situation is in Iran. Though my guys would do anything to get out of there, I must say that it really is a fantastic country: mountains, desert, a long, glorious history of culture. However, the government … Why else do you think I had to pursue a PhD in Malaysia? I am almost an old man. And still studying! Well, it gets me a visa.' He extinguished the second roach with a quick movement of his wrist.

The three sat silently for a few long seconds. Through the big glass behind them, they watched the lights on Penang Bridge moving swiftly outside, driving past inside car-cubicles.

Malik looked Asrul directly in the eye, still keeping that constant grip on his left knee. There was no need for further communication: Asrul understood it well, that the opportunity was very dangerous. He also knew he could not get out of Porthaksh's house alive were he to even contemplate refusing the offer. For sure, a drug kingpin wouldn't want one to know what his face looked like or where he lived if one didn't work for him. Asrul quickly understood that once again Malik had behaved like a boss. 'Abang' was what Asrul called him. Asrul felt more like Malik's slave than his brother.

'Well, I see that we have no option anyway: your friend has a gun, and I've already seen your face now and know where you live,' said Asrul. He wanted to show that he, too, had some balls. This was his grand moment of retribution. Malik looked surprised, and the grip on Asrul's knee transformed into a painful clench. Asrul jerked his leg away, setting it free. Mister Porthaksh sat silently. The other Persian was now standing behind them: Asrul already knew where he had put his hand, ready to pull out the gun and shoot them down. This was a life-changing moment for Asrul, and he thought of Alor Star. He thought of Siti's big eyes and her fascinating smile, and the way she had stayed close to him as they had watched the waves rock by against the Esplanade's low wall, the yellow cargo towers in the near distance, ruining Butterworth's flat shoreline. Then he thought of holding a gun in one hand and a lot of money in the other, wads of cash to buy himself a nice car and some good clothes. And maybe a new bass guitar to play in a band.

'Mister Porthaksh, I don't see why we shouldn't accept,' he suddenly erupted, his emotions flushing out as if they were getting sucked inside of a black hole's whirlpool. The Iranian released his smoke into the air without saying a word. He seemed quite relieved.

'Bring more nuts, Saheed,' he said, 'and tea … We have to discuss business with our new guys.' Emptying the table of the newspapers, he brought out a bunch of maps and some printed and neatly annotated paperwork. He never took the cigarette from his lips as he distributed the material amongst the three of them and started explaining what they meant.

8

THEY HAD BEEN DRIVING for the past three hours. Malik was at the wheel and was squinting his eyes to concentrate on the imperceptible objects that lay on the horizon. Mister Porthaksh had given them an old, battered Proton Saga, with a full tank of gasoline and a simple plan to follow: get in the car, leave Penang, take the North-South highway up to the Thailand border at Padang Besar, then stop at the parking lot up there. Someone would approach them. The two of them would have to do exactly as they were instructed. This detail sounded quite silly to Asrul; after all that carefully planned big-business bullshit he had experienced at Porthaksh's house, he hadn't expected any room for negotiation and compromise.

'Malik, do you think that guy's alright? I mean, are you sure we will be OK?'

Malik glanced at him quickly, turning his head to the left, and then immediately went back to concentrate on the highway's unfolding white line.

'Asrul, the man knows his stuff. These Persians are fine. He's a Muslim, too. Not the same kind of Muslim we are, but the hand of God is there, directing us safely along the road to success.'

Asrul did not want to continue talking any further, as the conversation was getting pointless, heading to the divine. They had just passed Alor Star a few moments ago; he had felt his heart thumping when he had seen the green signpost appear, first far away and then becoming bigger and bigger as the car had moved closer and closer. He was immensely glad when the Proton did not move into the left lane leading to the exit. Too many memories would have come flooding back, had they taken that turn, to disturb the quietness of the late morning, which so far had only been disturbed by the constant background drone of their car speeding on the highway's tarmac. He did not want to think of his past life and the black-domed mosque anymore. He did not want to remember the beating. He noticed the long, thin scar running across his left arm, and he moved his gaze away, concentrating instead on the long lines of palm trees stretching along both sides of the highway.

'Don't worry, Asrul. This will be an easy job. Just get there, park the car and wait for the courier. We don't even have to cross the border. Easy peasy,' said Malik calmly. 'Porthaksh wants to give us a try. We cannot screw this up.'

'And what if we do? What if the police stop us, and we are fucked?'

'Why do you always have a negative outlook on life, Asrul? I told you – God is on our side and we will not fail.'

'OK. Imagine that God forgot about us for thirty-five seconds. What then?'

'Then, we don't worry. Because we'd be safe anyway.'

'Why, Malik?'

'Asrul, I have got it covered. How in hell could you think I would put myself at so much risk if I didn't have any backup?'

'What backup?'

'Do not ask too much, Adik. I said I got it covered, so leave it. I'm talking about big, powerful connections, above us. I am not a fool, Asrul, always remember that.'

'Tell me then, Malik. I want to know, c'mon! I'm also deep in this shit, as much as you are!'

'In time, Adik, in time. You will know, I promise. And I already told you – big, powerful connections up there. Now leave it and relax, or you will piss me off. I have the right to keep some personal details to myself, cool?'

'OK, fine,' Asrul slumped back in his seat, bothered. He concentrated his gaze far beyond the highway, where a few water buffalos were plying the thick mud, walking slowly, moving their hoofs carefully, without any rush. Their freedom and oblivion made him envious. The view outside was changing abruptly from plain rice fields to a jagged, saw-toothed panorama of low limestone karst, thick rattans climbing down the rocks, looking like ancestral green beards. He remembered that his family had liked to go there on Sundays, hiking leisurely before having picnics at the base; his dad had loved to make up heroic stories about warriors and princesses, and the monsters who would try to keep them apart. Padang Besar was about thirty kilometres away; Asrul felt that slow, groping sensation growing again from the centre of his stomach, unrolling infinite, grey, thick anxiety-tentacles inside him, reaching into his bowels. He just wanted to get this thing over with as fast as he could, go back to the apartment and put his shaven head under a cold shower to rinse from his mind all these unlaundered thoughts.

Malik kept on driving, looking straight ahead, as if he didn't really care about anything but what was waiting for them at Padang Besar; this was the trait Asrul envied most in his more resolute brother.

'Perlis, Asrul ... This is where Kuasa Melayu came from, did you know that? This is great, isn't it, Adik? Here we go, to where everything originated!'

'I thought the whole thing came from you, Malik.'

'Oh no, Asrul. Perlis is the place, my friend.'

The next signpost advised that Thailand was close. The environment started to change, slowly, for the border was set over a street junction; the Thai side was a bit of a scruffy place, not very dangerous, but neither the kind of environment you would want to walk around alone in the middle of the night. Asrul observed a majestic wooden mosque emerge out of the village's tile-line as they zoomed past. It looked reassuring, and it may as well have been the last one they could see before they entered the Buddhist world. He immediately closed his eyes, shipping a few of his concerns up in the air to the attention of his great God. He realised that as of late he had been thinking of Siti way too much; he had even forgotten to visit the mosque for its call to prayer a few times. Her smile was so tantalising, and the shape of those immature breasts, protruding against the light shirts she liked to wear ... He opened his eyes quickly and stopped thinking about her. He didn't want to be disrespectful; he felt like he was pissing against the leg of God, like a mangy street dog, which only deserved to be instantly annihilated, crushed to death, squeaking.

'Are we there yet?'

'Very soon' replied Malik, holding the steering wheel tightly as if he were cruising the last of the seven seas on a battleship from hell.

'I think I need to piss; stop somewhere please.'

'Yes, Adik. Five more kilometres, and we are there.'

* * *

To: 0178575954
From: SITI
'I am free tonight. No work. Want to go out together? :-)'

He kept staring at his mobile phone's screen for what seemed like ages, petrified. The parking lot was a flat expanse of rubble and dust bordered by low bushes of scruffy vegetation that looked like they could cut when touched. The powerful image of a golden Buddha was looking straight at him from the other side of the fence, peeking into his soul with its tiny eye-holes, its head profiling against a background of foreign Thai characters. The symbols were strange and incomprehensible to Asrul; they looked like something one would make by scratching a diamond's hard edges on soft limestone. A swarm of people was buzzing around on motorbikes, shuttling all sorts of paraphernalia up and over the border. A tiny gate was before them, guarded by a concrete mound; it patrolled two lanes: one going in and one coming out.

And on either side, people were evidently leading different lives, marked by different codes of religious conduct. The veiled woman at the Malaysian immigration post had waved them through without any problem, smiling complacently and wishing Malik a safe drive. Now, they were waiting on a piece of land that nobody seemed to want to claim as their own. Asrul did not know what the hell he should type into his phone, as his reply to Siti; nobody had come for them yet, and he could not estimate the time of their return. Or if they would return, for that matter.

Malik was standing next to the car's trunk, staring blankly into the distance. Asrul could tell that he was not really at ease. The way Malik stood made Asrul quite nervous; his hands were planted at his sides and he was gently rocking back and forth on the heels of his army boots, covering them in a film of dust. Generally, Malik knew what to do. Not today though, it seemed. Asrul didn't want to ask him anything for the time being; he kept one eye constantly fixed on that intermittent cursor, which was waiting impatiently for him to spray a line of words across the phone's digital display. For sure, he wanted to see her. But not from behind a row of rusty prison bars.

'So, what are we gonna do now, Malik? What did Porthaksh say we must wait for,' he finally asked.

'We have to be good boys and wait, dear Asrul. He didn't say anything else. Just wait.'

'For what, Abang?'

'This is the point, Asrul. I don't know. I guess this is part of the test. They want to test our nerves, maybe. Just keep at it, and something will come.'

'Great,' Asrul pushed his arms up to the sky then dropped his clenched fists back against his thighs. The cell phone in his hand smacked painfully against him, striking his leg; he had forgotten he was holding it. He realised he was getting a little too tensed.

'Relax. That Iranian is a pro. He needs to be sure we are not bodoh, so just relax.'

They stopped exchanging words. From the opposite side of the parking lot, exactly where the gravel terminated at a step of fresh tarmac, which led to the Thai immigration booths, someone was finally coming down. He was hidden behind a thick layer of swirling dust particles held together by the reflection of the sun. As he drew nearer and the shape became more discernible, Malik squinted his eyes to see better through the blinding early afternoon light And Asrul held his right hand above his eyes to shield them from the sun. His cell phone was still blinking, abandoned in his left hand.

It looked like a young teenager was walking across the yard towards them, pushing something black, quite big compared to the boy's smallish size. The two skinheads did not really understand what was going on and moved a few steps in his direction. Beyond the parking lot, Asrul saw that border-life was as frantic as ever: a big Matahari bus pulled over and vomited a line of obese Malaysian tourists in front of the immigration checkpoint.

The parking lot's new arrival was indeed just a boy; his longish hair was combed neatly to the back, framing a high, royal forehead and two small, innocent black eyes. Asrul could not tell whether he was Thai or Malay. To Asrul, this boy defied any race, and he was aptly entitled to live with each foot planted on a different side of the border. But here and now, in this funky stretch of no man's land, he looked like he may have been the son of the local King. Malik had guessed right after all, Asrul realised: ever since Malik had seen him coming down the road from afar, he had concluded that the boy was pushing a car tyre. And now both Malik and Asrul were one hundred percent sure about this. The boy walked firmly, his left hand in his pocket and the right one just a few inches above the rolling tyre's surface, slapping it forward with his open palm as it gave the first hints of slowing down or was about to roll sideways. Malik suggested that, according to the big plan, he should walk towards the boy.

'Malik, wait, there is –'

He stormed off, without waiting for Asrul to finish what he had to say.

The young man and the even younger one met almost at the centre of the parking lot; it looked quite strange that at this time of the day, nobody had parked their cars there. The lot was only occupied by Malik's vehicle and by another van, parked a bit further back.

The boy looked at Malik intensely, a very strong eye contact that one would not expect from a teenager. He put his right palm firmly over the wheel, stopping its motion abruptly and capturing it with a firm grip. Malik didn't say anything and kept looking at the boy.

Then Asrul finally realised that someone else was also waiting in that van. He observed the sun's reflections making tiny flashes as they fell against a big pair of biker shades. Asrul understood this was exactly the time and the place for quick action. He knew that the man would fire his gun if Malik didn't do exactly as the boy told him to.

As Asrul walked to Malik, his friend stretched out his right arm and stopped him, holding it at Asrul's neck. Malik then moved past, smiling at the boy.

'Are you Mister Malik?' chirped the teenager. The sound of his voice further brought into question the nature of his sexuality, and Asrul thought that his long hair might have very well belonged to a little girl.

'Yes. May I know your name?'

'Not important, Mister Malik. You have to change a tyre, now. This is your new spare, as requested.'

Asrul looked at the dusty surface of the wheel's rubber grip. He didn't clearly understand what was going on.

'OK,' Malik went on, 'so you want me to change the tyre, here and now?'

'Yes. Change it or put this in your trunk, and then use the other one you have inside; I don't mind. As long as you get me the rear right wheel that is screwed on now, I am fine. If I were you, though, I would definitely change tyres, for it is by far the safest option. They wouldn't look for what is so obvious.'

'Right,' Malik turned and walked back to the car, leaving Asrul stranded in front of the little boy. He took the new tyre along, balancing the weight by bending a bit to the left, looking like he had suddenly become an older man. He opened up the trunk, took out the jack from underneath the spare pneumatic and put the newly acquired tyre against the side of the car. He began to unscrew the car's right rear-wheel and kept at it for a while. Then, with sweat staining against the front print of his black t-shirt, he moved back to where Asrul and the boy waited.

Asrul checked if Mister Sunglasses was still in his position: he was still there, smoking. Now, the man looked like he couldn't care less about being spotted.

'Thanks, Mister Malik,' said the boy, moving forward and receiving the tyre with both hands. He made it bump on the gravel with a sturdy sound, causing the limestone to shift to the sides as if Moses had parted that sea of minute stones.

'Anything else?'

'Not at this moment. Please go back, and have a safe drive. Give my regards to Mister Porthaksh,' the boy turned around slowly and started walking back to where he came from, leaving a new trail in the gravel where he dragged the tyre. He reached the tarmac and disappeared among the people at the border. They stood there for a bit, motionless in the scorching sun. The van's engine revved with a sudden roar that made Asrul's heart jump inside his chest, and the vehicle started moving slowly, bumping up and down on reaching the tarmac step. It joined the queue of vehicles on their way to Thailand, slowly sputtering as it inched forward, following another SUV. The Thais loved to own such bulky cars, Asrul observed; they must be rich.

Malik looked into Asrul's eyes again.

'OK, let's screw on this tyre quickly and get going. I feel weird.'

'Fine, Abang. Let's head back to Penang.'

In a moment they were beside their car. They spun up the jack, secured the tyre on the empty knobs, letting them slide inside, quickly working to fix the screws. Asrul guessed they would have had to do this again once they arrived at Sungai Dua, but he didn't bother about that; he just wanted to get out of the parking lot as quickly as he could. His neck was getting numb and was covered in wet pearls of sweat. He needed a shower already. He passed one hand over his shaven cranium, wiping away the watery broth that was spilling down his neck. Today was really, crazily fucking hot.

As the jack rocked down, the car sunk back into the gravel, ready to go.

'Let's move, Asrul.'

They revved the engine and drove off so frantically that a shower of limestone sprayed out from under the tyres and hit the front glass. As they reached the tarmac road, Malik slowed down, approached the jump and crawled carefully on the road, taking a right towards the South highway, and to their Salvation. He was so focussed on driving that when the Malaysian immigration officer asked for his ID, it took him a while to answer and hand it over stiffly from his window. Luckily, the officer seemed more interested in the slow stream of traffic coming through behind them, rather than in their new set of tyres. Malik had a quick glance at the new tyre as he got his ID back: to him, it looked like it was a completely different colour. Surely it was impossible not to notice that it was unlike the other tyres? However, the officer waved them on with a smile, wishing them a pleasant journey back home. As they drove off, a minivan carrying a bunch of foreign backpackers approached the border line: this time, the officer rushed out from the booth to stop the vehicle, probably sensing that some easy money could be made. As Asrul turned around to watch, he saw the officer standing in the scorching sun, smiling like he had just received some good news, and asking the tourists for their passports.

9

To: 0123445779
From: Asrul
'Sorry for delayed answer, was busy. Pick you up at 9 p.m. Bring helmet.'

HE ZOOMED DOWN the road, using the white line that separated the lanes as his own track, imagining that his bike was some sort of two-wheeled tram carriage. He loved to drive in the middle of the road; it made him feel powerful. Especially tonight, with Siti's arms tied around his waist, soft, and her precious perfume spreading all around him, he felt like the king of Penang's roads. In front of him, a car's tail lights suddenly transformed into two angry red eyes, and Asrul gently hit the rear brakes and steered to the left, wedging in between the high curb and the relenting vehicle. He sped up, carefully twisting his right wrist towards the sky, the doorstep of God, then rocked past the car and joined the white line again, followed it like a maniac.

'Go slow!' Siti said, giggling.

But he knew she didn't mean it. He increased the speed as he went past Times Square, his wheels eating metre after metre of Datuk Keramat Road, like a hungry asphalt cannibal. As he saw the red light, he started to slow down, carefully manoeuvring the bike into the geography of narrow metallic tunnels created by the casual scattering of exhausted, breathless cars, and Asrul soon reached the feet of the red-eyed Cyclops. He finally put his leg down to support his stand against the ground. The exhaust fumes had made the night as heavy as a mouth filled with Orangutan whisky-infested breath.

'Asrul, you scare me when you drive like that!' Siti cried out, punching his sides softly, in the way babies do when they want something very badly.

'C'mon lah, I am a good driver, Siti. Don't worry!'

'Yes, but I only have one life and want to live it, damn you!' she laughed, pinching randomly at his skinny sides, trying to hurt him.

He could see her beautiful sparkling white teeth reflected in the right rear-view mirror, and the inverted projection of the high tower of Times Square's shopping mall in the distance behind them. He was happy, and he didn't want to think of the job any longer. He felt safe now; there was no need to think about their first smuggling mission anymore. He had been very scared. Although Mister Porthaksh had orchestrated a simple task, Asrul felt a bit scorned because the man had wanted to test them. For sure, as Malik had said, the Iranian was a professional, but Asrul was not – at least, not until today. He couldn't stop thinking about the afternoon, about the way Malik had decided not to listen to him. After all, he had been so fixated on the boy that he hadn't cared for anything else that had been happening around him. Asrul was no fool, he had immediately noticed the man in the van. Sure, people may have told him off many times because he acted like a bit of a coward, generally. Although Asrul had had the sun's strong reflection in his face, he had still been able to observe that the man was sitting in the van's cubicle, holding a gun. It had been almost impossible to see that the man was in the car, through the vehicle's obscured windows. Asrul had been able to notice the gun only because he had seen the sun's light reflect off and gleam over the top of the gun barrel. And of course, a gun doesn't hold itself up inside of a car, unless someone has taped it to the front seat – a very unlikely and silly idea indeed. That was why he hadn't dared to move. It had been quite upsetting – he knew that the man had been there to control them, to see that no harm was done to the boy, and that the exchange ran smoothly. And for sure, he couldn't have been one of Porthaksh's people: his skin was too dark.

As the cyclopic traffic-eye turned a benevolent green, Asrul kicked the first gear down and leaned forward, pushing a perfect current of muscular steam into the accelerator's handle, turning it back with his right hand. The motorbike continued its mad run, sputtering puffs of white thick smoke into the night. He knew that, of course, the man was a Thai – there had to be someone organising and controlling the trade, didn't there? Or …

When he finally realised it, he nearly swerved off the road. It seemed like Siti hadn't noticed that he had almost hit a lamp post, for she continued to hold him comfortably from behind.

How could they have been so stupid? Really, he meant it. He

was uncertain whether or not Malik had understood this yet. The tyre, the one they had brought back from the border, was most probably the empty one. In other words, the tyre that they had given to the boy, the tyre that had already been screwed onto the car when they had left Sungai Dua had been, in fact, filled to the brim with syabu.

Otherwise, why would the boy have specifically asked for that particular tyre? And why had the Thai gunman been watching over them the whole time? Clearly, the Thais were buying the stuff, not selling it. It was all going into their country, not coming out. The Iranian didn't tell them this: he had made up the story about them having to bring a shipment back, so that they would have left Penang without a worry, loaded with drugs but with a light head. His first impulse was to drive back to Porthaksh's place with a crowbar and crush his face in. That smart motherfucker. This was not cheating, but it wasn't fair play either. Asrul felt used, thrown to the fangs of fate, almost kind of cheated.

When he parked the motorbike he was still lost in these thoughts: Siti now felt to him like an extra accessory for the night. He decided that he needed to get this sudden knowledge about their job out of his mind and enjoy his time with her, but he still felt cheated. She could see it too, as clearly as one might the first sign of the sun after a pouring monsoon rain.

'What's the matter with you, sayangku?'

'I'm sorry, Siti. I just realised I made a big mistake at work today. I don't want to spoil the mood, but it keeps coming back to my mind.' She immediately looked comforted, her face releasing itself behind a bright smile.

'Are you sure you want to hang out? If you have no time, it's OK; you can take me home.'

'No,' he stepped forward, reaching for her hand. She received it by opening her palm voluptuously. She was soft: the touch of her skin began to erase the afternoon's images as if they were pencil lines disappearing from his memory's sketchbook.

'So, you have a job now, right, Asrul? You never told me.'

'Well,' he said slowly. 'Yes, Siti. Exports for a foreign firm.'

'Oh, really?' she said with interest.

They walked down the esplanade; he led Siti past the food court, much to her surprise. His plan was to go a little further up, to that dark corner of the walkway he had recently discovered, and to sit upon the rocks, enjoying the nice, quiet view of the sea. He knew she would love to hear the sound of the waves; also, he had in mind another purpose for going there. He wanted to turn the day into a complete victory.

'Yes. Malik, my tall friend, remember? Well, he and I have to deal with the customers, directly. Sometimes in Penang; sometimes we even have to go up to the Thai border.'

'Really?' she seemed amazed that her new boyfriend could do that, could leave the island. That was the problem of living in Penang: it could end up swallowing your world into a soap bubble, if you let that happen. That was probably what had happened to her.

'Fantastic,' she continued, 'I am so happy for you, Asrul. So, one day you have to take me along, OK? I would *love* to see Thailand!' Her eyes brightened and she held his hand more firmly.

They soon arrived at his favourite spot: it was the end of a side road, opening up in a little circle, surrounded by low rocks. The sea was dark and quiet just below the low wall, crashing its waves gently against the shoreline. Asrul led Siti by the hand and helped her climb over the furthest rock, which was hidden away in the shadow of the palm trees.

'What is this?' she asked. 'A blind date?'

'Because it is too dark to see?'

'Exactly,' she laughed a bit and drew closer, hugging him and finding a comfortable shelter for herself, wedging herself under his right armpit.

The sea smelt fresh, and the breeze titillated their faces, made them close their eyes, awestruck. This was the right moment for Asrul to move his head downwards, his chin looking for her forehead. She quickly adjusted her face to let him press his lips against hers and then opened up her mouth: her tongue softly started battling against his. He hadn't kissed many girls before, but this one surely tasted like magic. The combination of the fresh breeze and the darkness, and the sounds of people cooking and drinking only a few metres down the slope made it all the more exciting. It didn't last forever.

'We can't do this here …'

'But we just did.'

She entered his mouth again, pushing her chest against his. Her tudong had slipped back across her head, and a long swirl of black hair fell out, rolled over the side of her face – it smelled of fresh shampoo and cold shower.

'Do you love me, Asrul?' she said, whispering in the short time she had to take in a breath.

'Yes, I do,' he said as his hand savoured her body, getting around her firm thighs, pushing her small and soft breasts.

Her breath was getting shorter; he could hear its hot sounds in his ear, sweet as sugar rays, warming up the inside of his ears. Without stopping the kiss, he pulled her gently to one side and supported her shoulders against his heart; only then did he slide his right hand down, patting lightly against her until he had reached her crotch. She let him do it. He unbuttoned her jeans and pulled them down a bit, giving just enough space to let his hand enter and press against her panties. She moaned lightly, purring like a cat.

'You want to …'

'Yes …'

'They will see us.'

'Relax.'

The next thing he touched was hot and wet and soft around his fingertip. The more he played with it, the more Siti's hands transformed into excited claws, digging into his back. She panted and became increasingly stiff, stretching herself against his body; then she turned into stone. As Asrul was about slide his hand out of her thigh's harsh denim, he thought she had suddenly petrified: she was mute, completely silent, and had her face pressed into his neck, her hot breath drawing steamy pools against his t-shirt's collar. At last, she leaned back, smiling. Asrul's neck was hot and wet, with a mixture of tears and saliva. As the fresh breeze hit that spot, he felt an immediate fresh relief. She swung her arms around his neck and kissed him again, under a silent half-moon that would keep their secret safe.

'I love you too,' she said, looking sweetly into his pupils and smiling without showing any trace of her teeth.

10

THEY WERE SITTING around three cups of steaming hot tea. Mister Porthaksh puffed cigarette smoke into the air, making it increasingly less breathable. He looked quiet and satisfied. Malik was waiting at the opposite side of the table, arms crossed over his chest, silent.

'Very well done, my friends,' said the Iranian as he fished out a few fat pistachios from a little saucer placed at the centre of the table. He inserted one in his mouth and kept another nut firmly gripped in between his thumb and index finger, as if it were a miniature precious trophy.

'How do you prefer to get your cut? I reckon a bank transfer would not be very justifiable, as you don't have regular jobs.'

'May we have cash?' asked Malik. 'That would be fine for us.'

'Fine,' Porthaksh slung his hand at his helper, who thus far had been standing silently against the livingroom wall; the helper immediately moved across the floor and disappeared into one of the bedrooms.

'I hope there have not been any problems at your end.'

'Not really. Nevertheless, we would have preferred to have known that we were carrying the stuff from Penang, and not the other way around,' said Malik with a hint of rigour in his voice. Porthaksh didn't answer, but only concentrated on his cigarette. He made the other pistachio rapidly disappear inside his mouth.

'OK, my apologies. I had my reasons, Mister Malik. The situation is not safe, and I couldn't risk losing the first shipment. What if you just drove off with my car and about 40,000 worth of drugs? Not a fun situation – especially if I have to find you.'

The following silence broke into the air like electricity. Asrul concentrated on a king bee that was rhythmically hitting itself against the closed window-wall behind Porthaksh's back. No way in, but too stubborn to turn around and get back into its own free, high-altitude world.

'I hope we have gained your trust now, Mister Porthaksh.' Malik still hadn't uncrossed his arms.

'Yes, you did, indeed. And if you need an explanation now, it is fairly simple, Mister Malik. We import from the Middle East and distribute over here: this is how the business works. The Thais buy from us. I import. You help distribute. It is as simple as that, really. I am actually very pleased with you, because you went quickly and returned on time, no questions asked. You see, some of my guys have felt the pressure and screwed up. Knowledge sometimes is a bad beast: makes them act weird and get caught before they even reach the border. This is why I preferred not to explain all of the details beforehand, because it was clear, since the first moment I looked at you Mister Malik, that you are still green to the business. And business is business.' Malik didn't reply.

'I hope you aren't too angry at me, and if you are, I'm sorry.'

'No, I'm not, Mister Porthaksh. It was a learning experience.'

The second Persian returned into the livingroom and offered a yellow envelope to Malik with both hands. It was bulging and fat. When Malik took it, the man let go and brought his right hand against his heart.

'That's 8,000 ringgit, your twenty percent. The tyre was only half-stuffed – you have my word, Mister Malik.'

As Malik opened up the envelope and looked inside, Asrul leaned over his friend's shoulder and saw a bunch of fat fifty-ringgit note bundles tied together with rubber bands.

'Next time we would prefer to see how you pack it, no offence. It is business, after all,' Asrul spat out, and Malik reinforced his friend's demand by nodding in consent. Porthaksh didn't react, he exhaled more smoke and relaxed against the couch's back.

'Fair enough. I think it will be done in about five to ten days – we'll give you a call. Remember, the number will always change, so please answer any unknown call you get. Someone will tell you that his child needs tuition classes. And you'll come here the next morning at nine a.m. sharp. Now, enjoy your success. And take it easy.'

'Thank you, Mister Porthaksh. I'm confident you will get to trust us as much as you do some of your best men.'

'It's a mutual feeling, indeed. So far, so good,' said the Iranian, his smile masked by a thin layer of cigarette smoke.

* * *

Besides two circles of white strobes fixed directly behind the small stage where Internal Vomiting was playing, there wasn't much light inside of the club: the guitarist, dominating the left side, was riffing heavily, accompanying the relentless cacophony with the rhythmic banging of his head. His long hair moved in a frantic whirlpool, as if he were under an attack of dementia. A skinny, black-clad singer was standing at the centre of the stage, screaming loud blasts of lung material into the microphone. At the back, the drum set was taking a severe beating, a guy carefully bashing its skins as if there was no tomorrow. The combined assault of the quick bursts of death metal and a grinding base was however not very convincing.

Malik looked bored. Waiting at the back of the pit, he pushed away each and every human bullet that happened to bounce against him, shot out of the mosh pit's savage spiralling motion. Asrul was beside him, helping keep the trench safe by pushing his arms forward.

'I don't like this band,' he screamed on top of his lungs and into his friend's ear. 'It's just a bunch of guttural crap.'

'I agree. This is nothing serious. There's no message, no revolution ... Let's get out of here.'

They moved out of the pit and went through the door into a smaller, smoke-infested anteroom filled to the brim with other metal heads and punks. Some turned their heads as they noticed Asrul and Malik's shaven heads, boots and braces. As they walked across the floor, pushing their way out, Asrul noticed a minority of the female kind; they were parked on some of the couches, put there by their musician boyfriends. Useless, unattractive hags dressed in fake rock attire, which would probably look better on the mannequins at Gurney Plaza's shopping mall if it were washed out of its after-punk crustiness. He felt like they were looking at him and Malik and giggling, passing a message from ear to ear, speaking a secret code in which Malik and Asrul had been made the prime subject matter.

'Are those bitches laughing at us?' he asked Malik who was almost out and heading down the stairs.

'Maybe, Asrul. Just get out. Let's not waste more time here.'

'Hey, did you say my girlfriend is a bitch?' a voice came firmly from behind. Asrul turned around to stare into a dark face looking intensely at him. The thin mug had long hair falling around it, and it was all pasted over a big neck. He was coming close to Asrul, trying to look mean and impress his bitch. As he sensed trouble, Malik came back, rushing up the staircase, and stood next to his friend, a solid rock made of flesh and muscle.

'You should teach your bitch some education, sir. It's rude to comment on people, you know that?'

The guy didn't answer immediately as he noticed that the room was emptying behind him, creating a space where he was the only actor, performing centre stage. Without losing the nerve that had made him speak up in the first place, he kept staring at the two skinheads.

'We don't want people like you here. This is a place for music and freedom. We don't like your views. We know you guys. People like you are better off in that shitty Perlis up north, not in Penang. No racism here, folks.' As he finished his monologue, every person in the anteroom was watching this scene play out before them. It had brought some fresh air into the dull, dead conversations they had been having until a second ago. Some guys at the side had clustered into a group and were mumbling amongst themselves, undecided about what they had to do.

'Racism?' Malik smiled. 'You are indeed being racist by telling us off.'

'You better go; Kuasa Melayu isn't welcome here.'

'OK, my hero. We're going.'

'Very glad you are; you're just ridiculous. Do you know what your main man actually thinks? Adolf Hitler. Take a look in the mirror tomorrow morning, man: you are *brown*.'

Malik was quick. He hit the guy only once, by slapping both arms forward, smacking him directly in the chest, a train wreck of muscles that made the guy fly across the room and crash on the floor a good couple of metres behind him. He hadn't expected it. All the punk faces instantly filled up with horror, their eyes bulging and their mouths opening, as if by hitting that guy, Malik and Asrul had opened the regulators of their feelings air-tanks and started an irreversible implosion process. Nobody spoke, and all eyes were fixed on them. The guy, still shocked and on the floor, was trying to get up, to react, but nobody came forward, neither to help him nor to take a stand for him. It seemed to Asrul that simple stuff like this didn't happen there often after all.

'Fucking dorks,' spat out Malik, snapping his knuckles together.

'We're going now. Any final remarks?' Nobody dared to say a word.

'Great, go back to your brainless activities. Piss off.'

As they walked out and down the stairs leading to Pengkalan Weld and into the seaside breeze, nobody in the club had the balls to do anything. This attitude was not rock and roll at all, Asrul thought to himself; he gladly followed the shaven head of his leader downstairs, and out into the night. It was time for the Nazis to turn again into werewolves and run amok under Penang's moonlight.

11

Work time was almost over, and the girls, who lived not too far away, had asked if Than and Nyan would walk them home.

'Just the other night, a group of people disturbed us on the street. First, they whistled at us and then started to make catcalls at us. It was unbearable. They got closer and tried to touch us. Now we're afraid of walking back home at night, but we have no other way to get home; the last bus was at 11.30 p.m. Can you accompany us?'

'No problem,' the men had answered happily.

The girls were from Vietnam and were indeed pretty – especially Cam. Nyan liked the way she smiled and tilted her head sideways, as if she wanted to follow the sound of her own laughter. These girls were different: he knew that after work they liked to go out and have fun, unlike the other women workers. This never happened back home in Myanmar; he thought that the girls there just didn't know how to spice things up. Nyan and Than had been working in the restaurant kitchen for almost a year when the girls had joined as waitresses; Nyan had overheard the boss saying that they were from Ho Chi Minh City, but one could never be too sure about this. Any Vietnamese girl would tell you that she was from the big city; it was as if coming from the countryside was a criminal offence to them. However, the girls were nice and always helpful – they had created some sort of secret alliance between the floor and the kitchen staff, and they knew how to sweeten the routine of any work day, to make it fun. They were very different from the others, the Malaysians, who were willing to stab you in the back as you turned, and were always ready to kiss the boss's ass, madly obsessed with climbing up the social ladder, even if it had to be done by sticking their tongues into some rich man's asshole. He was from Myanmar, but Cam and her friends didn't care; they were genuine, just needed the money to send it back home and help their families.

Why not walk these cuties home, Nyan considered. As he finished slicing the vegetables and threw them into a sizzling wok, he couldn't resist watching her from behind, through the thin window that separated the kitchen desk from the restaurant floor. It wasn't possible to ignore that plump, nice ass of hers, her hips shaking up and down before a bunch of busy, uncaring customers. Nyan liked to joke with Than about the fact that, in spite of being in the company of beautiful, expensively dressed women in high heels, whom they brought along to dine with, local men always seemed to have time only for their cell phone's screen. If he only had a little bit of extra money, Nyan would have shown these men how to treat a woman. He rolled the vegetables on their raw side, shook the wok forward a couple times to make them simmer in the hot oil, and another portion was ready to go.

It had been a long day. Nyan could still smell the burning

wok on Than's clothes, despite the night's open sky. Although the streets were almost empty, it wasn't yet that time of the night when it was just you and the moon on Penang Island. The girls were walking boldly along with them as if they really thought the two men could protect them from any form of street evil. Nyan tried to stay as close as possible to Cam, intentionally hitting his shoulder against hers whenever he could. She didn't seem to be bothered by it, but, instead, was looking at him, smiling. And she was smiling in that special way only beautiful girls could. He knew he could get somewhere with her, with a little patience perhaps ...

They left the edge of Georgetown and walked up on Burmah Road. Nyan loved the fact that one of the island's major roads was named after his homeland; he immediately felt more secure. Pulau Tikus was about a twenty-minute walk at moderate speed; that was enough time for them to convince Cam and one of the other girls into accompanying him and Than out for a kopi, or even a beer, if they felt like it. Perhaps Ngoc would agree to come along. She was very close to Cam; also, more importantly, she had very big boobs, and Than liked her.

'Hey, Cam, are you very tired?'

'Well, a little bit, yes,' she looked at him, smiling, showing the little imperfection of her front teeth. He still loved that as it made her look more real, made her accessible, within his league.

'Do you want to go out for a drink?' Nyan didn't have to ask her. She asked him.

He felt his heart racing faster, and once again he bumped against her; she didn't react, as if she really didn't mind.

'If we can get home, no problem, OK... I change clothes and we can go. Beer?' she smiled and elbowed him lightly in the ribs. Nyan felt immediately aroused by the proposal. He slowed down a bit and held her back from the group, pulling her arm softly.

'What about Than? I am with him, not alone ...'

Cam seemed like she held the key to every door; she knew all the answers already.

'Than can come along too. Ngoc is coming,' she smiled, crinkling her eyes a bit, and she elbowed him again, this time looking him straight in the face as she hit him.

There was nothing left to say. Nyan already loved the ways of these Vietnamese girls so much.

* * *

'Shit, those losers made me so pissed! I want to crack some heads now.'

'How, Abang? The other boys are not here.'

'Ah, forget about those losers, Asrul. Why do I have to be constantly surrounded by those low-life loser scum? Me and you, Asrul, we're different. As long as we're our own team, we're strong, Adik.'

Malik was walking quickly, cutting through the back roads of late-night Little India – a grid of silent, empty lanes that had stopped sizzling with life a few hours before. The pan had become cold already, it felt weird to cross Market Street and not hear any blaring Bombay dance tunes trying to scratch the paint off the walls. He was heading fast into the heart of Georgetown.

'Asrul, as I said, I'm so pissed I need to do something. To show those fucking creeps that we have the power. We have to do it, as soon as we can! Here and now!'

'But, it's just me and you, Malik. Where do you want to go? What if we end up going against a bunch of people and cannot fight them all?'

'Fuck you too! Don't talk like one of those losers.'

As he followed Malik, trying to catch up with his increasingly quickening pace, Asrul felt morally slapped. He was no loser. He had been there when the syabu shipment deal had been happening, from the first moment till the last. He had seen the Thai gunman first, before anyone else had. He was good.

'Malik, so what the fuck do you want to do?' he grabbed Malik by the back of his shirt and risked a hit in the face as his friend rocked his left arm back, rotating the torso, ready to punch Asrul.

'Are *you* questioning me now?'

'Yes, Abang, I am. You're losing it. They were just some fucking metalheads, Malik. Just forget it. They're not worth it.'

'No, Asrul, I don't agree, it's worth it and important too, because I don't like to look like one of them. I would never fall down and be unable to get back on my feet.'

He stopped and cleared his throat.

'OK, fuck it. The other day, when we were driving to Padang Besar, remember I told you I had it covered, right?'

'Yes.'

'OK, Adik. You wanna know the secret? OK, just wait and see.'

Malik pulled out his cell phone and started jabbing his finger against the screen, looking for a contact. When he found it, he pressed it and brought the earpiece to the side of his face, preparing to answer the call. He walked around and back a few metres, making sure Asrul remained where he was, nailing him to the ground with a precise stare. Don't come any closer, Malik's eyes commanded. He talked for about a minute in a low voice, making sure to keep his eye contact with Asrul. Meanwhile, Asrul felt as if he was being drilled by a screwdriver of curiosity.

'Now, wait and see ... They will be here in a minute. Come with me.'

Malik started walking towards a dark back-alley, heading in the opposite direction to the Goddess or Mercy temple. He walked a few more metres and then stopped in front of a prewar house that had seen much better days, its facade fractured into clouds of concrete and cobwebs of old, decrepit paint.

'What are we doing, Abang?'

'We're waiting.'

After about five minutes, a car entered the lane, its headlights slowly piercing the darkness. It shuddered along as if it knew that they were waiting, but couldn't clearly see where and had to touch familiar objects in the dark to find its way. As it drew nearer, Asrul took in the chequered motif on the front wing and couldn't believe what he was seeing. The car ground to a halt right in front of them.

The cops had just arrived.

* * *

Ngoc was dead tired but still had to do this to please her friend. She had put on a nice little dress and was walking in her new pair of sandals, her feet hurt badly and she felt really unattractive. The only place she wanted to be now was in her own bed, and alone. She had been running up and down the restaurant floor since 5 p.m., taking orders and trying to understand what the customers said. Yes, she still had problems with her English, and the way Malaysians pronounced it only made things worse. She especially couldn't stand nor understand those who tried so hard to act rich and posh, with their fake, inbred British accents. Most nights she would just return home with a splitting headache, unable to keep up with making all those mental ties across languages; today was one of those nights. But when her friend Cam had taken her aside as they had walked back with the boys and had asked her about coming out tonight, in Vietnamese, so that the guys couldn't understand what she was saying, she hadn't been able to refuse.

Cam had insisted she come because, finally, one of the cooks, the one she liked so much, had asked her out. She had been pestering her with details about him for a few weeks now: he was so handsome; he was so nice; he was the best guy in the restaurant. And Cam, who despite her strong appearance was quite a shy girl, had asked her to come along and help entertain Nyan's friend, Than. She had talked to him a few times and had found him quite silly. Moreover, she knew that whenever he had talked to her, the only thing he had seemed interested in were her tits. Sure, Mother Nature had been generous with that, but this was the first and foremost thing that put her off. It made her feel as if she was only good for sex; she couldn't stand it. She had a degree in Economics and had to attend tables in this stupid country of Malaysia only because the pay was twice as good as what she'd be paid in Saigon, even if she worked in a firm. Now, walking to a bar, in these damn sandals, with her dolled-up friend who was looking for love, she knew she should have bought another pair, for the laces were too tight around her feet. She just felt like the most stupid girl in the world. Plus, she didn't share Cam's passion for Burmese muscles. She felt sticky, hot and bothered, and just wanted to go home. But no, they were going to a bar instead. Suddenly, she started pondering the terrible possibility that Cam might ask Ngoc to let her use their shared room with Nyan for a while. She immediately felt a sharp sensation crawling up from inside her womb and exploding directly into her chest; she wouldn't go that far on a first date, would she?

A few metres ahead, Cam was laughing and pulling at Nyan's arm. She seemed so happy. Ngoc felt a tip of burning envy poking the lower side of her throat. Why did she always have to feel like that? So successful and so selfish? Ngoc did not know whether she couldn't stand her friend's behaviour, or if she was plain jealous because her own life, on the contrary, was just boring, a different kind of mess.

'Cam!' she cried out loudly to make sure she was understood. Her friend stopped walking and looked back, her expression fading into a dying laugh, her flashy fake handbag hanging on her right hand like a decoration from a Christmas tree. Ngoc sped up, running on her toes, feeling the handicap of those shoes. As she ran to her friend, she started lamenting in their Vietnamese code.

'I want to go home, Cam! My feet hurt!'

'So why did you wear those shoes? Can't you see I'm doing well with him now? Help me!'

'Where do you want to go?'

'To the bar, like I've already told you. I want to drink a couple beers and then go home.'

'We go home alone, right?'

'Sure, what are you thinking? It's the first date. Do you want him to think I'm a cheap slut?' Cam looked pissed. Than walked up to them from behind, giving Nyan the look of someone who clearly did not understand why he was being dragged into this.

Ngoc suddenly realised she was acting like a baby, and immediately felt horrible.

'Cam, sorry, I'm just very, very tired.'

'It's OK,' her friend said, touching her lightly on the right cheek under the low illumination of the street lamps.

'Try to relax and have some fun, OK? I'll buy you ice cream tomorrow, OK?'

'Don't treat me like a child.'

'Well, you are being one. Relax! I'm sure having some fun with Than will not do you any harm,' she smiled, broadly.

'Is everything OK, girls?' Nyan came in and broke the Vietnamese spell with his flexuous English, 'Any problems?'

'No,' Cam smiled. 'Let's go. Ngoc needs to sit down; her shoes are very new and her feet hurt.'

'Sure, the bar is just a couple hundred metres away. Or shall we call a taxi?'

'No,' said Ngoc, frustrated. 'Sorry, I don't want to be a pain. I just need to sit down a bit,' and as she said this, she thought to herself how tired she was of all this lame acting. If truth be told, she had had enough and wanted to sink her nails into Cam's neck, and scream as loud as she could.

12

As they turned into Jalan Kelawai, they realised how nice the island could be when the roads were empty and the sound of the night low, imperceptible. The engine buzz seemed like a distraction from the outside reality, which unfolded slowly as they proceeded along the large, semi-deserted lane. A loner on a motorbike rushed by and as he saw their car, he reduced the speed and disappeared quickly into one of the side roads.

'Idiot,' they said from the front seat.

This wasn't what they were looking for, they would have to scan the scene a bit more before finding the kind of fish they sought. It wasn't long before the officer in the passenger seat cried out suddenly: 'Over there.' Asrul's heart was racing, for he didn't have any idea about what would happen now. Normally, he was always quite nervous before any attack – they would hide, would wait for the right moment to strike, and then come out in bigger numbers than their prey. But tonight he was sitting next to Malik in the back of a police car. This was Malik's dirty little secret: Abang had such connections, he was friends with the police. Or, at least, with these two officers, who looked as spirited and ready for a fight as Malik was.

'Over there' had meant the side of the road, Asrul saw, not very far from the junction leading out to Tanjung Tokong. There were two couples there. Two men, not too tall, with quite dark skin and carefully combed hair. Not Bangladeshis, definitely. The girls were pretty; he saw that their long black hair reached almost down to their lower backs and knew that they were Vietnamese. The classier immigrant girls were always from Vietnam. As their car moved closer and pulled over, a few metres ahead of the group, Asrul saw a look of horror spreading across the girls' faces. One clung to the other, grabbing her arm and hiding against her side: the flashes of the flashing lights designed a beautiful light show over the girls' fair and carefully shaven lower legs, their dresses interrupting the show just above the knee.

'Nice catch,' Malik finally interrupted the silent trance he had fallen into since Penang Road. 'Give some food to these hungry dogs!' His face was gleaming with excitement.

The two guys looked around in a frenzied attempt to find an escape. However, if they wanted to remain the chevaliers they had been, they knew they wouldn't be able to run too far with those high-heeled beauties in tow.

The police car's doors opened quickly, and the two officers got out. Malik followed them, while Asrul sank back in the seat, not really knowing what to do. He felt awkwardly unable to move a single finger. What a miserable role model he was for the Nazi youth, he thought as he glanced at Malik's back through the windshield. The only thing he could do was stay here, within the security of the car's backseat, and watch the events unfolding outside.

One of the policemen flashed his torchlight into the face of one of the two immigrants, blinding him. The man turned his head to the side to escape the probing ray; the light then fell on one of the girls. She was a mask of silent terror: her face was shocked, trembling like an emotional pool whose surface was about to be shattered by the big, engulfing tsunami of her fear. The two looked like they both knew this would end badly for them. They exchanged a mutual gaze, without saying a word. To Asrul, it seemed like the man wanted to apologise for something he didn't commit, while the girl accepted his regret, gulping down. A second girl was clinging to the arm of the first, trying to hide behind her friend. Asrul couldn't yet see her face clearly, but he noticed how her generous cleavage rocked up and down, trying to contain her agitated breathing.

'Show me your passports, please,' said the first officer.

Asrul watched as the four immigrants slowly grouped together, their hands fishing inside pockets and handbags. The first man finally moved closer to the officer, clutching two little maroon books in his hand.

'We have only two, Encik. The girls didn't bring theirs. They have left theirs at home.'

Asrul heard these words knock against his side window as if a phantom limb had hit the glass with cold bone knuckles.

'Well, I can see we have a violation of the immigration rules here, Mister,' said the officer, grabbing the two passports and frantically turning its pages.

'Where is your visa?'

'Let me show you, Encik … I have work visa.'

Asrul saw that as the man tried to get closer and point to the right page, the policeman drew back and beamed the flashlight straight into the man's face, blinding him again.

'Do not move! I didn't tell you to move, you asshole!'

'We both have work visa ...' the two immigrant men gestured at each other, but the policeman seemed uninterested. Asrul saw how he kept glancing at one of the passport pages, letting time slide inexorably over the blade of the night. Asrul tilted his head to the left and saw Malik standing there, tall, his bald head upright in the dark, the skulls on his t-shirt shining in the dark, his hands thrust into his pockets. He was next to the second policeman and looked impatiently fierce, very out of place in that crime scene.

'I reckon you have to follow us to the police station.' Asrul turned back to see the officer's face blazing with weird anticipation.

Dear God, give me the power to decide what to do – the mental command didn't work. Asrul was still stuck inside the car, his legs completely unresponsive. He was seriously concerned. What if these immigrants made a police report and said that they had seen him and Malik hanging out with the cops? Things were going very wrong, and all because of Malik's need for an adrenaline rush. They had just gotten involved in the syabu trade; it was completely retarded to show their faces to the police now. He didn't understand how Malik could be so foolish; sure, they had some money to give to the cops, if that would settle it. But still, he was feeling like somebody had given him a bunch of soaking wet clothes to wear after a nice hot shower.

'What are you still doing in there? Come out!' Malik slapped his open hand against the roof of the police car. Asrul had no option but to get out, for he was afraid that his friend would probably drag him out otherwise.

'It's time to get out of that car, Asrul.' The voice sounded like an imperative command. Asrul decided to step out, trying to keep his face out of the flashing light's radius.

'Why are you so chickenshit, Adik?'

'Nothing. I'm scared.'

'Of what?'

'They are cops, Malik.'

'You see, Asrul, this is why you are and always will be a pussy. These cops are my friends. They think like me and you; they don't like this immigrant scum, and they aren't afraid to show it. What is wrong with that? They are on our side, Adik. Why do I have to explain all this to you like I was your fucking mother, Asrul? Open your eyes! Kuasa Melayu exists!'

Asrul felt, as usual, like the doormat Malik used to rub his boots clean on. In a way, he thought Malik was right, but on the other hand, he just hated him. He wanted to prove that he also had guts and balls; but so far, his every attempt had gone awry.

'Good. Don't answer me. I want to carry on with my mission, Asrul. Come along or watch, it is up to you. Either way you will be as responsible as each one of us; we are all involved.' Malik stormed off towards the policemen, leaving Asrul to stand by the side of the car, his face intermittently red in the car's flashing lights, looking like a clumsy clown from hell.

* * *

'Maafkan kami, Encik, but our documents are at home. We forgot, so sorry,' Ngoc tried to cry out in vain. She was shivering lightly, but not for the cold. She could feel that the two men were looking at the curves of her body, compressed under the tight dress. She felt so stupid for having decided to come out tonight, about not insisting that Cam meet Nyan in the daylight, somewhere safer. She knew how the Malaysian police could be damned evil, could ask for a bunch of money she definitely didn't have. Cam was standing behind her; she could feel Cam's arm getting cold and sticky against her back. She didn't dare looking at her, as she wanted to stay strong enough to cast away the officers' inquisitive stares; she was feeling their gaze unpleasantly running along her body, fondling her with their eyes.

'I'm sorry, lady, but you're asking me to avoid protocol. I said you come to the police station. Get in the car.'

'But, Encik, we have regular jobs and visas. I can prove that if you just let me walk back home …'

The cop shook his head slowly. 'You see, if I let you go now, I wouldn't be obeying the code of conduct, the protocol. What do your officers do in Vietnam, eh? I suppose that where you come from, the police don't do their jobs properly, for sure, as you are asking me to close my eyes to the law. You see, bribing a policeman is another very serious offence,' he laughed openly as he looked at the other policeman. Ngoc was confused. She saw two other guys standing behind the policemen, arguing. But they were too far for her to make sense of what they were fighting about. The strange thing was that they looked like anything but cops: they had shaven heads, wore boots, and one of them had sort of funny-looking braces fixed to the top of his t-shirt, which made him look like a big schoolboy. Had she been in another situation, she would probably have laughed at them; but now, the only laughter she heard was coming from the cop's mouth, a clattering of teeth thrown into a raucous throaty sound. She measured the distance between the cops and the corner, and she damned herself for having decided to put on those high heels to show off her freshly painted toenails. She had paid quite a fortune for it too, sitting at the shopping mall salon, her toes held by the rubber-gloved fingers of a Chinese girl in a face mask. Her shoes were traps; they wouldn't help her run, for sure. Shit. Why had she decided to be beautiful tonight? People are never beautiful on the day of their death, she thought, shuddering against Cam's slimy cold skin.

Than noticed that one of policemen was busy with his cell phone. Shortly after, another car came in and stopped just in front of the first one. Only a few hours ago, he had been very happy to know that Ngoc was also coming out with them for drinks; he thought she had a fantastic ass. And those boobs – oh my, he reckoned he had never seen anything like them in all of Mandalay. But now, the feeling that was slowly replacing his mental hard-on was of another kind: it was creeping, devouring fear. He had heard stories from his other Burmese worker friends: he knew that the cops were real pigs around here. Sometimes it was just about paying a small bribe, but other times, people had gone to the hospital because of them. They had been given cracked skulls, stitches, broken ribcages, even jail terms. Burmese didn't have much opportunity for retaliation, after all; what action could they take against the authorities when most of them had fled into Malaysia illegally from Thailand? Locked up in storage tanks and loaded onto boats, crossing the sea and landing at Langkawi. Or hiding in the back of freight trucks and bribing their way into Malaysia. They had no rights, and the police knew this very well. The cops loved this, apparently.

Two other men in plain clothes came out of the second car and approached the group. They wore nice clothes and shiny shoes; one of them moved to the side of the road with one of the police officers and started discussing something. As the man lit a cigarette, his face looked ghastly in the darkness. Judging by its shape though, Than recognised that the new arrival was another Malay man. The detail was confirmed when he overheard some of their exchange and found that they were speaking in Bahasa. The plainclothes man kept sucking fire from his cigarette in a relaxed way – small clouds of smoke were exhaled into the night, disintegrating quickly as they flew up.

'I'm sorry, but did you really ask me to avoid protocol? I said, you have to come to the police station. Get in the car, now.' The voice broke through Than's thoughts. As Cam started walking slowly towards the open door, Ngoc was dragged along too, as if she were the dead part of a pair of Siamese twins, attached shoulder to back. Than tried to walk towards them, but a cop ordered him to stop, extending his right arm just in front of Than's face.

'Nobody told *you* to get into any car. Stand back, I have a gun.' The man reached for his belt and extracted a revolver with his right hand, as he pointed the flashlight in Than's face with the left. Than immediately closed his eyes, stepped back and brought his hands up to his face to shield himself from the blinding light.

'What do you think you are going to do? Give me back my passport! I am a regular worker with a visa.' Than tried to fight back, still blind, but four hands grabbed him from behind. When he felt that he was being pushed down to the ground, he tried to resist by screaming and moving his arms about frantically, until a strong punch to his stomach's mouth tore the breath away from his lungs. The second strike hit him directly in the face and put him to sleep. He didn't know where Nyan was; he just blanked out, like a light bulb does when someone hits its switch.

* * *

When Nyan finally woke up, he felt like his whole side was bulging with pain. His hands had been tied together with duct tape; when he tried to move his legs, he realised that they had been given the same treatment. The two plainclothes officers were in the front seats, driving the car up a slope. He had been put in the back seat, wedged between two young men; one looked like he was in his mid-twenties. He looked quite muscular and had on a black t-shirt with pictures of skulls on it. Nyan had seen similar things back in Yangon – groups of teenagers playing loud music with electric guitars, something that had been becoming quite popular in Myanmar before he had left to work in Malaysia. On his right side sat another young man, similarly dressed, leaning against the window. His eyes were lost in the outside darkness, watching the palm trees that seemed like the eerie fingers of giant, protruding skeleton hands. Nyan noticed that both men had very short, shaven hair. This was not so common among Malays: Nyan had observed that when they started going bald, they generally wore a songkok.

Than wasn't there in the car with them, Nyan suddenly realised and his heart started thumping faster. He then thought of Cam. Where was she now? And why in this world had he accepted to walk her home that night? He kept pretending to be passed out, his eyes almost shut, letting his dead weight bounce between the young men's shoulders as the car rampaged uphill. After a few minutes, the car stopped as the terrain became flat once again.

'Here,' said one policeman, and they switched off the engine and got out, slamming the doors behind them.

The bigger, older man got out from the backseat first, leaving Nyan to rest against the other distracted man. After a heavy moment, Nyan was pushed to the side, and a noise of slamming plastic and metal informed Nyan that he was now alone in the backseat. Cold sweat ran down his back as his thoughts slipped down the sides of his brain, hoping to find a surface where he could cut the tape off his wrists. Instinctively, he moved his tied hands to the lower metallic extension of the front seat's sliding grid, rubbing them up and down, trying to break the tape open. As he was busy with this, trying to be silent and discreet, he heard the trunk open up with a metallic clank. He lifted himself up slowly and peeked through the rear window. The four men took something out of the trunk, then moved quickly towards the side of the road. Nyan looked out of the window, still trying to stay as hidden as he possibly could, and he could not believe what he saw. They were carrying Than, holding him by his four limbs. Than looked motionless. As the group approached the side of the road, Nyan realised that it opened dangerously over the edge of a deep cliff. He couldn't really see how deep the drop was from the inside of the car, and because of the pitch black darkness outside. The four men rocked Than's body back and forth a couple times and then, without a moment's thought, let him go. They threw him off. Nyan's felt his heart stop for a painful moment as he saw his friend's figure disappear into the night's unknown. He didn't even know if he was still alive. As he passed his tongue against his dried out lips, he realised they had no feeling anymore.

The four turned back and moved towards the car – to get him, he was sure. He quickly decided to pretend to be unconscious again. He hadn't still found a sharp enough object to tear the tape and free himself.

'OK – number two now,' said a voice. Nyan kept his eyes closed, thinking of Buddha, praying for his soul to be saved from certain death. He felt forty fingers pulling him off the seat, lugging his weight against a sea of air, parting and holding his limbs spread eagle. As they approached the cliff, he did not dare to open his eyes; he just kept silent, immersed himself in prayer. 'C'mon, move it … One, two …'

Oh yes, Lord Buddha, if I can get out of this alive, I will pray to you even more, every day, please help me now … I don't want to die, Nyan promised.

'… three …'

As he felt that his body was flying in the black air, Nyan instinctively brought his arms and legs into a foetal position and prayed again, for the cliff to be shallow, for its rocks to be as soft as those Chinese-made down jackets sold at the Mandalay Sunday Market.

* * *

Ngoc stopped crying. She realised that crying was just plain useless. She needed to contain herself, try to look tougher now. Otherwise, these two would crush her like an insect under their shoes. The car was slowly driving back from where the cops had stopped them along Burmah Road. She could see that the policeman in the passenger seat was looking at her from the rear-view mirror, without saying a word. Cam was holding her hand: the reflections of the passing lamp posts drew zebra lines across her face, disappearing intermittently. Ngoc saw that her friend still looked beautiful, even if she had fear spilling out of all her pores.

'Are you from Saigon?' the driver broke the silence and lowered his window a bit, letting some fresh breeze come in and slap Ngoc directly in the face.

'Is that important?' she said. Cam kept still and silent.

'OK, OK, I'm just trying to have a conversation here … So, how do you know those guys?'

'Work,' she looked outside. The profile of Datuk Keramat Road's police station was getting closer.

'Are you really going to take us to the police station?'

'Yes, of course. Where else would you like to go, ladies? Clubbing?' the cop laughed and looked at his colleague.

As Ngoc grew resigned to having to deal with the authorities, the car suddenly steered into a side alley and pulled over in an empty parking spot. As the driver turned off the engine, Ngoc's heart started beating faster. She looked at Cam, gulping down. 'What are we going to do?' she whispered in low Vietnamese.

The two policemen turned and looked at them with two pairs of inquisitive eyes.

'Going out with that Burmese scum is bad, not respectable for ladies like you. Don't you like Malay men?'

The two girls did not answer. The air was getting thicker. Ngoc could feel its electricity running up her nostrils at each breath.

'I said, don't you like Malay men? Malay men like Vietnam women, for sure.'

The two girls didn't reply. Cam tightened her grip around Ngoc's hand.

'So,' Ngoc finally regained some inner strength and talked in a soft, almost imperceptible voice, 'aren't we going to the police station?'

The driver laughed. He sounded mean. In Ngoc's mind, she stabbed him right in his eye with a knife and watched him die as she pushed the blade down into his skull, penetrating his brain. 'We can go. Of course we can go. But I'm giving you a good option, ladies. Police station means you go to jail. That's no good; will cause you a lot of problem. Work permit problem, everything problem. Otherwise …' he didn't continue, leaving the sentence open to an obvious interpretation.

'Otherwise, what?' Ngoc demanded, as if she didn't know.

The two policemen looked at each other and then smirked right into the girl's faces.

'Ladies, we have no time to waste. We're asking for a fair exchange. You see, we could throw you in jail and give the keys to the dogs, if we wanted. Also, we could decide to get what we want without asking for your permission.'

Ngoc's hand kept exchanging sweat with Cam's. The situation didn't seem real – it seemed like the kind of thing that they might overhear from someone else, who had been working in the country longer than they had. They would have never thought this stuff may just happen to them one day.

Cam finally spoke up. 'What do you want?' was all she could say, in a voice broken by the ripples of an oncoming outburst of tears.

'Ah, these Vietnamese girls are so stupid, lah!' the driver sighed at the other policeman. 'OK, I'll help you understand this: jail is bad, and my friend told me that when he travelled to Vietnam, the girls there can suck it very, very well. Now, we also want to give it a try. Understand, OK?' He didn't wait for an answer. He revved the engine, started driving into the night, as the other cop took out the gun and pointed it at their faces.

'And be very careful. Suck does not mean bite.'

Ngoc sank into the backseat, finally exploding in a suffocated cry. As she felt the salty tears dripping down her face, she felt much better. However, she couldn't stop sobbing as the car sped to a place she didn't want to remember for the rest of her life. As she looked straight at, and got sucked into, the cyclopic eye of the gun barrel, she knew this had to become their dirty little secret.

13

ASRUL HAD BEGUN to feel more comfortable each time they visited Mister Porthaksh's apartment. He started to kind of like the idea that on entering the premises of the apartment block and surpassing the security check-post, pushing the buttons to call upon the ever busy elevator, he was entering a Middle Eastern world tucked away inside his own. He loved to think of it as an Islamic matryoshka, a smaller box inside another bigger box. He had also started to feel more relaxed in front of the man himself.

'Well done, my friends,' Porthaksh wore a shiny blue silk shirt that conferred him the look of a marine creature, as if he belonged to a rare species of hairy fish floating in the livingroom's darkness. The great expanse of ocean outside the window reinforced Asrul's impressions, and he couldn't help but smile.

'I'm glad to see that you're getting accustomed to the job. Did you experience any discomfort so far? I need to know if you have any remarks about or suggestions for the operations.'

'Well, Mister Porthaksh ...' began Malik hesitantly.

They had been toying with this idea for a few days now, and they had agreed that it was time to throw it on the plate and see what the Persian had to say. He was the boss, after all.

'Mister Porthaksh,' Asrul erupted, exuding rare confidence, 'we do actually have a suggestion, if you don't mind listening to it. We have been discussing this idea for a few days, and would like to know your opinion: don't you think it would be better if we try dealing directly? I mean, we could increase the customer base through bypassing the area dealers?'

Porthaksh looked at him briefly, then thrust a hand into his pocket and pulled out a pack of cigarettes. He lit one carefully, raising the flame to the tobacco tip and sucking the fire smoothly.

'You mean, you want to sell on the streets,' he said, weighing the words.

'Yes, that'd be the idea, in brief. I think we have the right connections to make it worthwhile.'

'I'm not sure about that, Mister Asrul. It's a dangerous thing to do in this country, very careless.'

'We know,' Malik broke in, 'but we were also thinking, of course in your interest, that we could help you reach where you haven't arrived yet. We could help you sell more.'

'How?'

'We know many people, Mister Porthaksh. Youngsters, friends of friends, even outside of Penang.'

Porthaksh took the cigarette out of his mouth, puffed the smoke out like an impatient dragon, and leaned forward across the table, looking at them straight in the eyes.

'Let me be honest and clear, Mister Malik. I don't like this idea. It doesn't work like that. We're not a distribution company, let alone a bunch of unprofessional amateurs.'

He stopped to inhale a long drag of smoke, tightening his eyes. 'The business already kind of works as a distribution, if you wish, in the sense that we bring the drugs to a few ... well, let's call them "centres". People can go directly and get their bags. I'm not interested in developing this any further as it would be foolish at this point. You see, there are other forces working here, parallel to us ...' he suddenly stopped and retracted, puffing a white cloud in the darkness.

'Isn't the money I give you enough?' Porthaksh then asked. Malik and Asrul looked at each other and then back at the Iranian.

'Well, yes. This isn't really for the money. We're doing great now. Malik even bought a new car,' Asrul patted his friend on the back, emphasising this detail. 'We just thought we'd like to get more involved, Mister Porthaksh. That's why we came up with this idea, which you don't like. I think we kind of deserve to step up a bit. Driving to the border is frankly becoming a bit boring, if you know what I mean. We're hungry for growth.'

'I understand,' Mister Porthaksh relaxed against the couch. 'Sounds fair enough.'

He paused again, cupping his left hand under his chin, thoughtful. He then crushed the cigarette's roach into an overfilled ashtray. 'I can find something else for you guys, if you are really keen about moving forward. Let me explain how it works, and let's see if you think you can handle it. There's a catch, obviously: if you want to step up, you have to be careful and follow our rules, or you are out of the game.'

'But ...' Malik tried to speak, but Porthaksh, like a verbal executioner, cut off his voice.

'I'm afraid, there is no but. That's the first rule. If you want to climb up the ladder too quickly, you ought to fulfil your duties perfectly, Mister Malik, and take responsibility for your actions. That's how it works, at least back in Iran.' Porthaksh paused for a moment, looking first at Malik and then passing his gaze over to Asrul. He scanned them as if they were two lumps of raw opium, and he wanted to ascertain their correct market value.

'OK,' he finally erupted, fiddling with the top of his cigarette pack, without lifting his eyes from Malik and Asrul. Asrul was beginning to feel slightly disturbed on receiving such severe attention.

'If you really feel you are ready for something new,' Porthaksh continued, clasping a cigarette by its filter with his thumb and index fingers, 'there's something you can do for me tonight.'

The Iranian paused again. This man knew exactly how to build to an intense crescendo, Asrul thought. At the opposite side of the table, Asrul was waiting for more, trying to hide his anticipation.

'And that something is …?' Malik broke the silence, while sinking back into the sofa. Asrul noticed how his friend, too, was waiting for Porthaksh's further instructions.

'Well,' the Iranian puffed out a thin line of smoke in the air before them, 'I have this situation in Upper Penang Road. You know the place, right? It's where all the fancy clubs are.'

'Sure,' Malik nodded, while Asrul was still trying to locate the place on his mental map.

'Go to a club called Milky. That's where most of the clubbers go during the weekends. The place has got a sophisticated, rich, young crowd ... It's one of our most profitable distribution centres.' The Iranian leaned back and closed his right hand around his mouth, a cigarette nestled in between his index and middle fingers; he sucked at it leisurely. Asrul was so focussed on the man that he could almost taste the smoke in his own mouth, feel it go down his own lungs.

'There's a guy working there at the bar. He's our link, a Chinese bloke named Yew.' Before he went on, Porthaksh leaned forward to drop his cigarette's ash into a clean ashtray sitting on the coffee table. As he moved, he gazed intensely at Asrul for a short moment. Asrul felt his mouth grow dry, and he instinctively leaned back to put a more comfortable distance between his face and the Iranian's. The two skinheads remained sitting against the couch, without speaking a single word.

'Look for this guy,' Porthaksh's voice exploded again, washing Asrul with words that felt like molten lava flowing down his back of neck. 'Bring him to me, here. I want to ask him a few questions, as he's been later than usual with his payments.' As he said this, the Iranian leaned forward again and looked intensely at Malik. Asrul felt his friend squirming against the back of the sofa. Then, Porthaksh slowly shifted his gaze to Asrul again: under the direct illumination of the lamp, Asrul saw how powerful the man's eyes were.

'Bring Yew here, do a clean job. Very simple instructions. This is the next step up the ladder you're climbing, boys.' Porthaksh sanctioned their pact by crushing his cigarette into the ashtray. As the fire died away, sizzling against the dark ceramic, Asrul felt as if the Iranian was rubbing the cigarette's flaming tip against his spinal cord. His legs twitched before he could stop them.

* * *

It all seemed quite simple to Asrul. The drugs arrived from the Middle East, somehow. Porthaksh didn't want to tell them more about this for the time being. Some of the biggest buyers were Thai, and that was why they had to take the shipments up to the border regularly. He didn't know where the stuff ended up once they left it at Padang Besar. In addition, the organisation used some public places where customers could go to and buy the drugs directly; Porthaksh had explained that his people controlled a few nightclubs and a couple of massage parlours. And, surprisingly enough, there were a number of supermarkets involved as well. It was a small web of retailers scattered all around Penang Island and the Prai: one at Bayan Lepas, one at Air Hitam, a small one at Batu Ferringhi, some in Bukit Mertajam and, of course, in the city centre of Georgetown. In a way, Asrul's conscience felt dirtied with sin – he felt like he was poking God straight in the eye by being involved in this trade. He was helping spread the sin, the Devil's intoxicants.

'How do you feel about this, Malik?' he asked his friend, as they drove out of Sungai Dua, on the coastal road to Georgetown. Malik had bought a nice used car with the money he had made thus far, and there was still quite a lot left over in the bag.

'I mean, how do you feel about doing the Devil's work?'

'What do you mean?' he overtook an old lorry that was buzzing along the middle lane.

'Well, we're helping this man deal drugs all over this country, Abang. Syabu is a super intoxicant, isn't it? We're going against our own faith … don't you think so? I can't help but feel dirty.'

Malik cracked into laughter as Asrul said this.

'Don't you think we'll be punished for this, Abang?'

Malik looked at him for a moment before concentrating on the road once again, manoeuvring the car around the hundreds of cars that came in from all directions in the usual late-evening traffic jam.

'I think we're serving God by crushing all these infidel scum, sending them back to where they belong: into the trash. Think about it this way – are we using the drugs?'

'Hell no!'

'Exactly. We're giving this stuff to feed those same people who don't follow our God, dear Asrul. It's all part of the great plan, for ultimate Islamic domination. The day I see you using that shit, Adik, I swear on God's name that I'll tear your head from your neck and eat your bowels directly from the hole. You've been warned.' He kept driving; Asrul thought that everything Malik had said made perfect sense. He glanced at the car's digital clock and saw a '6.53' shining in green flashy stick-lines.

'Stop the car, Abang,' he said, looking happily at Malik, feeling comforted.

'Why should I?'

'See, we're next to Tesco. Please turn into the parking lot and go to Bukit Dumbar. There's a nice mosque over there. Maghrib is in about ten minutes. I want to stop there and pray.'

'OK, good idea, Adik …' Malik put the signal to the left and entered the elbow junction just in time, speeding up the hill as people pushed their carts through Tesco's sliding doors, following their own calls for materialistic prayers.

When they had finished kissing the floor, Asrul met Malik back at the car.

'Let's go home. I want to relax for a while before we get going tonight.'

'Fine, Abang. Give me a couple of hours though. I need to go and see Siti …'

Malik didn't say anything, but only stared through the windshield, concentrating on the people moving swiftly in and out of the mosque's main entrance, filling the floor space with their scattering shoes.

'You should not mess with women before you fight, Asrul.'

'Well, I have to see her. If I don't, she might suspect I am up to something strange. It's Saturday night.'

'I see that you are getting hard headed, Mister Goat – a good and a bad trait, that is. Remember, we have to get to the club at midnight. We need to catch the guy as soon as he finishes his shift. If he's gone when we arrive, it means we have screwed up completely, and we are done for.'

'I know. I'll not be late, Malik.'

'I hope so. I will not sit here and watch you shatter an empire just because of some tits, Adik – remember that. If that happens, you'll become my enemy. We'll no longer be friends, I warn you.'

As Malik started the car and drove out of the parking lot, joining the line of vehicles buzzing down the hill, Asrul realised he had had enough of his friend's constant nagging. He silently leaned back in the passenger seat and let his mind fly high into Siti's arms, disconnecting his mind from the body trapped in Penang's evening traffic un-flow.

14

HE SHOWERED DOWN the last few glasses into his mouth nervously, letting the water create a whirlpool inside him: this had become his closing-time cleansing ritual every night for the past couple weeks. Never trust a friend: that was the moral of his stupid story. He had trusted his good friend Tan Moe with all this because he had said they would be stronger working together. Tan Moe had promised that they could turn their portions of mongrel's food into a much fleshier, saucier leg bone. All they would need to do, Tan Moe had suggested, was to keep a few bags off every shipment, cut them with chemicals to mount the syabu and then sell it privately to other customers. And, that's exactly what they had done. Nobody had realised that they were making money off Sio Sam Ong's stuff by lacing it. The club's customers hadn't complained either, and neither had the couriers. Tan Moe's plan had indeed worked. And then, Tan Moe had come up with the idea to retain one full shipment, cut it with their shit, and shave off the extra profit, keep it for themselves. Yew had never fully understood why his friend had wanted to do such a thing. Yew had been afraid of biting the very same hand who'd been feeding them for so long. He was more comfortable keeping up with the dutiful and ceremonious licking he was used to, having his wet mongrel tongue caress the expert old hand of the drug trade. He knew the hand would slap them hard if they messed with it, crushing them like mosquitoes.

'Wait and see, bro, this is going to be huge!' Tan Moe had insisted though, and had pushed him into committing treason day after day. It had seemed like Tan Moe was being pressed down by some other problem, which he didn't want to spill out to Yew. Yew was sure that someone else was breathing down Tan Moe's neck – breathing a sticky, black breath that was tainting the white of his friend's eyes and was forcing him into doing such things. Tan Moe, however, had convinced Yew to look at it from a very logical perspective – it was just a matter of taking a cut of the profits. They were paying back the organisation their forty grand as they usually did, and were only keeping the extra sauce for their own pockets. Though, on the one hand, Yew knew very well that the job was a dangerous one, on the other, he felt like Tan Moe was right. He had finally caved in when his friend had offered to take care of doing all the selling outside the club.

'Just let me handle it, and cover my shifts at the bar,' he had said, adding that he would pay him the balance of what was due to Sio Sam Ong in a week's time. Yew could earn his share anyway by staying put at the club, Tan Moe had said.

The problem was that Yew never saw the bloody cash. And now he was extremely late on his payment. He had not been able to pay them back for two weeks now. The first time, they had come in after two days. They had sent a girl. She had looked like a foreigner to him. She had come in and sat at the bar, had ordered a strong drink. He had never seen her before, but from the way she had nodded cheerfully at whatever he had said, he had thought he would get lucky that night, that she might help him forget all this shit for just one night. She had been waiting for him until the end of his shift, hooking him in with those big brown eyes and their flesh-melting powers. And when she had followed him to the back and he had motioned for her to take a seat at the back of his new bike, he had felt a winner. Then, she had simply smiled at him and politely asked, 'Why you didn't pay them yet?' Yew had pretended that he had not understood what she was saying. So, she had said it again. And she had told him that he had better hurry up, or the next time, they wouldn't want to be so nice, wouldn't send over an angel to warn him. The next time, they would send in a demon from hell, with iron claws ready to tear his heart out. After that, Yew had tried to get hold of Tan Moe. First, he had gone over to his place to look for him but had found it locked. He had returned to the house again, every bloody day, at different times, for more than a bloody week, but Tan Moe's place remained locked. Yew had then decided to contact Tan Moe's girlfriend. He had driven his motorbike down to her place, an apartment she shared with a Chinese girl who worked as an event promoter.

'Let me in!' Yew knew she was in there. He had stood at her door, knocking intermittently for a few minutes before he had finally heard a sound. That girl. He had never liked her. Yew knew that she had been the main reason why Tan Moe had taken up the whole drug thing so seriously. This was a costly habit, and it seemed like she could never have enough of it. When Yew had first met him in high school, Tan Moe had not been like that. He had been a regular guy, one of those people you would never notice until he had accidentally stepped on your foot. In fact, Tan Moe had been such a wallflower that when Yew had to move to Kuantan to go to university, he had quickly and completely forgotten about him. Upon his return, and upon joining his old circle of friends, he had met Tan Moe again. But it was like he had met a completely different person. An alien from outer space.

'So, how have you been in Kuantan, Yew?' Tan Moe had asked him, taking off a pair of sunglasses that Yew could have never imagined being appropriately placed on top of his friend's conventional face. But that mug, it was not the same anymore – Tan Moe had turned into the kind of guy who could walk into a dark room wearing those sunglasses, and still look cool. Something had changed about him, something big had turned him inside out. It was as if even the contours of his features had changed, had become abruptly sharp, as if his muscles were tied up over a set of bones that were made for a man of bigger size. Tan Moe looked like his profile could cut through things, like it was a shark's tooth wrapped inside of a black leather vest.

'Tan Moe? It's been a long time ... you look so different,' that was all Yew had been able to say when his old friend had come closer, put a hand on his shoulder and burst into short laughter. His goatee looked so inappropriately stapled at the end of that sharp chin, Yew had observed.

'I was lucky man ... I've been to Australia ... One year Down Under. Well, it changed my perspective. Completely. Can you imagine that?' Tan Moe pulled back his arm and smiled. 'Would you like to hear some stories, Yew? You look shocked, man. Come, have a drink with me ... We have a lot to catch up on.'

And that was when Yew had met this creature, the one that had just opened the door and stood shaking before him. Back then, she had looked gorgeous.

'What do you want?' she muttered, leaning against the door, her pale body shaking under a white shirt and a pair of cotton panties. She was in dire need of a few bags. Yew gave her some to calm her down, before asking his questions. Apparently, their fucking friend had disappeared, couldn't be found anywhere, and had left her there, in the worst dump she could be in. That bastard, she kept saying. They both thought Tan Moe had fled somewhere for good, with the money he had made from all that lacing. She knew about their plan because she'd had been helping all along. She had many friends. Girls. Models. Dancers. Regardless of the sales, Yew was left with less than half the cash he needed to pay off this round to Sio Sam Ong.

'So what? What do you want me to do? I've got no money to give you, dear Yew,' she told him, hissing like a snake as the syabu started to turn her skin back into its usual colour, and life was slowly reignited within her intoxicated centre. He needed 40,000 ringgit. It wasn't an incredible sum, but he couldn't just walk into Maybank and ask for it, damn it.

He had been controlling the club's door every night and had informed the bouncer to alert him whenever a Middle Eastern-looking person entered the premises. 'Don't ask me why,' Tan Moe had told the bouncer. 'Just do it.' There were some small windows in the toilet cubicles, which could take to the back lane and the parking lot behind the club: he could easily sneak out through them. In fact, he was skinny enough to let himself out through the club's air ducts if he had to. He needed to be extremely careful. He should be like Tan Moe, he had decided, should just fuck everyone and flee the country. He couldn't just go to Mister Chang and say that he had screwed up, had handed out the bags like free gifts. He would, at the very least, have his fingers cut off. Tomorrow morning, yes. He would apply for his passport; he had finally decided to do it. The 40,000 ringgit he owed them was not worth suffering so much for.

* * *

'Please, this way. Have fun.'

The bouncer showed them in. A swarm of high-heeled, miniskirted Chinese teenagers, their hand bags rocking on their arms, rushed in, along with him, through the club's doorway, showing far too many centimetres of their perfectly beautified legs. Asrul had rarely seen so much naïve poshness before. It was so different from the growling apes he was used to head-banging to and with, and he felt a little confused among the towering stilettos and the curves barely contained by the small, tight dresses. Some of the girls were so young that they could hardly walk straight on their foot-binding torture towers. Their skin was as white as pure milk; Asrul couldn't help but notice this as he entered the doorway and descended the stairs into an increasing volume of pounding techno beats. Although he hated the place, he was mesmerised by its smells of fresh shampoo and party-ready body odours. The room was lit in red, a big strobe intermittently spraying light waves on the dark walls and the frantically shaking female bodies. It seemed that men, if present, had preferred to chameleonise themselves into the walls and let the room be the realm of a tribe of sexual sirens. This was so unreal, captivating and different from what Asrul had experienced so far.

'Here he is,' Malik pointed his thumb at the bar. A Chinese guy was quickly manoeuvring glasses under the cover of the cocktail-making station.

'That's our boy.'

They pushed their way through the side of the dance floor, navigating between dancers and hands carrying drinks. At the centre, groups of ladies danced by moving their upper bodies to the thumping rhythms, their feet planted firmly on the chequered aluminium platform beneath them. As the strobe bulb flashed with electric life, their moves transformed into a frantic, open AK-47 machine gun fire of black and white photograms.

Meanwhile, the bartender washed his hands, pulled his apron off and slid out of the aisle.

'Quick!' Malik screamed to make himself heard over the thumping low frequencies. Yew was heading to the restrooms. The two swerved off, breaking the seal of two foxy mini-skirted Venuses holding hands and rushed to the men's room without apologising. They knew that the guy wasn't heading in there for a quick piss.

As they had expected, the restroom was empty. One chubby guy peeked at them from a mirror distractedly, as he finished washing his hands and moved out. Asrul quickly closed the door and blocked it shut by placing a mop under its handle. They walked softly in front of each and every cubicle, carefully listening to every sound. As Malik neared the central cubicle and noticed it was locked, he heard a clatter coming from inside it. Without thinking twice, he slammed into the flimsy door, charging at it with his right shoulder; the lock broke open. 'Come back here!' Malik thundered as he disappeared into the cubicle, and Asrul heard another voice cry out loudly. Asrul ran to the door and saw Malik pulling a guy by his legs, taking him down, for he was stuck halfway in the air-vent window just above the toilet seat.

Malik pulled the guy down until he fell to his knees, slamming his chest against the toilet. He remained there, hugging the toilet bowl and lamenting pain. A good couple of minutes passed before he regained his senses.

'Who the fuck are you both?' he cried, holding his chest.

'Batman and Robin,' Malik laughed, grabbing him by the neck and pushing him back against the wall. 'Who do you think we are?'

The guy protected his face with both hands, shaking. Asrul stood at the doorstep, making sure his spread legs blocked any exit from the cubicle.

'Why did you want to run away, Mister? Don't you know is very impolite to do so?'

'I am sorry ... Really, fuck, I came here just for a piss before I got off work. What do you want?'

'So why were you trying to escape then?' Asrul burst out in the most menacing tone he could manage.

'What would you do if you heard someone closing the restroom door and check out each one of the cubicles? I was scared, of course!' He answered as Malik tightened the grip, suffocating the Chinese guy with his own shirt collar.

'Don't fuck with me!' Malik head-butted the guy in his forehead, and he slid from the wall to the floor as his legs got instantly stripped of their control.

'No, please! I'm sorry. I didn't want to do it. It's Tan Moe's fault; you have to get him, not me, please …' He was crying. Asrul moved a step forward and put his head inside the cubicle, as if this could help him better understand the Chinese guy's accent.

'Who the hell is Tan Moe?' The guy curled himself up on the floor, without saying a word, shaking.

'Now, you better talk,' Malik said and kicked him lightly in his side, just to make him react. 'We've got no time to waste with you here. Where is the bloody money? You get it to me, and I walk out of this shit dump right now. You don't, and you're going to cry.'

'I don't have the money. It's Tan Moe –'

Asrul looked first at Yew, and then at Malik. The expression draped over his friend's face did not clarify the situation any further. Malik remained still, looking down at the Chinese guy on the floor.

'OK, no money? Give us the drugs back then,' Asrul suggested.

'How do you know about all this? Who are you? You are not Persian …' The Chinese guy's eyes became bigger as he made this vain observation. Malik, who until now looked like he had been petrified, finally broke his silence.

'We are the new kids on the block, and we've come to get what is ours, or to kick your ass. Now ...' Malik bent down and got very close to Yew's face, '... if you don't want to co-operate, I will be forced to hurt you more. Do you understand?'

The Chinese guy coiled into the corner between the wall and the toilet. The window was still open and brought in a nice breeze from the outside, his lost chance for freedom. The thumping music echoed from the other side of the cubicle, shattering in waves against the cubicle's plywood walls.

'Abang, let's get going,' Asrul said. 'We can't leave that door shut for too long, or people will understand what's happening, and the bouncers will be on us!'

'Sure, let me just teach some good manners to this cockroach here,' he squatted down and took the metallic cord of the toilet hose in his hand.

'You see, I told you. We like swift, cooperative people.' Malik grabbed the guy by the hair and pulled him down as he rolled the hose around his neck. He started tightening the cord's noose with both hands. Yew's face became cyanotic, and he tried to grasp the metal hose with both hands. But he couldn't; he was suffocating.

'Abang! You're killing him!'

A gurgling sound came out of the Chinese's throat as his eyes dilated and his face turned almost purple.

'Not yet Asrul. The best is yet to come.'

* * *

'Why you closed the door for so long? I need to piss,' a chubby guy shouted at Malik and Asrul just as the door opened. 'What the ...' the man froze as he saw the two skinheads push out the breathless Chinese man, his shirt torn, his body dripping wet from his knees up.

'Move on, fatty. Now you can go in and sprinkle. Piss off.'

And then there they were again, hurling themselves into the frenzied madness of shaking hips and promises of casual sex and rides in expensive sports cars being whispered into deafened eardrums. It seemed to Asrul like they were too small to make any impression among all those electrified bodies.

'Come in the front. Don't make it obvious,' Malik ordered Asrul.

They moved quickly to the far side of the dance floor, pushing against the soft bodies, disentangling the newly formed acquaintances of limbs, steamrolling their way through the pungent clouds of perfume. Asrul could see the exit. He started thinking of what to say to the bouncer once they had reached the top of the stairs. At the same time, he scanned the bar: it looked like nobody had noticed yet that Yew had left. He had finished his shift, after all. Malik was pushing Asrul from behind, while he held Yew's arms crossed at the back, handcuffed into his own hand's grip.

'Go, go, get out of here ...'

They were about three metres from the stairs when two black guys barred their way. They stepped in abruptly from the side, looking down at them: they had nice clothes on, and one of them wore shades even though he was inside the club.

'Stop there, bro,' thundered one of them, 'the guy's ours.'

'What do you want?' Asrul retraced a few steps, and Malik stopped pushing him, while holding Yew back. This man was their trophy tonight, and they didn't want to hand him to anyone else.

'I said, move along and give us the guy. He's ours.' The black guy spoke in a slurred, heavy accent. Asrul was almost sure that he was African. He saw Malik roll Yew under his armpit and stand there staring intensely at the new arrivals. Some girls passed by chattering, and for a moment, Asrul got lost in their blinding perfume and plunging necklines.

'Listen, Chocolate, do you really think I'll come here, do all the dirty work and then hand this man to you? It's not yet Christmas, my dear … May I know who the fuck you are?'

The Africans tilted their heads back, insulted.

'Give us the guy. Don't get us angry.'

'You don't understand,' Malik smirked, his voice almost submerged by the club's bass frequencies. Asrul's stomach buzzed with retro static waves.

'This is our catch. Piss off and get out of my way.'

One of the two African guys stepped closer and Malik promptly shielded Yew, stretching his right arm over the man. Asrul advanced in defence, but felt a bit goofy, pins and needles impaling his feet – however, he knew he didn't want to let go of their catch, didn't want to act like a loser anymore.

'Fuck off,' said one the black guys and rushed in headfirst.

Malik quickly threw Yew into Asrul's arms, grabbed the African by his jacket's collar and pushed him back towards the exit. The other black guy, who had been standing silently until then, dove in to help his friend, pushing him back into Malik –

the five men obstructed the entrance to the dance floor, engaged in a strange kind of tug of war. The people around them began to sense that things were about to go really wrong in the club.

'Move it!' the black guy punched Malik in the side of the head. Malik retraced and then blasted forward, headfirst, head-butting the African between the nose and the upper lip. The man was thrust back, a sleek line of blood flew into the air and then splashed against his nice outfit. He stood there holding the lower part of his face, blood sprouting like black petals from the cracks of his closed barrier of fingers. Asrul understood that Malik had probably broken the black man's nose, and he started feeling a sense of excitement warming him up, rising from the tips of his boots. He pushed forward. This was a chance to show his worth.

'Now, get out of our way,' Malik gripped Yew's shoulder more firmly and went forward again, hell-bent for the exit, thrusting into the men like a battling ram. He hit the wounded African in the chest, pushing him down against the other one, who fell to the side. Asrul and Malik moved forward even as the two black guys got back on their feet and ran after them, angrily, like bulls running to the red cloth.

'Don't move!'

Asrul heard a thundering voice from behind and turned just in time to see what was coming. He immediately grabbed Malik's neck, pushing him down to the floor. The African had a gun, and it was directly pointed at their necks, only two metres behind them.

'Down! Shit, get down! He's got a gun!'

The detonation made them both deaf. Malik flew forward,

crashing against a bunch of sofa chairs. Asrul was still on the ground when he saw that the gunshot had cracked open the sanity shell of that place, as if the African had shot in front of a lake full of migratory birds. Panic exploded like a nail bomb in the club – everyone inside was hit by shrapnels of terror. Girls started screaming and running for the exit, their high heels clattering against the aluminium floor. The bouncers didn't know what was going on and were uncertain about what they had to do, their eyes rolling about in spirals. It was a good moment to exploit, to get the hell out of there.

They saw that one of the two Africans was still holding out his gun, his other hand still pressed against his bleeding face. The other man stood there, lost, bouncing against the flow of screaming souls rushing to the exit.

Yew was lying face down on the floor. A black hole spat blood from his upper back, soaking his dark shirt in a brownish colour. A stream of red was stretching from his side, growing like a red shadow, funnelling down the tiles' edges into a small pool.

Malik got up.

'Shit!'

As Asrul got back on his feet and reached for Malik, a screaming girl ran into his chest and fell back, hitting her head on the floor. Her friends gathered around her, blocking the wave of people trying to get out. The African was about to shoot again. Malik, who was busy getting out of the bunch of chairs he had crashed into when he had fallen to the floor, was the target. Asrul acted fast. He grabbed a stool and rushed forward, pushing it at full force into the African's side. He didn't know what he had hit for the second explosion from the man's gun rocked him back again. He heard the black man screaming. When he raised his head, Asrul realised he may have broken the gunman's wrist, as he saw him holding it tightly, while bleeding profusely from the nose. They didn't have enough time to understand what was happening.

'Malik! Get out! *Get Out!*' Asrul grabbed his friend's shirt and pulled him towards the door, thrusting against the column of mad people who were in a rush to get to the outside world. He pulled Malik as hard as he could, moving up the stairs and knocking down a few girls who fell back, slipping off their platform shoes, spraining ankles, showing panties. As the night's fresh air punched him in the face, Malik came to his senses again, became functional.

'Shit, who the fuck were they?'

'I don't know! Run! Just run!'

As they moved quickly towards Penang Road, dispersing into the crowd of bar hoppers, white backpackers looking for a piece of Asian love and street beggars parked next to sleeping rickshaw drivers, they heard the police sirens closing in. They ran through the junction and across Red Garden's parking lot, quickly dodging the notes of the Chinese karaoke band playing a terrible rendition of 'Saturday Night Fever'. The not-so-young dancer threw forth a set of stiff moves that reminded Asrul of a cop directing traffic. And then they were in the darkness of Muntri Street, running out into the night. They were free. With no bullet holes on their bodies.

15

Mister Porthaksh looked extremely worried.

'You are saying that two African guys came out of nowhere, wanted to get the Chinese guy from you, and when you refused, they fought back and then started shooting?'

'Yes, exactly in that order,' said Malik. Porthaksh looked for a cigarette inside its packet and couldn't find any, so he crushed the packet within his clenched fist.

'Nigerians!' he spat and then fell back silent, his face growing paler and more worried.

'What about Nigerians, Mister Porthaksh? You never told us anything about them. They had guns. They wanted to kill us!' Asrul sprayed verbal bullets across the table. 'Dying was not included in our fucking contract!'

'They're my rivals. They're also controlling part of the drug trade, those smart motherfuckers. Well, the cake is too huge for us to be the only ones baking it, if you understand what I mean.'

'OK, Mister Porthaksh. At this point you need to tell us what the hell is going on. Or we can't be sure where we might have to go with this story.'

The Persian assistant came out of the bedroom with a new pack of cigarettes and then deposited a clean ashtray and lighter on the table. Porthaksh slid one out of the box and lit it up, his hands shaking lightly.

'The Chinese. The problem is there. That club had two bartenders; they were our dealers. The place is very popular. We had always been able to sell a lot of bags through that outlet. Mister Chang is my guarantee there, a highly qualified professional. But you see, something went wrong with those two small fish, those bartenders ... Well, if you're telling me that one of them is dead, where is the other one?'

'Good question. How could I possibly answer you if this detail is being disclosed to me only now, after I risked my bloody ass out there?' Malik spat out.

'You see,' Mister Porthaksh continued, 'the Chinese, so far, had been of great help. They are the biggest consumers in the state, and they also distribute outside. Sio Sam Ong – have you ever heard about that?'

'Nope.'

'It's the local Triad group. Bukit Mertajam was a hotspot for them up to the late 1970s. Back then, you would never have been able to do anything on this island if you didn't go and ask for their permission and give them their share. I'm from the Middle East; I need to cover my back. They have been a trustworthy organisation to deal with so far – they work neatly, no problems with money whatsoever. Well, as long as they are paid on time ...'

He sucked on the cigarette, pausing. Asrul and Malik were listening with rapt attention, like school kids enhancing their involvement into the criminal world.

'They generally sell our stuff from that club. The people who dance there like syabu a lot, they give it to the girls and make them all hyped up for sex. You know what I mean ... that's a thing with their type. Generally, we collect our share every two weeks. I send a man there, and the bartender gives him the money. During my time here, we have never had any problem with this – until about three weeks ago, that is. Our guy went in as usual, and the bartender made excuses and gave him only a little bit of cash. He said there had been a problem with the shipments, which I totally didn't believe – Sio Sam Ong doesn't work like that. They are extremely precise because they require your total precision in return. I suspected that one of those two small fishes wanted to jump the gun, you know what I mean? Who knows what goes through their heads; they are the last ring in the chain. I didn't want to report this to Mister Chang. Not yet. But now, I'm afraid I have to, because we have a fucking big problem. One of them has turned up dead ... Did you know that the police are on the hunt now? Do you realise what have you started?'

'We? And hold on, sorry, but who is this Mister Chang?'

'A gentleman whom you would not want to meet, dear Asrul. Because if you do meet him, you will be surrounded by guns and knives. What you just went through at the club is fucking kindergarten.' Mister Porthaksh crushed the roach in the ashtray. The edges of his mouth sagged, as if old age had come about abruptly to claim its toll.

'Now, we have three problems. The Nigerians are onto something. Mister Chang will want some explanations, and that's my business. And, last, the police are after you. I'm sure somebody at the club must have given out your description, as you're always so unmistakably dressed like that ...'

Malik smiled, softly. 'The police are not a problem. I have connections there.'

Mister Porthaksh did not look surprised. 'I know. Why do you think I chose you?'

Malik's smile transformed into a small circle of surprise. 'How do you ...'

'Did you really think I hired you without doing my own homework? Mister Malik, Asrul. Don't dream big; learn to sit firmly in your present chairs, before you try to sit where you are not supposed to. Trust this old man – the wrong chair can grow fangs and eat your asses off. You still do not really know who you are dealing with. Somebody has already jumped the gun, and if he's not dead yet, he will be soon. This shit is serious and you are wading waist deep in it by now. Once it gets to your neck, it's like quicksand: there's no way out.' He looked at the two skinheads with a paternal expression. 'I like you two because you do what I ask you to, and you do it right. This situation was utterly unexpected, and I am extremely sorry about that. Now, we have to get this behind us, and make sure that things go on smoothly henceforth. I already have a good plan. Malik, tomorrow you fly to Johor Bahru. I have already booked a ticket for you.'

'Eh? I'm going down there for what?'

'First, to be safe and to stay away from Penang for a while. Don't worry, you'll be taken care of over there. And second, you need to help my man, Mamouhd, take care of some shipments up to the Singapore border. It's a learning curve, Malik; Johor Bahru is not as easy as Padang Besar. You wanted to move up the ladder, right? Here it is then, your golden ticket.'

'So we are going to Johor Bahru?' burst in Asrul, excited and worried at the same time.

'Nobody said you were going along,' Mister Porthaksh broke the spell. 'You are, in fact, going to Kuala Lumpur.'

'What? KL?'

'Yes, is that a problem?'

'No, it's just that I've never been there …'

'… and, also, you don't drive, do you?'

'Not really. Malik bought the car; I have no licence yet.'

Mister Porthaksh looked amused now. 'OK, I know you're a good boy. Besides, you have proved yourself very valuable tonight. Just take a bus to Pudu Sentral, and I'll send a man to pick you up when you get there, OK? You'll be taken care of.'

'Thanks. And what do I have to do there? Bring some bags?'

'Nothing like that. You're going to the airport to pick up a lady.'

'A woman? For what?'

'Be very careful with this assignment, Asrul. She's a very special lady, and very valuable to my organisation. You better take care of her and help her get settled into the country. She's from China.'

'Ah … A Chinese woman?'

'Yes. Please treat her with great respect. You can learn a lot from her; she's a very able professional. I will see you both back here in about a week. Report to me every day – I'll give you a special SIM card, just for our own communication. Be careful with how and what you speak there; don't act like kids, please. My men there will help you out with whatever you might need. Meanwhile, I'll try to calm the waters around here. And Malik ...'

'Yes?'

'Don't even think about informing your contacts regarding what happened tonight, or about where you are going, OK? If you do, I will know in a matter of hours, and you will be in big trouble. Please understand this: those people are fine as long as you just need them to beat up some poor immigrants but in the situation that you two are in now, they are as useful as toilet paper is when one doesn't need to shit. Am I clear on this point? Don't mess things up more than they already are. By the time you both come back, I will have settled everything.'

'OK,' Malik answered, scorned.

As they were putting their boots back on, ready to step out of the house, Mister Porthaksh offered them a final piece of advice: 'Please grow some hair on those heads of yours. Try to look different. Your style has been way too recognisable so far. Stop acting like stupid teenagers.'

Malik grunted as he tied the last string around his left boot. The two of them headed out.

KUALA LUMPUR

16

HE HAD NEVER been to Kuala Lumpur before. As he stepped off the bus and walked out of the shiny gates of Pudu Sentral, moving down the buzzing escalator and getting deposited at Jalan Pudu was quite a thrill. What he saw popped the cherry of his city life experience: the shapes of skyscrapers condensed into that tiny road, the revving engines, the attacks of a million ticket sellers, taxi drivers and general sidewalk practitioners on the prowl for something kampong. And the last one was totally like him, Asrul thought.

'Butterworth? You going to Butterworth? Bus ticket?'

'No, thanks. I have just come from there.' He needed to find his driver, as Mister Porthaksh had instructed he do.

It was not long before the driver found him.

'Asrul?'

'Yes ... And you are?'

'Azad, Mister Porthaksh's chauffeur. Please follow me.'

Asrul walked to the roadside, where a nice BMW was waiting for him. The engine was still on, the car's side lights still flashing.

'Please, get inside.' The driver, a short Persian in a black jacket and a silky maroon shirt, pressed a button on a small remote he held, and the doors unlocked automatically. Asrul took a seat at the back. It was cosy and comfortable, and he felt a bit out of place sitting there in his unkempt shirt and jeans. The car left, immersing itself in the stream of traffic ahead. The driver manoeuvred along the city centre and finally took a road going south, disentangling himself from a line of waiting vehicles. They were moving in the direction of Kuala Lumpur International Airport.

'What time's the flight supposed to land?'

'At 2 p.m. We still have some time. You can't drive, can you?'

'No, not really. Planning to learn soon, actually.'

'Ah, OK,' Asrul liked the way the forest, still looking potently green, had been pushed to the sides of the concrete strip they were driving upon. He wondered if every capital city in the world was like this. Azad glanced at him through the rear-view mirror and continued chatting.

'It's a big mess up in Penang, right? Don't worry, I'll take care of you here.'

'You've been informed of everything, haven't you, Azad?'

'Certainly, Asrul. And I'm glad you are still alive, by the way. Those Nigerians are a problem: Kuala Lumpur is full of them, too. It seems like they never want to go away. Those rascals enter the city on student visas and as you may guess, not many end up in the classrooms. The girls, most of them, you can find at Bukit Bintang, fishing for clients or hidden out in most of the brothels. The guys, well, you have seen what they are capable of doing …'

'Yes, I'd never had a gun held to my face before, I can tell you that.'

'Doesn't feel good, does it?' Azad overtook a passing lorry and approached the highway exit for Subang Jaya.

'So, do you know anything about this lady?'

'Who? Miss Ming Fei?'

'Is that her name?'

'Oh, yes. She's a pro, Asrul. She has already become a great asset for our business.'

'From China, right?'

'Yes. She's flying in from Chengdu, but I'm not sure where she's really from. China is one big country, you know, three or four times the size of Iran ... And Iran is quite big by itself.'

'You said she's a pro ... A professional in what though?'

'International relations – let's just put it that way,' Azad broke into a low laughter that painted two rows of good teeth across the rear-view mirror. Now that the heavy traffic had dispersed, the car was speeding on the highway; Asrul buzzed with anticipation in the back seat, looking forward to knowing more about his new assignment. Perhaps, he hoped, he would have some time to get to know about the capital city as well.

* * *

The airport was more shiny and posh than he had ever imagined it could be. He had been at Penang's airport once, but this one, in comparison, looked like it belonged in a futuristic world. He was waiting before the Arrivals sliding-doors, holding a paper sign with 'Ming Fei' and its appropriate Chinese characters emblazoned on it, surrounded by a flock of dispersing humanity. Airports gave him the impression that one was about to enter into timeless zones where the boundaries of nationality, ethnicity and borders dissolved like lemon drops wrapped under a tongue. Every time the doors slid open, a group of people came through them: a few Arabs clad in the traditional thawb walked out, their bodies furnished with solid fat in all the right parts, making them look powerful and sturdy. They carried more luggage than Asrul could even think about taking on a two-year cruise around the world; this thought cracked open a smile across his face. A few busy foreigners, talking in different tongues into their cell phone earpieces, zoomed out and disappeared into the quick comfort of taxi cubicles, as if the contact with the foreign soil had no effect on their senses. They walked stiff, cold, like androids in suits and ties.

It was 2.30 p.m. when Asrul started to feel a bit drowsy because of the strong air conditioning and the sweltering 34°C heat outside. Did she have any trouble at immigration? That might have become a big problem for her indeed. Eventually, when the doors slid open again, a woman walked in, lavishly swinging hips as she put her every step in line: big shades were planted on her soft East Asian nose, covering most of her pale face. She was pulling a plastic trolley cart with her right hand and held up her elbow in midair as if an invisible man was walking with her arm in arm. Her figure rose up from a pair of high heels, to become a slim and firm body, and when it reached up to the top of her head, it was crowned by a graceful sock bun. She looked like she had been scissor-cut out of an outdated popular fashion magazine and pasted onto the airport's tarmac with some cheap glue. Asrul knew she was Ming Fei even before she had halted for a moment and turned about twenty degrees from her trajectory, looking directly at him, curling her lips in a small, welcoming smile.

'You must be here for me,' she said in English but with a pronounced Chinese accent. This stuck him a bit odd as this was the first time he had heard such a sound. She was a modestly tiny woman, probably around one metre fifty in height without the high heels, and he had to tilt his neck down a little to look at her in the face. The dark lenses of her sunglasses contrasted starkly with her pale skin and the red lipstick she had put across her mouth. Although she was still standing behind the metal fence, Asrul could feel a powerful energy radiating from her.

'Yes, I'm Asrul. Pleased to meet you.'

'The pleasure is all mine. Shall we?'

'Of course.' He walked along with her until the fence opened and then grabbed her trolley bag.

'Thank you,' she said, zooming past him, making him follow her. He was unsure whether this was an attention-catching strategy, or if he was just over-thinking it too much, but he would have sworn that she had walked ahead of him in order to give him a better view of her small, firm ass, shaking to the right and left every time she took a step. As the sliding doors opened and the air-conditioned comfort imploded against the early afternoon sun, Asrul's forehead beaded with drops of sweat. He couldn't decide whether this was because of the sun or the spell this woman had just put on him.

* * *

'Are we going to the hotel? I'm a bit tired, would love to have a shower.'

They were driving back into the city. Kuala Lumpur seemed a strange place to Asrul: there was an expanse of greenery fractured by rows of identical two-storey houses lined in neat rows all along the Klang Valley belt, radiating out of a pumping heart of concrete, which did not really seem quite in place there, encaged at its centre.

'It has changed quite a bit,' Miss Ming Fei said slowly. She was looking outside the window, still wearing her shades; they had heavy frames that covered her face almost over her temples. Asrul couldn't see most of her face.

'Have you been here before?'

'Yes, I had a job here a few years ago. This is not an easy country for my business though,' she nodded, finally interested in what was happening inside the car.

'And I've heard that the Twin Towers are not the tallest in the world anymore! What a shame ...'

'Yes,' replied Asrul, still a bit hypnotised by the new, unfamiliar sounds of Ming Fei's English. There was something about this woman he could not describe, but it was there, trying to stab him hard in the eyes and poke out his rational thoughts, once and for all. She was in her early thirties, he guessed. Her body's structure suggested so.

'This place looks so much better than any Chinese city, you see. All of this greenery ... In China, we have very big, modern cities. I like China, of course, but all these trees here ... They're cute.'

'KL is a very modern city, too. Has a lot of big buildings.'

'I know. Have you ever been to China?'

'No. Actually, this is my first time here.'

Ming Fei turned to him and finally lowered her shades. She did so as if Asrul had said something that qualified him as a new species of human being, something that had to be further studied. She stared at him, revealing a pair of dark, shining eyes, and a low, delicate nose: it seemed like she was looking for the good vein from which she could drain a blood sample for her analysis.

'You're kidding me. You're *Malaysian*.'

The way she said this word cut a line across Asrul's stomach – his guts were ripped to shreds, inundating his crotch with blood and dark, smelly liquids. Ming Fei had superpowers, he was now one hundred percent sure about this. Perhaps she was a bomoh; in China they must have female bomohs certainly. He sank into the seat, savouring the caress of its fancy leather against his neck. She broke into a giggle and went back to looking outside the window. Asrul kept ogling at her, at the line that curved along her breasts, pressing softly against her silky cream shirt, then going down to a flat, inviting stomach, continuing along her thighs, covered in a short black skirt, and then down again, from her upper knee and to her ankle, her skin opaquely translucent under maroon nylon.

'What are you looking at?' she said without shifting her gaze from the unfolding concrete highway. Asrul didn't know what to say.

'Well, I just noticed that you are wearing stockings. Aren't you hot?'

She looked at him again, lowering her sunglasses, as if the experiment had yielded some unruly results she had to take account of. It wasn't a disgusted or annoyed look, but, instead, quite a self-complacent one.

'In China, it's not so hot now. It's the month of March,' she uttered, slowly, moving the verbal knife in and out Asrul's open sensorial wounds. 'Does it bother you? OK, wait a minute.'

She sank her bum into the bottom of the seat and rolled up her skirt over her thighs, showing the dark red lace on the top of the stocking. The exposed piece of skin between the stocking and the line of her dark underwear was paradisiacal, as white as the snow that Asrul had seen at the peaks of the Himalayas in his schoolbook's pictures. That's what winter must look like, he thought. He felt like his crotch had been just pressed by a giant foot; his throat got drier.

With the shades slung forward over her nose and her eyes looking directly into Asrul's, she started toying with the stocking's lace edge, and then pulled it down to her calf. Her eyes looked completely dark, with no clear separation between her pupil and iris. She set her right foot on the edge of the seat and pulled the nylon off her toes, slowly, still nailing him with her powerful dark stare. Asrul felt like he needed a drink. His throat felt like a desert. Then, she started it all over again, with her left leg. Not surprisingly, he saw that Azad's eyes were on the rear view mirror, not the road. May God help them reach their destination safely, Asrul prayed.

When she lavishly pulled off the last centimetre of nylon from her left foot, she put on her shoes again, unconcerned that, by moving her legs over the backseat's tiny space, she was giving him a full frontal view of her silky black panties. She unrolled both legs of her stockings, folded them and put them inside her handbag. Throughout, she had not stopped looking into the inside of Asrul's skull, not even for a single moment.

'Are you happy now, Mister Malaysia?' she spat out. 'Now, is this hotel very far away? I want to shower and rest for a while.'

'Not far, Miss,' said Azad, his contented eyes still fixed on the rear-view mirror.

'Great. And after my shower, it's time for some shopping.'

Asrul didn't dare speak a word. However, he did notice that she smiled at him before she fell silent and immersed herself again in the moving-highway TV series that was playing out on her window. Professional or not, she had just showed them that she was boss.

* * *

Ngoc looked at Cam straight in the eye: this meant 'well done'.

'Fine, let me get this straight. According to your statement, you are claiming that two police officers, whom you don't know by name but could recognise by face, forced you to perform oral sex on them.'

The air in Tanjung Tokong's police station was heavy; the words fell on Ngoc and Cam like bricks thrown down from a building's twenty-fifth storey. They nodded softly, in unison.

Mr. Cheah relaxed on his chair, putting both palms on his

desk and looking at the girls inquisitively. 'You know, this is a serious claim and constitutes an extremely punishable offence. Are you sure you want to go ahead with this? I cannot be sure, but this might even get you expelled from this country, despite your regular visa status. Do you have any witnesses?'

Cam gulped down her saliva before she could answer the officer.

'Yes, we do. But only if they can make it out of the hospital,' a tear crawled down her cheek and disappeared below her chin.

'I understand,' Mr. Cheah continued. His face seemed contracted from the inside, sucked into some sort of vacuum of police pride. When the officer released his facial stiffness and spoke again, he looked straight into their eyes.

'Do you know that only a few days after your incident, there had been a shootout at one of the poshest clubs on the island; it had left a young Chinese man dead.'

Ngoc received the message without much surprise. Something small and dark was still swimming inside of her, kicking against the walls of her intestines as it tried to find its place within her. She imagined it looked like an amphibian foetus of forgotten origin, something dirty, which left a slimy trail behind its tail as it crawled across her entrails. Ngoc didn't answer until Cam patted her over her thigh with her cold, wet hand.

'No, we didn't know that, sorry,' Ngoc replied in a soft voice. Every time that little amphibian thing moved inside her, she felt the aftertaste of sweaty flesh and urine coming back to her mouth. She had to tilt her head to one side and cough to avoid gagging into the face of the police officer. He wouldn't know what a policeman's cock tastes like, would he, she thought to herself.

'Penang ... It isn't anymore the place it used to be,' Mr. Cheah said, as if he wanted to apologise for what happened to them. But his words were not enough to penetrate Ngoc's mouth, reach into her stomach and pluck that obscene thing out of her body. 'I will do what I can within my power to help you. Here's my card. Don't hesitate to contact me if something happens, if you get any suspicious visitors or receive strange phone calls. Please call me. I will provide you with an escort in such cases.'

'Thank you, Officer,' Cam said as she accepted the man's business card with both hands.

'It's my duty. Now, please, go home and try to forget about this. I know it is hard, but you have to move on. The outcome could have been much worse, trust me.'

Ngoc and Cam left the room, arm in arm. They didn't speak to each other until they had reached the exit of the police station, had left its air-conditioned comfort and accepted the sticky embrace of the afternoon's sweltering heat. As they headed to the bus stand, their dresses, soaked in their perspiration, began to stick to their bodies. Once they had taken a seat under the soft shade of the bus stand's shelter, Ngoc turned to Cam and finally spoke, her voice mixing with the sounds of the cars zooming past them on the highway.

'Don't you feel like something is crawling into the depths of your stomach? Don't you still taste it, the aftertaste of what happened, on your mouth?'

'Yes ...' She paused, wetting her lips. 'I can't describe how I feel, Ngoc. Since that night, I can't sleep anymore. It's in my mouth, every second of every fucking day, and as much as I brush my teeth and try not to think about it, the aftertaste is always there.'

Ngoc didn't say anything else, but move closer to her friend, reached out for her hand.

'It will be OK. We've been lucky, after all. Have you heard from Nyan?'

Cam stared absently at the fabric of her pants for a long time before she answered.

'No. He's still at the hospital. Yesterday, when I went back to work, the boss said they both had been missing since that night. He didn't know anything about where they were, of course. In fact, he was completely oblivious. He was furious. He complained that his kitchen was empty.' Cam's lips stretched back into a forced smile. 'You know what?'

'What?' Ngoc asked, sheltering her eyes from the sun rays with her left hand.

'I'm going back to Saigon. I don't care about getting better money here. I don't care about anything anymore, actually. I just need to go home. I can't even think about bumping into those two pigs again. I don't know what I would do, then. Just the thought of it happening gives me the creeps.' Cam closed her legs and started patting over her thighs with her hands, trying to kill her nervousness with that simple beat.

Ngoc hadn't expected to hear this, but in her heart, she had strongly hoped she would.

'Do you have a ticket yet?' she asked.

'I'm going to get it later today, I think. My visa will expire in a couple months anyway …'

Ngoc rolled her gaze away from Cam and onto the road, where four lanes criss-crossed into each other, directing a mass of traffic back and forth to Batu Ferringhi. She felt like she didn't belong there. Her eyes moved to a big advertisement that pictured two smiling, young girls dressed in fancy suits: 'Come to study with us. Your future is in business. Most recognised degree in the United Kingdom.' She couldn't let her future be jeopardised. Not by getting a dick forced into her mouth.

'Would you mind if I came along?'

Cam tilted her head towards Ngoc, her mouth blossoming into a smile. She reached for Ngoc's hand, covering it like a mother does with her child's.

'Of course not.'

They stayed like that for a while, exchanging comfort by looking into each other's eyes, as if they were two lovers sitting on a bench in a quiet, secluded place. When the bus arrived, screeching to a halt before them and sending the smell of hot gases and dust into the air, they almost forgot to get on it. As they sat themselves on its orange seats and let the cold air conditioning blow over them, they felt the dirty aftertaste in their mouths become a little less acrid.

17

'When are you coming back?'

'In a matter of days, maybe a week ...'

'Aw, why do you have to be in Thailand for so long ...'

There was a pause.

'Work has been hard, Siti.'

'You must have met another girl over there, haven't you? I knew it! Thailand's famous for that!'

Asrul felt the weight of the roof caving in over his shoulders. He didn't know what to say to Siti anymore.

'Trust me, Siti. I'd be into your arms right now if I just could!'

Another pause filled his phone's earpiece.

'OK ... I miss you,' she finally muttered.

'I miss you too. Talk to you soon.'

And she hung up. Asrul realised Siti was not happy with him at all. He had left Penang without any explanations. Moreover, the turn of events during the past few days had taken Siti away from the centre of his thoughts. He felt quite bad about it. The hotel room smelled of sterile deodorant mothballs, and the bed sheet he was sitting on felt fresh but stiff. However, Mister Porthaksh had put them up in a nice hotel, he had to admit. Ming Fei had disappeared into her room about an hour and a half ago, and he had had time to watch some TV and also take a shower. He was surprised that there had been no mention of the club's shootout on any major newscast.

While he was lost in his thoughts, someone knocked on the door, three times, firmly. He got up and opened it: as he had expected, it was Ming Fei. She had no shades on and her face looked like a snowflake. He noticed again how her dark eyes created a stark contrast against her skin, making her small nose stand out strongly and giving it a regal quality. She wore a casual light blue dress and had no shoes on.

'Can I come in?' she said, looking over his shoulder to scan the room.

'Sure, why not ...'

They entered and she sat on the bed, while Asrul pulled up a chair for himself.

'Where is Azad?' he asked.

'Ready to take us anywhere we want to go,' she answered, looking quietly at the carpet.

'Do you need to go anywhere?'

'Well, I guess we both do. Has Mister Porthaksh spoken to you about it, by chance?'

'I guess not ...'

His phone rang exactly as he said this. It was Porthaksh.

'Is it him?' Ming Fei asked, crossing her legs, and then swinging her right foot in the air.

'Yes.'

'OK, answer the call. I'll wait here.'

The cell phone was still buzzing. Asrul decided to answer it, in spite of the woman being present in his room.

Mister Porthaksh's voice sounded crisp and quiet, as usual.

'Good afternoon, Asrul. I suppose you have received Ming Fei already. Now, listen very carefully: in my world, favour pays back favour, and in order to get your ass back here safely, you'll have a new job to do – and you'll have to do it carefully and swiftly. If you do decide to help Ming Fei finish this job, things'll clear up for you and Malik here. You can both safely come back.'

Having said all this, he paused.

'OK, I understand,' Asrul agreed.

'Is Ming Fei there with you now, by any chance?'

'Yes.' Asrul thought this seemed like too much of a coincidence.

'Now, please pass the phone to Ming Fei. She will instruct you on the procedures. And remember this: keep it cool. I guess if you want to talk to me again about this, it'll be in person, and after you have successfully completed your mission. Good luck, Asrul. I'll be happy to welcome you back here.'

'But –'

'No buts, Asrul. Give the phone to Ming Fei now, please.'

Asrul handed the phone to her. She seemed as if she was expecting it. She didn't look surprised, at all. She listened carefully for about a minute and then said, 'Yes. I'll see you there, bye bye,' and thus ended the conversation. Then she lifted her eyes from the display and looked at him with the hint of a smile.

'OK dear, I guess you are not ready for the news.'

'What do you mean?'

'I mean ...We just won two free tickets to Taipei! Woo hoo! Are you happy, little Asrul?' she exploded, her mouth spread into an unnatural grin.

'What?' Taipei? Where was that, anyway? He got off the chair. 'I don't understand what you mean,' he said, baffled.

'OK, baby, chill. Sit down,' she was laughing openly now, patting the bed with one hand and covering her mouth with the other.

'Let me tell you, you got caught up in quite a bad situation back there in Penang,' she said, regaining a placid seriousness. 'You see, one person is dead; people saw you and your friend there; and those Nigerians are, of course, from a rival gang. Do you think they'll let you walk away freely after you got their target killed?'

'Wait a minute, wait a minute ... How do you know all of these things?'

She looked at him again, opening her mouth as if she wanted to say something but had then decided to say something else.

'Asrul, do you know who I am?'

'Well, yes. Miss Ming Fei, from China.'

'That's it?' She brought her right hand to her mouth and covered another low, giggling laugh. 'I'm sorry, Sweetie. You're just so adorably naïve, that's all. I like you. OK, let me explain something here. I know Mister Porthaksh pretty well; I've worked for him over the past couple of years, mostly in China and, of course, in Taiwan, where we're bound tomorrow.'

'Wait, wait ... Worked in Taiwan? What the hell?'

'Did you really think that Porthaksh's reach only extended

till Iran and Malaysia? Well, Asrul, Mister Porthaksh orchestrates an international traffic from Malaysia. Hope you already knew that?'

'Yes.'

'Perfect. And do you know about the Three Little Emperors?'

'What is that?' Ming Fei seemed to get slightly annoyed at this point. She stopped swinging her foot and put it down, uncrossed her legs.

'Sio Sam Ong? Did he tell you anything about that?'

'Oh yes, now I remember. He said something about Mister –'

'Chang,' she cut him short. 'Yes, he's the organisation's boss. I met him once when I was here a while ago. Well, Mister Porthaksh relies on them for the trade. They give him free action space, and he supplies them with fresh stuff coming in from the Middle East. A fair exchange, yes – you got it?'

'Yes,' answered Asrul, sinking deeper in his chair. Everything was getting confusing.

'Now, I have helped Mister Porthaksh many times. He's an honest man, pays well, is generally better than the others in this trade, but he really likes clean jobs. Normally, I deal with him from inside of China. I collect the stuff and then travel within the country. Easy job, good pay. But sometimes he needs me for bigger assignments, and these are definitely worth the trouble. The money is pretty good.' She paused and curled her leg, reaching down to scratch the back of her foot. 'But I don't have to tell you the story of my life now, do I? You're here to do what I tell you to do, Asrul. So, we're off to Taipei – no questions asked. It should be quite an easy job. Besides, I speak the language.'

'And why I'm supposed to come with you?'

'To watch over me, and to look useful to Sio Sam Ong, of course. This is your trial, baby. Not that I need someone like you to get this done.'

She put down her leg and looked at him again, her face serious.

'The fact is Mister Porthaksh thinks you and your friend can blend in locally, as you are Malays. This country, as far as I know, is all about the skin, Asrul. What do you think?'

'This is our country,' he spat back. 'It *belongs* to us. Those Chinese and Indians, they came here! *We* are born here!'

'Please spare me the bullshit propaganda, Asrul. I don't care about what you do with your friends over the weekends. To me, you are just small, stupid, ignorant delinquents. That's all. You just happen to be on the lucky side of the game.'

The remark made Asrul feel bad, small. It shut him up. But she was not finished yet.

'You have to watch over me to prove yourself, Asrul. This way, Mister Chang won't come looking for you when you are back in Penang, and might even grant you protection from those wild ass Nigerians out there. How can they be so stupid? Firing their guns inside a club, with all those people there, for chrissakes? The police, they will be, of course, looking for those Africans by now … Three Small Emperors has a very neat, clean work ethic. They don't do this kind of stuff, not anymore. You'd better learn to get on their side; they have been in Penang longer than your great-grandfather had taken his first piss in his pants there, trust me. Why else do you think we're going to Taipei? They're everywhere in the Chinese world – everywhere.'

At last, Asrul's mind started to put together the jigsaw's pieces.

'You do know that someone has run away with some money, don't you Asrul? They know it's not you. However, the Nigerians think it's you: they want you and your friend. So you better prove yourself right. Porthaksh wants to make sure that you two are loyal, before he can decide if he has to throw you to the sharks and just close the matter, or to protect you. You've nothing to lose.'

'I don't get this.'

'Those Nigerians think they can just come in here and disrupt the order that Sio Sam Ong has maintained in the trade for centuries. The two gangs are at war. To make things worse, someone, a young link like you, has jumped the gun on both sides, Asrul. They might just throw you to the Nigerians, let them eat you alive, rip your heart out and cook it in front of you while you're still alive and watching. It's all about money. It's money they're after, baby,' she took a small metal box out of her pocket and extracted a tiny cigarette. She lit it slowly, closing her eyes as she sucked in the first smoke. 'We all are …'

'So … are you going to take bags up there?'

She smiled, her cigarette in-between her lips.

'Asrul, I'm a mule. That's how I make my good living. I'm just like you, maybe just a bit more valuable and trustworthy.'

'A mule? What does that mean?' She looked at him as if he were a funny-looking thing that had just stumbled into the room from a different dimension.

'I carry it, Asrul. Inside of me.'

He was still confused.

'I eat capsules full of drugs and then get on the flight and go across the customs, and wham-bam, lunch's ready! This is why they have sent you in, to help me get through this.'

'This is ridiculous!' he said, getting up from the chair again. 'You mean, we're smuggling drugs internationally? On a plane?' He realised he was raising his voice. 'Shit, this is too much. We're fucked.'

She stared at him, bringing her left leg back over her right knee. From where he was standing, he could see a little up her dress, see a piece of her black lace panties, an inviting twilight zone.

Ming Fei looked bored. 'OK, it's your call. You don't want to go? Don't go. Take a bus back to Penang and wait for the guns to shoot through your bones. I don't have to care. Why am I still here, wasting my time?'

She got up and walked towards the door, stopping to put her head inside the bathroom and throw the cigarette roach into the toilet before she opened the room's door. Asrul noticed that a little ash from her cigarette had spilled on the ground between Asrul and the bed she had just occupied with her sensual presence.

'If you decide to put some sense into that shaven shit head of yours, I'll be in my room for a while. They have a nice show on the National Geographic Asia Channel now. It's about reptiles. You can join me, and we can watch it together, if you'd like that. Tomorrow, you have to be up at six o'clock in the morning. We gotta check in early, baby. Bloody Air Asia, they never let me sleep eight damn hours straight.'

He didn't answer her. He was sinking his nails into his palms as he watched her walk over the doorstep and down the corridor. He was feeling increasingly worried, and the aseptic aroma of his hotel room only made him feel worse. As she slammed the door shut, he wondered if the inside of a casket might have smelled the same.

TAIPEI, TAIWAN

18

THE AIR INSIDE the cabin was fresh and smelled of artificial perfection. They had taken off about an hour earlier, and he had duly enjoyed seeing the view of Kuala Lumpur as it had tilted up at forty-five degrees under the plane's wing. Looking at all of those untouchable, miniscule buildings underneath him and the micro cars buzzing along the highways had given him the strange sensation of looking down at a miniature theme park while sitting atop a Ferris wheel. Ming Fei was sitting next to him, scanning through the pages of the in-flight magazine. Its glossy cover had a picture of an old town city centre, probably one of those European destinations that Asrul had never seriously thought about visiting before; the cobbled streets looked inviting, shining in the cabin light's reflection every time Ming Fei moved the magazine closer to read better. She was extremely quiet, seemed calm. Asrul, on the contrary, felt a growing pressure rise up from his lower stomach. He couldn't imagine himself being in Ming Fei's situation, getting onto the plane while completely loaded with foreign objects. She hadn't told him about what drug and how much of it she was carrying; he only knew that each passing minute of the three remaining hours that they would be trapped midair would pass slowly. It felt like an aching pain that would never go away.

'Are you OK, Asrul?' she asked without taking her eyes off the magazine. She was reading an article about a bull festival: Asrul saw a few illustrations of people smeared in red running along small alleys, chased by free, wild bulls. It all looked quite crazy, really.

'Spain ...' she murmured, distractedly. 'Relax, Asrul. There's nothing to be worried about.'

The night before she had come back to his room and knocked at his door around nine. I have to talk to you, she had said. Asrul had opened the door and she had slipped in. She had wanted to explain the next day's plan: the flight would have left at 10.30 a.m., and the journey would last around four hours; upon arrival, Asrul would have to queue up regularly, get his passport stamped, go through customs and wait for her at the luggage carousel.

'Aren't you coming with me? You said I have to protect you.'

'No, don't worry about me. There is a gatekeeper at the customs, someone we know. He'll let me in. You just go ahead: act naturally, and don't attract any unwanted attention. Just go and wait for the luggage. Once we are out of the airport, the problem's solved, and everyone's happy.'

Asrul had learned that, apparently, Sio Sam Ong had connections with the airport staff. This had calmed him down a little, but, still, he couldn't feel completely at ease.

'What are you thinking about, Asrul?'

'Nothing, nothing much really ...'

'Try to act normal. Pull out a magazine, relax. It'll be fine.'

The airplane zoomed through the clouds, and he could not see anything but white around them anymore.

* * *

When the undercarriage hit the tarmac, the sudden contact with the ground broke the spell he was in. Asrul's mind snapped open. Here they were, he thought. The plane reduced its speed, and they rocked against their safety belts until it came to a gradual halt. Lights buzzed on and people got up, started to move about frantically, although there was still no sign of a free path to the exit. Overhead lockers snapped; arms grabbed bags and trolleys; only a few passengers stayed back in their seats, waiting.

'OK. Now, baby, we'll get out of here as soon as we can. Just act natural. Did you fill in your immigration form?'

'Sure.'

'OK, great.' Ming Fei unfastened her belt and adjusted her skirt over her knees. She looked casual and composed, like a perfect tourist. They walked down the airplane's aisle and when the flight attendant smiled at Asrul, he regained all of his internal balance and tried to give back his best dauntless expression to her.

'Thank you.'

Soon they entered the arrivals terminal. It looked clean and modern, and people were queuing up in an orderly manner behind the immigration desks. The air was filled with the vague sounds of stamps chopping passport pages.

'You can go now. See you later. It will be OK.' Ming Fei smiled at him and then stood back.

As Asrul queued with the others, he saw her moving towards the women's restroom, looking around briefly, and then disappearing inside. The line was moving forward quickly, pushed on by a regular thumping sound, the striking of hard rubber against soft passport paper. Once he had arrived at the yellow line, he didn't dare to look behind him. His heart began to race faster, and he felt stupid – he had to transform himself into a totally legitimate Malaysian tourist, who had just arrived in Taipei to take in a slice of the city's life.

As he approached the immigration counter, a middle-aged man with weary eyes and black hair, combed back over a forehead already covered in a layer of brown wrinkles, stared at him – first, into his face and then, into its paper reproduction.

'Ni hui bu hui shuo Putonghua?'

'Ah?'

'English?'

'Yes, sir.'

'How long are you staying in Taiwan?'

'Three days.'

The clerk flipped through his passport pages, looking for other stamps: he found none inside. Asrul's bloodstream had a rush. Finally, the clerk's hand lifted and hovered over the stamp's handle, dropping down slowly, like one of those mechanical arms you have to manoeuvre in order to fish out stuffed animals or plastic watches from a vending machine. Finally, the mechanism worked like Asrul wanted it to: Asrul's mental hand pushed on the joystick, and the clerk's hand went down, grabbed the stamp and came down on his passport, at the upper centre of a shiny new page.

'Welcome to Taiwan,' the man said and then sent a welcoming gaze to the next person in line. Asrul took back his passport and proceeded at a normal pace across the gates, moving in the direction of the luggage carousels. Attendants on golf carts went zooming past him, shuttling about oversized bags and chattering quietly. He was in. Now, he needed to wait for her.

When he arrived, he found her already standing at the side of the carousel. One of their bags rolled in at that exact moment, and she bent down to reach for the handle – there was something surely beautiful about her body.

'OK, Asrul. Let's get the bags and get out of here. We have a hotel room booked; I need to get there quickly.'

The other luggage arrived less than a minute later. Asrul loaded it onto a trolley cart and started pushing it towards the exit. Ming Fei was walking beside him, and he could see from the stares they received that they must not have looked like a run-of-the-mill mixed couple. There weren't too many foreigners around, he could tell; he could spot only a handful of white folks, waiting for their backpacks by the carousel line. It felt as if he had stepped into a world where his brown skin was something unknown, something strange. Everywhere he looked there were Chinese-looking people around him, pushing their carts, pulling their bags, waiting, laughing and hugging their friends and family. They went past the outer customs control, and Ming Fei got closer and took his arm.

'Walk through the green lane. Don't look them in the eye,' she whispered.

He kept pushing the cart, looking forward towards a pair of sliding doors in the distance, beyond which there was freedom.

'See, we could catch a taxi and get to the city centre and see the Taipei 101. What do you think, Sweetie?' she said in a tone of voice that could be easily overheard.

'Fine, that'd be great. Let's go to the hotel and have a shower first.'

As the sliding doors opened and they rolled through, he was sure none of the cops had taken the time to raise their eyes off their reports or their lips off their coffee mugs. And when the doors closed shut behind them, the light zooming in from the airport lounge hit him in the face and made it feel like the hand of God was still shielding him from everybody's eyes. And then it was the tarmac again, and screeching taxis, and a quick ride to their hotel room.

* * *

To: +60178575954
From: SITI
'Tried to call you, but no answer. Where are you? Still in Thailand? Miss you :-*'

Asrul had been staring at his cell phone's display for about ten minutes, thinking, not knowing how to answer. He had to be cautious; she didn't have to know about why he was in Taiwan.

Ming Fei had been holed up in the bathroom for more than an hour now. She had said it would take her a while. These things, she had said, sometimes don't come out quickly. When Asrul stood by the door and tried to listen very carefully, he could hear, at times, a squirting sound followed by running water. Asrul had tried to picture the scene that was going on inside: he had imagined her squatting at the centre of the bathroom, a bowl under her rear. It was not appropriate for him to think about a woman emptying her bowels into a container, but that was what he pictured was happening behind that white plastic door.

Finally, it unlocked with a click, and Ming Fei rolled out. She looked exhausted and nauseated, and shrubs of hair stuck to the sides of her sweaty cheeks and temples. She rolled onto the bed and assumed a foetal position, putting her head under the pillow, lying there motionless.

'Wait a while till you get in there, or use matches,' was the last thing she said. Asrul decided to go out and get a coke. He left her there and walked downstairs, where he saw a vending machine. Nobody was in sight. He played around with the new foreign currency, trying to insert the right coins, and finally pushed a button, wishing that the strange character emblazoned on it meant 'drink me'. The can got ejected from its row and fell down into the tray; it felt cold against his palm.

When he returned to the room, Ming Fei was sitting on the bed, her back against the wall.

'Can I use the loo now?'

'Sure,' she said, 'good luck with that.'

The room smelled like spray perfume and matchsticks. She had probably lit a couple to make the smell of shit melt away, Asrul reasoned. Placed at the side of the shower base was a metallic bowl filled to the brim with bulging multicoloured capsules, still sprinkled wet with water. They looked clean, as if they were a bunch of newborn, limbless puppies with no eyes. Asrul thought there might have been close to a hundred capsules there, as the bowl was literally filled to its edge.

'Shit.'

Under the sink was the trash bin, with a plastic bag inside it: Asrul saw that it was full of something soft, something that was shining in the neon lights. He got closer. Condoms. It was full of torn, broken, floppy condoms that had turned their natural transparency into a mess of brownish stripes and stains, scattered with small dots of black blood. He felt an acid reflux pushing up to his lower throat and then instinctively retract, disgusted. How could a lady do something like that? He couldn't capacitate himself and kept on thinking of Ming Fei squatting there, pulling out slimy condoms out of her stretched anus, as if they were the worst, dirtiest version of those porn toys he had seen on the internet, plastic balls tied together with a string for soft cavity torture.

He finished passing urine and got out. She was still sitting there, hands crossed over her stomach, white legs spread against the soft grey blankets.

'Yes, I know. It doesn't look too good,' she said with the hint of an apology. She lit up a cigarette and motioned him with her hand towards the other side of the double bed.

'C'mon, lay down. Rest.' She got an ashtray from the nightstand and put it on the patch of dress between her legs, evidencing the shape of her thighs and crotch. Asrul switched the air conditioning on and sat on the bed. Why did they give them a double room? As he lay down, he could comfortably see the tip of her toes, moving up and down softly. The nails were painted in a beautiful red colour, and a stark contrasting white line ran down from their upper edges like a curling vine.

'Done. It is always such a nightmare passing all that out, and excuse me for say this …' she muttered, sliding onto her left elbow and getting closer to him, watching him closely in his eyes. Asrul could sense that her piercing stare was finally gone. Her eyes were still dark and penetrating, but lacked the intensity they had when they had first met the previous afternoon.

'I can tell,' he said, looking at the roof. He felt a bit awkward being so close to her, in the same bed.

'Later tonight, they'll send someone to collect them. And then, we will be free to go for a ride. Taipei's a nice city, Asrul. Good restaurants. And you can bet I'm hungry, I haven't eaten in almost eighteen hours …'

She came a bit closer and started toying with her finger against his right shoulder. Asrul felt strange, immediately, as if she had a little emotional spearhead attached to the tip of her finger.

'What can we eat here?'

'Anything you want, baby: Western, Chinese, street food, anything really… You're also very hungry, right?'

'A bit.' As he felt her finger roll down to his side, he became stiff.

'Look,' she said softly, moving her lips to his ear and letting a vent of hot breath curl up against his lobe, 'I kind of feel hungry and empty now …' The finger had transformed into an open hand

and was combing his chest, softly.

'Do you think you could help fill me up a bit?'

'Well ...'

He wasn't fast enough; nor did he want to resist her. She had already rolled herself towards him and had mounted him, her legs wrapped around him; he could see her white thighs opening along his sides, her black panties held as the final wall between her and Asrul. Her panties contrasted starkly against the surrounding tunnel of white flesh. He felt like he was about to be vampirised: her face looked as pale as a Pontianak's, and her black hair, finally released from her sock bun and running down her shoulders. She tilted his neck, to find a spot to sink her fangs into, and then started sucking away Asrul's life. Arching her lower back, Ming Fei rubbed her snatch against his stomach several times. She was so hot down there, Asrul thought, radiating hypnotic hooks that had already secured him to the bed, had entered deep down into his flesh.

'You know, I like you? You have this puppy-dog face, and you're so clumsy ... You are irresistible. You always screw things up, but it looks like you do that with a special power, Asrul, like you could save anybody at any moment ... And at the same time you are the most stupid criminal I've ever met ... C'mon, you know that ... Let me get a bite of you,' she said in a low, bowel stirring purr, and the room changed colour and everything became soft, wet, her words rubbing off from his mind the image of those bulging, watery capsules floating in a bowl at the side of the shower.

After they had been at it for a few minutes, she stopped, still on top of him, and stretched her muscles around his erection and looked straight into his eyes.

'Don't tell me that this is your first time …' Asrul didn't say anything. He grasped her back, keeping his eyes closed.

'Oh shit …' she said, before her face disappeared into the skin between his neck and right shoulder.

His cell phone rang again and he knew from the sound that it was Siti, but he didn't consider stopping to answer her call.

PULAU PINANG
(once again)

19

Sitting on his knees still hurt; that sharp pain in his ribs seemed like it never wanted to go away. He had gotten out of the hospital three days ago, and it was only then, on that morning, that he had felt like he could even get off the bed and walk straight. It had felt natural to come here and ask for help: the rage was making him blind, constantly pushing at him from the back of his eyes, urging him to get out, possessing him, making him want to kill. Probably they could help him to make sense of all of these burning feelings.

'I see …'

The monk reclined on the back of his chair. A cluster of bamboo was shaking in the light breeze behind him, across one of the open windows of the Dhammikarama temple's wall. He took some time to think over his story, without talking. Nyan's side was burning in pain, but he tried not to make it too evident; he closed his eyes and murmured a mantra. Finally, the monk leaned forward and spoke again.

'Why so much violence? To what purpose?'

'I don't know. As I said, I'm confused. I don't know what I should do.'

'Where's your friend?'

Nyan didn't answer. The mental movie starts to roll, and then cuts to the first scene abruptly. He, the protagonist, wakes up in a bush. His back is slouched against a rock. It feels as if the pain is directly radiating from the soil, the stones, the grass, the little debris and dust of the hill side. It takes him some moments, which seem more like ages, to regain some balance and get into a sitting position. Looking up, he realises that he has flown down for about three metres and has luckily bounced against this particular flat space. His body is still stiff, but he finds that nothing is broken. Where is Than, his friend? He can't see him from where he's sitting. He starts climbing towards the right side of the mountain for he remembers they have thrown him down there. When he finally finds him and sees the black blood coagulated on the grass at the side of Than's head, Nyan thinks his friend is dead.

The movie makes a sudden jump to another scene. The screenwriter has switched the time to later, has switched the location to a hospital: the doctors tell him that his friend is not dead. But it seems like Than's in a coma: he dreams, and he doesn't want to wake up. Towards the end of the movie, Nyan has to put down a month's salary in order for the doctors to take care of Than. These are the rules, they say, as the closing titles roll in from the left side of the screen.

'My friend can't be here right now. He just can't,' he finally said, sighing. The monk's face became darker in a grim, silent understanding.

'You are saying that the police and two young men attacked you without any plausible reason, took away your girlfriends, and threw you off a cliff ...' The monk adjusted his position and enveloped his body with his robe, then dropped a foot down to the floor and got up from his chair. He placed a hand on Nyan's shoulder. 'Come with me.'

He followed the monk across the hall and behind the shrine. They walked back across the passageway, where the life of Siddhartha had been dissected and framed in heavy, dark coloured wooden pictures that hung all over the sides. They finally turned left and reached the main hall, where a tall Buddha statue stood, placid and contemplating the eternity, holding out a white, open palm. His golden robe created a dramatic, divine contrast against the more sober interiors of the Burmese temple of Penang.

'This is a tough call,' started the monk. Nyan was still following him, slowly, limping around. His legs hurt, and his waist was a bit strained, his sides intermittently burning with electric pulses of pain, depolarising him in flashes along his ribcage every time he took a step. 'But I guess I could give you my personal, human point of view, if not a divine one ...' They stood in a beautiful, warm silence for a while. Nyan could feel the gaze of Buddha upon the both of them, for the air around them spiralled in particles of blessed light; he was sure this was brought forth by the monk's presence.

'As a monk, I would tell you to forgive, and forget. But as a Burmese man, I would tell you one thing only.'

Nyan waited for a long moment to listen to the resolution. It seemed as if the monk wanted to wait until they had walked out of the reach of Buddha's hearing in order to confess his secret. When he felt the daylight beating up against his chest again, the monk was already at the doorstep.

'I think you should punish them. As a man, this is my suggestion. Look around for others like you, and give them the justice they deserve.'

The monk stood there and did not say anything else. However, Nyan knew there was more, for he noticed the sea of feelings stretching beyond the monk's eyes, painted red, the colour of blood, and darker than the maroon of his robe.

* * *

When they arrived, Malik was already waiting at Porthaksh's table. He was sitting at his usual place, just across the Iranian man. Asrul followed Ming Fei and then took a seat next to his friend, while she sunk into the other side of the couch, crossing her legs and adjusting the edge of her skirt. Malik didn't say anything, but Asrul could feel that the arrival of his new friend had caused some sort of anxiety in Malik.

'Mister Malik, this is Ming Fei, an esteemed colleague.' Porthaksh made the presentations. The two exchanged a quick glance and nodded at each other, but that was it. The Iranian pulled out a cigarette from his pack and then reached forward, across the table, to offer one to Ming Fei. She didn't refuse.

'Welcome back,' he exhaled a cloud of smoke. 'I'm happy to have you back here.'

'Thanks, Mister Porthaksh.'

'Let me explain: when you were away, I had a chance to meet up with Mister Chang,' he paused and looked so austere it was impossible not to give more attention to his discourse, 'and the verdict is positive. They have found their man, and the money. They send you their apologies and welcome you back to the island.'

He kept silent for a long moment to give more emphasis to the fact that he had resolved their problem. The news took Asrul by surprise. Did Malik know anything about this? Asrul still didn't know what had happened in Johor Bahru. He instinctively turned to Malik, expecting to find his usual condescending face; he wanted to exchange a mutual friendly gaze with Malik, something they hadn't done in a while. But Malik was not interested. He kept staring at Porthaksh, his eyes stretched under his furrowed forehead, looking like a mastiff that was waiting to bite into the man.

'So, welcome back and good job. As always, I am proud of you two. I'm very happy to have you in the gang.'

Ming Fei smiled, 'And thanks for arranging my Taiwanese visa, sir. It's always so much paperwork for me, and I can never think straight when I'm doing it.'

Malik finally tilted his head and gave Asrul a weird glance that, Asrul knew, could mean only one question: did you go to Taiwan? Asrul answered it by lowering his stare and fixing it on the centre of the table, between the ashtray and an empty cigarette pack.

'Hold on a second,' erupted Malik in a low, thunderous voice, shocking the livingroom's quietness, 'what about those gun-totin' Africans? You haven't said anything about them, have you?' He gave the three of them a cold look, one by one, as if he were looking at three serial murders lined up before him. Porthaksh received Malik's verbal bullet and then reloaded his own vocal rifle with an effective clearing of his throat.

'They've been taken care of, Mister Malik.'

'How, may I ask?' he insisted.

'Well, once Sio Sam Ong found the man, they got together and questioned him, then arrived at a fine solution.'

'What does that mean? The guy is dead, and they split his body into equal portions of food for their pigs?' Malik's remark didn't make anyone laugh. The air was getting thick with smoke and sonic electricity.

'I'm sorry, but I can't disclose any more details, Mister Malik. These are confidential dealings between my organisation and the other players on this island. You should just be happy with the fact that you're still alive, don't you think?' He crushed the roach and stared at Malik. Their gazes collided in mid-air and created a silent detonation above the table.

'OK,' Malik said, getting up, 'then I guess I have no business being here anymore, Mister Porthaksh. If you'll excuse me, I would like to leave.'

'Sure,' the Iranian said in a firm voice, 'I'll contact you soon about your next job. And about your pay, of course. You did well down south, Malik. I'm proud of you – remember that.'

'Great,' Malik said without the slightest excitement. He grabbed his vest, which had been hung over the back of the couch, and headed out, letting Porthaksh's man help him out the door.

Asrul looked at both the Iranian and Chinese before him, and could not glimpse any interest running through their bodies, limbs or faces.

'I think I have to go and talk to him,' he finally said.

'Yes, you probably do,' Ming Fei's remark cut across the room like a lawnmower's blade, taking out with it all the emotional furniture Asrul had felt building between them in their Taiwanese hotel room. She was curled on the couch, her body leaning forward, holding a half-burnt cigarette in one hand. This could be the last time he saw her, he thought as he walked to the exit. In that moment, however, this thought didn't disturb him too much. He needed to speak to his friend.

He reached Malik as he was about to drive out of the building's parking lot; he waited for him at the barrier gate next to the guard's cabin. Malik shot him a deadly glacial stare from behind the car's windshield.

'Gimme a lift?' asked Asrul.

'What for? To get spied on by the Communists? Fuck off, Asrul.'

'Why are you acting like this? Lemme get in, I need to talk to you.'

Malik revved the engine and looked away, somewhere to his left, where an Indian woman was walking, carrying shopping bags with a trotting child in tow.

'Get in, you asshole.' Malik unlocked the door, and Asrul crept in as the gate lifted. Then, they were out on the road, together again. Malik was nervous.

'So what do you want? I haven't got much time.'

'What's the matter, Abang?'

'Don't call me Abang anymore, Asrul. Not after you started

fucking around with those bloody Communists ...'

'What are you saying, Malik?'

Malik decelerated and drove the car into a vacant parking spot. He kept the engine on and started the air conditioning.

'Who's that woman, Asrul?'

'She's part of the organisation; her name is Ming Fei. I had to help her transport a shipment of drugs to Taiwan. It was all a last minute thing. It just happened!'

'I knew you liked to chase skirts, for sure. But I didn't know that you could stomp over your motivations for some pussy, kill your own beliefs for it. Was her cunt any good, Asrul? Tell me. That Communist cunt, how does it taste?'

The air conditioning had created a solid wall of humming frost between them. It felt like the windows might shatter any moment now.

'Why do you want to accuse me like this?'

'Because I know you fucked her. I can tell from the way she acts, Asrul. I wasn't born yesterday. I have told you this from the beginning: trust *me*. But it seems like you'd rather trust them.'

'Well, we've no choice, Malik ...'

'No choice? Asrul, maybe that's how it is for you. But not for me.'

'What happened in JB?'

'Well, nothing much. This guy, Mamouhd, I had to help him control a few shipments into Singapore. That border is tight, Asrul. But they always make it. They even used a kid; let's see if he can pass, they said. They glued and tied the stuff around his legs, and listen to this, they sent him off with a Singaporean woman.

Thank God they got through. Can you imagine that, Asrul? They used a kid! When I saw that, I felt like shit.'

'I was afraid too, Malik. When I arrived in KL, and I picked up this gal, Porthaksh called and told me to follow her instructions, and then he wanted to talk to her too. It turned out they already had the tickets to Taipei ready for the two of us, but I didn't know anything about it.'

'And then, you went on and fucked that Communist bitch's ass, right?'

'Malik –'

'God, you're not just happy fucking some Indonesian immigrant scum, are you? That's exactly the sort of scum whose ass we should kick. But fine, I closed my eyes to it because she is Muslim, at least. But this Communist bitch, Asrul, what the fuck are you doing, man? Red pussy? How can you even think of it? Tell me one thing, Asrul: can you trust her?'

Malik was looking at him through the air conditioned haze.

'Are you one hundred per cent sure that she's any good for you, Asrul? Wasn't it clear enough to you by observing the Chinese in Malaysia, that there's money behind whatever they do?'

Asrul's thoughts began to race. All that flirting in Taipei, her wanting to have sex with him so suddenly, the drugs – something did not seem completely right. Perhaps Malik had a point after all …

'OK, Malik, it happened. She jumped all over me, you understand? We had the same room in fucking Taiwan. What do you want me to do? It wasn't like I could just get out and sleep in the park, right?'

'Whatever, Asrul …'

The following silence made it clear that the conversation had come to an end.

'Go away, Asrul. I've things to take care of. This Santa Claus here is getting a bit sick of taking care of your ass, you stupid fuck. The situation here stinks, and it's definitely better for us to part ways for a while. So good luck, man.'

'What? And what about Kuasa Melayu?'

'Don't worry about that. If I were you, I would worry more about who I mingle with and about this whole shitty situation I've gotten myself into. It has started to stink here … Like I said, it's better for us to part ways for a while.'

'But, Malik, you've put us both neck deep in this crap. Do you get that?'

'Get the fuck out of my car.'

Asrul got out and sank again into the intolerable late-afternoon heat. As Malik zoomed away into the highway, Asrul started to think about where he could find the closest bus stop.

* * *

To: 0123445779
From: Asrul
'I am back. Coming to you soon. Have to catch a bus. Can't wait to see you. Love u :-*'

It was the first time that he had found nobody else waiting for the building's elevator. He went up all alone. He still remembered how cramped, sweaty and suffocating that cubicle could get during peak hours. Tonight, though, the immigrants had been kept at bay by the wee hours of the night and by the fact that they would have to start working again early in the morning.

As the number 18 glowed brightly on the elevator's panel, the cubicle stopped moving and the door opened with a buzz – the alley he saw before him was the same old, neglected, mouldy and humid concrete intestine clung to his former floor. But now, all of his doors were shut behind their rusty gates, creating such a stark difference. Night and day, this place looked like two different locations: Asrul quite liked the damp quiet of the late evening. He walked quickly to her door and knocked three times, firmly. He didn't have to wait too long.

'Hey you, finally!' Siti said from behind the protective bars, manoeuvring her key into the slightly rusted padlock. She wasn't wearing her tudong and her long hair ran smoothly down her sides, covering her figure down to her breasts. Asrul had never seen her like this before. In his eyes, she was beautiful: her dark complexion, freed from the tudong's restriction, was irradiated by the moon's light and glowed in the darkness. As she opened the gate, he rolled his arms around her waist and kissed her.

'C'mon, not here, come on in …' she whispered, giggling.

She closed the outer gate and then pushed the door shut. Quickly, she returned into his embrace and gave him a long, wet kiss. He could feel something move in his lower stomach.

'I missed you. A lot.' Her eyes were tender and stared into his. 'Why did you have to be away for so long?'

Asrul had rehearsed this scene all afternoon. He tried to pull out his best performance.

'They have transferred me, baby. They sent me to KL for two days, then back here again, only to be sent up north for training. I didn't know how long it would take, for real, and was so busy, with my boss breathing down my neck all the time. That's why I could not call you, understand? Like, you know when you really want to call someone, and you know it will take a minute or less, but you just cannot, because you know, it's just not possible. Sorry.'

She didn't say a word, but simply caressed his face. Her mouth slowly turned into a large smile.

'It's OK. The important thing is that you're here with me now.'

Wow. He didn't know this was so easy?

She took his hand and directed him across the small room to the other side of the apartment, towards the bedrooms.

'Shhhhhhh!' she held up a finger in front of her closed mouth, hissing lightly. 'My friends are asleep in that room, so be quiet. Come, let's go into mine.'

Asrul's blood was running quickly as she pulled his hand across the moonlit darkness and into the doorstep of her room: a ceiling fan was buzzing low over a single bed set placed against the right wall. The night entered, blowing in a fresh wind, from an open window on the other wall.

'Sorry, it's a very simple place. I feel kind of awkward,' she said, 'Now that you have a good job, I mean. Maybe this isn't enough for you. I'm sorry, Sayangku.'

'Don't even think of it,' he replied as she pushed him onto the bed and then curled up next to him, hugging him from the side. They stayed like that for a long moment, letting the night's breaths whisper sea-salt infused tales all over their faces and bodies. It felt good, as if a protective spell has been cast under the fan's moving blades, which cut comfort into the thick, sticky night's heat.

They kissed again.

'Asrul, I love you,' she slurred into his right ear, breaking away from the act of sucking his lips and tongue. Her words felt hot, like a fireball had rolled down his eardrum, transforming into a drop of acid and destroying everything inside him until it had reached his crotch.

'I love you too,' he replied mechanically, cupping a hand over her right breast. She didn't resist; instead, she slung herself backwards, pressing into the flimsy support provided by her shaky bed frame, and took him down with her.

'Oh, Asrul,' she kept hissing into his ear, making him taste her vitality, letting the pounding of her organs flow straight into his aural cavity. He was running his right hand under her shirt, feeling her flesh grow warmer and tremble softly, excited.

'Promise me one thing though,' she asked suddenly between their exchanges of saliva, 'that you will accompany me to see my cousin out in Balik Pulau tomorrow? Please?'

Asrul stopped and gave this a thought. Why not? Malik had given him the boot anyway? If this was something he could do to make her happy and continue with what they were doing, why not? 'Yes,' he said and dived forward into her, again.

The moon peeped in through the window, like the iris-less white eye of a giant pervert, to watch what passed between those two bodies. The crossing of arms and legs and the pounding of muscles against meat and bones developed like a silent movie before the Cyclop's creepy eye. Asrul had not felt like this, as if wires were tearing his soul apart, in that aseptic hotel room in Taipei. Possibly, this was why the cosmic intruder had not wanted to miss witnessing such a unique and stirring act, and had chosen it as the most interesting performance of that Penang night.

20

'You can't stay here. My roommates, they would know …'

It was almost 3 a.m., and the streets were totally dark; not a soul was around. It seemed like someone had removed Penang Island's batteries and the toy had stopped working. He kept walking along the side of the highway, trying to reach the edge of Pengkalan Weld; he would then take up shelter in some mamak stall, drinking teh tarik and waiting until the 6 a.m. bus to Sungai Dua, where Malik had rented them a new flat, something that was located closer to Porthaksh's place. Asrul couldn't afford to pay for a cab with the last few crumpled notes he had left in the bottom of his pocket.

It sucked so much that Malik wasn't there to help him out. He really needed a hand now. He was tired, but, at the same time, the kick that comes after you get your rocks off was pulling on his spine benevolently. He kept on going; the traffic light was not too far away. He decided to cross the road and cut through the maze of small lanes that made a grid between the sea and KOMTAR, find his way to Penang Road from there. As soon as he had entered the dimly lit area, he felt strange. His brain started playing scenes from a movie that he had acted in a few years ago, titled 'Hospitalised by the Indians'. In the movie, Asrul had starred as the central protagonist, and the plot had him walking back home alone, very much in the same way he was walking now, and had him getting assaulted and severely beaten. He ran his right index finger along his left forearm and found the scar. It was still there, pulsating foreign flesh sewn under his skin.

Something started feeling eerily similar to what had happened before; the lamp posts began to buzz, their neon light suffering under the night's pressure. As he approached the juncture of Lebuh Melayu and Lebuh Bridge, he saw a figure come out from the end of the road, limping slightly – the figure stopped suddenly in the middle of the road. The closer Asrul got to the junction, the more he thought he had seen this man before. But he couldn't tell from where. Asrul's heart began to beat quickly, exactly as it had on that night in Kedah.

The man was only a few metres ahead of him. Asrul could sense that he was not alone; the shadows at the roadside were buzzing with hidden eyes and limbs. The man finally cleared his throat and called him out.

'Hey you!' he shouted across, 'You're alone tonight, eh? Your friends are not with you?'

Asrul stopped walking and tried to carve a memory out of the voice he had just heard. It was still not completely clear, but it started ringing some internal buzzers. Where had he met this person before?

'Do you remember what you did a couple weeks ago?'

Asrul opened his arms in the dim light, shaking his head

slowly and retracing his steps.

'You don't?' The following silence filled up the lane with a grave, unstoppable carriage of anticipation. Then, two rows of shadows emerged slowly from the street corners behind the first man, entering the road's space as a human wedge of limbs. At first glance, he could count around five pairs of hands, all of them holding out sticks.

'I'll help you remember, my friend. Burmah Road ... you came with your police friends.'

What the hell! It came back to him all of a sudden. Asrul clutching the Burmese guy by the collar and carrying his weight together with three other men towards the edge of a cliff. Asrul not watching but doing the dirty job with his eyes closed, because he didn't want to feel responsible. Asrul releasing the catch, then opening his eyes to see a body flying into deep darkness, going down, thumping against rocks. He had thought they were both dead.

'Well, this time, I brought some of *my* friends over. I hope you won't mind.'

Asrul rocked back on his feet and steered to the left, running as quickly as he could. He thought that if he could manage to go back to Pengkalan Weld and run up towards the final stretch of Lebuh Chulia, he would be able to sneak into a side alley or a mamak's toilet, throwing them off his trail. He knew this was easier said than done. He started running at full speed. They were behind him, the sound of their shoes slapping against the pavement with full force. Asrul didn't care too much about what was happening behind him and kept speeding up along the dark alley, trying to blend his figure into the potent shadows that cast darkness along the alley's outer edges. Pengkalan Weld wasn't too far away now. One stick swung in the night behind him, blowing a fierce circle of air just two inches from his neck. He leaned forward and increased his speed; the aggressor behind him lost his balance and cracked his staff against a flimsy wall.

'He's moving fast!'

'Shit!'

Unlike the other night in Kedah, tonight Asrul's body was rushing with adrenaline, reacting differently to the same, dreadful event. His legs were proceeding steadily thanks to the grip of his boots; for the first time, he was glad to have stuck to the skinhead style of wearing such shoes, for they were helping him gain more and more ground, and the main street corner was just a bunch of metres away.

The group trotted behind him at different speeds, slowed down by the heavy weapons they carried.

'Come back here!'

Taking a final leap forward, he found himself around the corner of Pengkalan Weld. Unable to stop his mad rush, he kept mowing down slices of the night breeze as he spun his knees forward, his heart already numb with pressure. He kept running as quickly as he could, listening to the sound of their footsteps coming up from behind him, increasing in pace as the group clustered into a compact collection of pounding limbs. They felt to him like a carriage of vengeance thrown at full speed down the night's road, which had been left deprived of its usual metallic traffic.

If he kept going like this for much longer, he knew he would have to give up and surrender himself to the sticks and fists. His sweat was not running down his body yet, but it was surely there, blocked under his skin, ready to come out in a flow as soon as his legs would stop moving. Then, like a slow, peaceful pachyderm crossing its boundaries and emerging from the depth of an ancient forest, there it was. It was coming towards him, chugging its way down the road, sluggishly, ready to swerve into Lebuh Chulia and get lost into the bowels of George Town. The garbage truck.

He ran faster as the vehicle started turning left; one man sat sleepily behind its wheel. This would be his only chance to gain some ground and save his ass. He started moving to the right, shifting from one side to another, creating a scythe-like trajectory to mislead the mob behind him, yet trying to direct himself towards the back of the truck. As he neared it, an intense, pungent stench, of fermented lives squashed into dark, tropical sewage slime, raped his nostrils and froze his brain into a cobweb of disgust; but he knew he had to get on it. He concluded his run exactly as the truck was turning in, jumping his few last steps and finally getting close enough to be able to grab onto one of the handlebars and pull himself up.

'Fuck! Get him!'

A hand clutched his ankle and pulled him back, making him lose balance and almost fall off the edge of the loading hopper. Asrul held onto the truck with both hands and kicked back, feeling a chest under his boot. He regained his balance and knelt inside the hopper, feeling his whole lungs tremble, trying to contain the impulse to vomit: the steamy smell of rotten trash numbed his head, and he felt his knees get wet with unspeakable mixes of lurid juices.

'Shit,' he thought, without saying it loud. The truck wasn't going at full speed, but it was enough to put some distance between them and him. He was about to smile seeing that they were growing smaller and smaller as the truck kept on with its motion. But when it stopped at a lonesome traffic light, Asrul felt like his blood had just frozen. The group, left disarmed by the sudden luck of their prey, realised that the vehicle had stopped. Two of the men motioned their arms in Asrul's direction and then started running towards him.

'Go, go, go, get him!'

Asrul kicked the inside of the metallic loading hopper to produce a sound and convince the driver to keep moving, but this was in vain.

'Move the fuck on, c'mon!' he screamed. The men were drawing closer: he could see their swollen, angry faces. He wasn't in the mental condition to recognise any of them, except for the man he had personally thrown off the cliff in Air Hitam.

'Get him! I want revenge!' that man shouted on the top of his lungs while gesturing madly at the truck.

They got so close that Asrul had to start swinging kicks at them to keep their heads away from him, and it was only then that the truck buzzed forward, almost knocking Asrul off his feet and down into the regurgitating mass of stench that lay behind the hopper.

The traffic lights finally switched to green.

As the truck started to gain speed and distance itself from

his aggressors, Asrul grabbed whatever he could find around him and threw it at them. He hit a man in the chest with a box full of undecipherable dirt, making him fall and crash against a couple of others. The screaming mob was losing ground again, and Asrul was getting closer and closer to the perennial lights of Chulia Street and its depraved population of transgendered sex workers, drunk white foreigners and random rugged street dwellers. He knew he might have to get off the truck and find another hideout – a tough decision indeed, as he knew the mob might follow the truck he was on. As the truck kept rolling, he passed through a Kapitan restaurant that offered some of the best tandoori chicken in the city to a rarefied bunch of middle-of-the-night drunks. Their stares came alive and shifted from their hot cups of teh tarik and plates of roti canai to the weird view of a shaven guy in army boots and pants, soaked in slime, hitching a ride at the back of a trash compactor. But as soon as he was gone, the wretched souls of late-night Penang preferred to forget the small oddity they had just witnessed and nonchalantly returned to their crispy night bites.

As the truck slowed down to edge its way out of a line of parked vehicles, Asrul dismounted it: he fell down at the side of the road, exactly one metre away from the five-foot way that sheltered Chulia Street's night creatures from the powerful neon lights of the twenty-four-hour minimarts. A girl in a sexy black dress was looking at him from the shadows, marking time with the clicking movements she made by pressing together the handles of her bag.

'Hey love, you surely stole the scene by jumping in here like that!' she said in a strange voice that sounded like her sexuality had been mixed in a blender and poured out, minced into a smoothie.

'Yes, thanks,' he replied, more concerned about what was happening behind him. This time of the night, it wasn't easy to discern who was out to offer transgendered love and who was out there to buy some. 'I need to go,' he apologised, trying to find a safe way out of there.

'Hey, hun, why don't you come up to my room? I can massage you. We can stay together, can play on the bed ...'

'Sure, maybe another time.'

He remembered there was a small, dark hole of an alley just at the side of the Air Asia office. It connected to Muntri Street on the other side, following a sewage channel down a low wall: he thought that place would be just dark enough for him to set roots and hide out for a while. He didn't know where they were, but Lebuh Chulia wasn't that long a street; he rushed across the street and found the entrance to the alleyway, moving on into the darkness, not listening to what the ladyboy was saying behind him.

He reached for a secluded corner that opened into the darkness, the sewage channel continuing down below and then disappearing perpendicular to the alley. He squatted down and pulled out the cell phone from his pocket. The battery was getting low. He scrolled through his contacts and then pressed the number. He sat there, waiting for the dial tone to break into the start of a conversation. No answer. His heart had found its place in his chest once again, thumping blood up to his neck and into his ears, making his head pound. He dialled again. After about ten intermitting rings, a sleep-encrusted voice answered.

'What do you want, you fool, at this time of the night?'

'Malik, you gotta help me. I'm fucked, Abang ...' he whispered, still scared.

'What's going on, Asrul?' Malik had finally broken through the wall of his sleep.

'They're following me. The guy we threw off the cliff. Fuck. And a bunch of others. Burmese, Bangladeshi, all evil bastards. They're coming for me. They have sticks; they want to kill me, Abang.'

The following silence was, Asrul knew, Malik's trademark way of racing his thoughts around the apparently empty walls of his head.

'OK, where are you?'

'You know the Air Asia office, in Chulia Street?'

'Right.'

'I am hidden out in the alley next to it. I'm scared shitless. They're around here somewhere.'

'OK, stay there and stay cool. I'm coming to pick you up.'

'When?'

'Gimme twenty minutes at least. I'm at my dad's place.'

'Where is that?'

'Nevermind that. Twenty minutes, Asrul. Keep your ass safe. Call me if you change location.'

'I'll surely try not to.'

Asrul tried to grow smaller within the darkness and mix into the shadow of a nearby tree branch: it separated the moon from his face, casting a cobweb of dark shadows all over his cheeks, as if a painter, while trying to clean his brush, had splattered some black colour onto his face.

As his phone rang again, he saw a car's headlights shed their light onto the end of the alley.

'Come out, I'm here.'

'OK, I'm on my way.'

He emerged from the shadows and ran to the waiting car. As soon as he got closer, he recognised the hairless shape of Malik's head inside it. He looked around before stepping out of the alley. Nobody suspicious was in sight.

'Get in,' Malik's voice said from the car's door, which opened for him briskly.

Asrul didn't wait for another moment; he took a leap into the car and lay back against the passenger seat and then pushed it down, so that no one could see that he was in the car.

'Go,' he said. The bulbs of the light poles outside, seen from where he was lying, looked like orange flowers blooming out of the dark terrain of the night sky. Then, they were on the coastal highway, and he finally felt the sweat coming out powerfully against his clothes, soaking them.

'Fuck, you smell like rotten cunt juice, Adik!'

'Yes,' Asrul said. That was all he could say as he readjusted the seat to its normal position. Sitting beside his friend, he finally began to feel safe again.

21

MALIK WANTED TO KNOW everything, but there was not much to be told, really. Asrul had been visiting Siti, and then, because he had no transportation and it was late at night, he had been left with no choice but to walk back to the closest place where he could wait for the first morning bus.

'So, they just came out of nowhere and attacked you?'

'Yes, I was taking a shortcut through the back lanes behind KOMTAR, and there they were. The first guy, the one we threw off the cliff, he just came out of the corner and started talking to me. I just fled as quickly as I could. They might have been a dozen men, but I'm not sure as I couldn't count them properly. Well, I was running. They had sticks, perhaps more weapons too. I'm just surprised that they found me so easily, that they came out of the blue like that and attacked me …'

'Well, Adik, I would do the same thing if I found the asshole that pushed me off a cliff. The next time, we should make sure they are dead. What about the other one?'

'Not sure. Perhaps, he was in the group … I didn't see him, sorry.'

'It's OK. Now, you need to take a shower and then get some rest. We'll discuss the rest of your story tomorrow.'

'I'm actually busy tomorrow, Abang. I promised Siti that I'd accompany her to Balik Pulau, to see her cousin.'

'Mmmm, OK ... How are you going to go there?'

'I guess by bus.'

'Fine. Be very careful. It'll be daytime, so you should be fine. But try to come back home before dark. Be safe, you fool. These women will bring you down dead,' he broke out laughing for the first time.

'Thanks for saving my life, Abang ...'

'Well, I owed you one. Now we're even. You helped me first, remember?'

'I wouldn't have let you get killed by those Africans.'

'See, this is what I like about you, Asrul. You're one hell of a hard-headed, sometimes ultra-dumb motherfucker, but I can trust you like I trust my own self. After all, you're a pro, Adik. I'm impressed you made it this far tonight. And, I apologise for having acted like an asshole earlier today.'

'Really?'

'Yes, I guess so, but I won't tell you twice. Please, be careful, and put a leash on that dick of yours, once and for all!'

They both burst out laughing, and the darkest night began to fade into shades of grey.

* * *

'Let's get off here,' she said, pulling his arm.

The bus was practically empty when they got off at Balik Pulau's main intersection. The forest watched them intensely from the surrounding slopes: hills covered in thick foliage had taken the place of the usual mass destruction of the city's high-rise buildings, the bee hives of men.

'Wow, this is so beautiful,' he remarked, looking at her in awe.

'This is the best part of the island, I think,' she continued. 'I come here quite regularly to see my cousin. He works as a logger in a plantation around here. One time, he drove me around on his motorbike – it was so fantastic! The natural beauty here, you can't find it anywhere else in Penang.'

'Cool. Hope he'll give me a ride on his motorbike too.'

'If he feels like it. Let's go now,' she took his hand and smiled, proceeding to walk across the road and along the sidewalk, and past the entrance to a mosque.

Asrul stared at a few people walking in, taking their shoes off and then directing themselves towards the ablution pool. He had an instant memory of the men bending forward and kissing the floor with their songkoks in Alor Star, and he felt a bit strange. He felt like something bad was about to happen. He focussed on the road again, fixing his attention on the curves of Siti's swinging rear stretched into her denim jeans and following the rubbery clatter of her flip flops. She took a side path that branched off the main road and across a field, and she pulled him after her; the palms and banana trees had created a natural sun-shelter spanning the whole length of the field. They continued walking down the path until they came to a sudden slope, and then they twisted to the left to go deeper into the jungle.

'Is his place still very far?'

'No, not too much. I told you, he's a logger. He lives close to a small plantation; that's why we are walking into the forest, don't worry!'

'OK,' he said, feeling the grip of Siti's hand become firmer and a bit moist.

The afternoon sun was not strong enough to fry the insides of their heads, but it was still strong, and he felt like he was walking inside a boiling egg yolk. They walked on, further downhill, until they came to a clearing bordered by a neat line of trees. At the centre, a house rested on a row of low stilts, with an old car parked underneath it. The corrugated iron roof had some sun-bleached patches, making it seem as if the house itself was getting old and balding. The main entrance was connected to the ground with a wooden staircase, whose handrails had surely seen better days: they now stood pale, grey, after many hands had rubbed the paint off their wood. However, apart from a bit of wear and tear, the house still looked powerful and as beautiful as only a place surrounded by an expanse of greenery, sun and earth could look.

'Fantastic,' murmured Asrul, 'it kind of reminds me of my grandmother's home, up in northern Kedah.'

'Promise me that you'll take me there one day,' she answered and then got onto her toes, shortening the distance between her lips and Asrul's, and planted a soft kiss on him.

'Now, come on in … I'm sure he has some tea ready.' Again, Siti pulled his arm towards the house and into the courtyard, and then they were on the staircase. The steps creaked when he walked over them in his boots. Facing the door, Siti leaned out over the handrail and peeked into the house through a dusty windowpane.

'Wait, maybe he's not home now ... I have a key.'

She fumbled in her handbag until she had extracted a small, metal key and shoved it inside the hole. The door opened easily, into a dark corridor. Asrul could see a door; it possibly led into a bathroom, he thought. Next to it, the passageway branched off in two opposite directions, most probably into a bedroom and a livingroom. Siti had already stepped into the house.

'Please, come on in,' she called him in by flapping her fingers into her palm, her inviting smile still stuck on her face.

He followed her and went further inside, letting her close the door behind their backs.

'So, where's your cousin?'

'Probably still at work, or maybe he went out to buy some food for us. He knows we are coming.'

'Ah ... do you think it will take him long? It's getting pretty dark here.'

'Probably not. I think he will be here soon.'

The blow hit him strongly just under the nape of his neck, and the house caved into a spinning darkness, which left him drowning in a darker than dark, all-consuming sea.

* * *

He opened and closed his eyes slowly to get acquainted to the dim light, but he could only see as far as the wooden floor ahead of him. His neck was still very painful and had been pushed into a downward position for too long for him to be able to turn about and take a look around. As his limbs slowly regained their sensitivity, and the numbness slid off them, falling between the floor's cracks, he found that he had been crammed against the wall – his outstretched shoulders ached for having been under such tension for so long.

He realised he had been thrown onto the wooden floor of a small, dark room with no windows. Considering the house's architecture, which he had observed from the outside, he thought he was possibly sitting in the basement – the car should be parked exactly behind him, at the opposite side of the wooden wall he was tied to. In front of him, a doorstep announced an inviting path that would lead up to a staircase and out through an open door at its end. But he could not pull himself up and off that wall.

Where was Siti? When he finally could lift up his neck and take a look around, he saw her naked feet suspended at the upper corner of the doorstep in front of him. Her feet were placed at the end of the staircase, in the space where the two doorsteps connected into a third dimension. She was standing at the end of the corridor they had used to enter the house, waiting for something. Or someone.

'Siti!' Asrul screamed.

There was no reply. However, it seemed that after the scream, all the things around Asrul had become stiffer and more silent, as if producing an allergic reaction to his frustration. A few long, silent moments gave him a chance to study his new surroundings better; he now had the impression that he had been parked in what he thought might have been a laundry room. A bunch of scattered furniture and old chairs loomed in the darkness to his right: their menacing wooden parts weren't long enough to reach out and grab him, to carry his body away to a dark corner to devour his flesh, undisturbed. Halfway between where he sat and where the doorstep stood, there was a dog bowl, filled with the remnants of some brownish food, looking like an un-flushable toilet full of the morbid, floating outcomes of a midget's defecation.

The room smelled powerfully of humid wood. Its flimsy walls were held together by bulging planks that rubbed together at the corners. The only light coming in was from the open door at the top of the staircase, flowing in from the upper floor.

They had done him in: he was down like a freaking clown. He tried to think and put the pieces together, to reason why Siti should have been involved in this mess. He was frustrated and disillusioned. They had made love only the night before. She had told him that she loved him. Emptiness soon found shelter inside Asrul's body – it entered through his mouth, and adjusted itself in a supine sleeping position, like the corpse of a small child encaged by his own bones. It took him a while to kick it out of the way and onto the floor, screaming to scare it off and make it crawl away into the outlying darkness. This whole story could not end like this, with him dying in front of a bowl of rotting food.

He was thirsty. Luckily, by his side, there was another green plastic bowl he hadn't noticed before. It had a little water in it. He bent down as far as he could, checking to see how freely he could move away from the wall. Surprisingly, he found that he could easily reach the bottle's plastic rim and pulled it closer with his teeth. The liquid inside didn't taste like water, but it surely helped him regain some lucidity and pushed him towards the understanding that, if he ever wanted a chance to get out of there, this may as well be it. He looked behind him, and saw that his wrists had been secured to leather straps chained to the wall. The job hadn't been done very professionally, he thought, basing his suspicions on the knowledge he had gained from films. There was a gap between his left hand and the strap, and he started toying with it. He pulled his arm down as much as he could, until his shoulders creaked. Taking his thumb out would be the hard part. He started pulling, feeling the leather become increasingly hot against his hand, his blood congesting under the pressure. He kept at it for a few minutes, until his thumb finally snapped out, sore and pulsating. Taking out his other four fingers was easier. Halfway released from the binds, Asrul got up on his knees to better examine his right wrist, which was still tied to the wall: it was secured with a belt. He wondered if they had done this because they had not had any better material to tie him with. Probably, they had assumed that he wouldn't wake up before they had returned. These thoughts were irrelevant, he told himself;he needed to work on the buckle as quickly as he could. Untying a belt with the left hand wasn't as easy as he had thought it would be. Asrul struggled a bit with his cramped fingers before he could unroll the belt from his wrist and push the buckle's pin out of the leather hole.

When the immobilising fornication of leather and flesh had been finally broken, he was back on his feet. Still feeling drowsy, he took a look at the surroundings and saw that the room he was in opened to another, small empty anteroom that led to the staircase.

On top of it, another door had been left open, light pouring out of it, briskly illuminating his environs. Some undistinguished chattering sounds tried to splash their way towards him, from beyond the source of light, but they were too feeble to reach his eardrums. That was his only way out, at the moment. He looked back at the grubby room he had been thrown in: there was a small, obscured glass window at the top, too high for him to reach and too small for him to crawl through. He resigned himself to the idea that, considering they had put him here and had kept him alive, they wanted something from him. Hell, he didn't even know how many of them were involved in this.

While he was thinking, some louder noises directed his way made it clear that they were about to visit him downstairs. Instinctively, he buckled under the belts once again, making sure to leave a loose space for him to easily slide his hands out of, and went back to his submissive position against the wall. The upper floor's doorstep was obscured from his sight for a moment as two figures stood against the light, and then two pairs of feet started their careful descent. Asrul figured out that a man was leading, and that Siti was following him, her hair let loose and cascading down her shoulders. As he reached the entrance of Asrul's prison, the man blocked the light with his body, his face concealed by the backlighting; Asrul noticed the clear shape of a long rattan stick protruding from the man's hand.

Siti was right behind the man, peeking over his shoulder, struggling to stand on the top of her toes.

'Is he awake?' she asked in a different tone of voice, a dry one Asrul had never heard coming from her pouty red lips before, a voice that felt as sour as taking a bite into a bad green apple. Asrul felt something breaking inside of him. A lot of his memories were instantly erased, as if they had formatted his brain's hard disk by putting him into that cell room.

'I guess so … Are you, mister?' The man swung the stick forward and across the room, touching Asrul's leg and nudging it. On hearing his voice, his accent, Asrul understood immediately that the man was Chinese.

Sio Sam Ong. But why was Siti here? What was her business with the Chinese mafia? Asrul's thoughts raced like swerving drunk horses in his mind's turf club, but he still pretended to be half unconscious. Then the stick whacked his side pretty hard, and he had to pull out a little scream.

'Wake up, c'mon …' The Chinese man kept prodding and pushing at his lower legs. At this point, Asrul pretended to wake up. He opened his eyes, and the man he saw before him looked young and had a small, light goatee crawling out of a sharp chin.

'What the hell …'

'Oh, here he is! He woke up,' Siti cried out. How could he have dared to kiss her?

'Yes, I am, you fucking bitch!' Asrul thundered in rage, and the stick hit him hard on the ribcage, taking his breath away. He jerked forward, so hard that he almost slipped out of the belts. He had to be careful and keep up with the show for a little longer.

'Do not talk to my girlfriend like that, asshole! And this,' the man landed another hit just over Asrul's right shoulder, violently. Asrul felt his bone absorb the impact and release a discharge of pain cells across his torso, exploding at the arcs of his ribs in a stampede of black and white stiffness. 'This is for having fucked her. I hope you liked it, because there won't be any more sweet pie for you, dear Asrul.'

'How do you know my name?'

When Siti laughed, he realised how stupid his question was. Those two had been together from the start, and they had cheated him so perfectly well. Asrul had really thought Siti was falling for him.

'You aren't that smart, are you?' the guy let the stick rest over Asrul's shoulders, ready to strike another bone-shattering blow.

'Yes, Tan Moe,' Siti chirped out, leaning over the man's shoulder. 'Asrul's really bodoh. Look at him. It has been so easy!' She buried her face into his neck and made him giggle.

'What's this all about? Who the hell are you?'

'Yes, sure. I guess after all you deserve an explanation – although you are just a small, insignificant cog in the big scheme of things. We knew you would have been perfectly dumb for our plan! This is why this fantastic girl chose you,' he looked over his shoulder at Siti and planted a solid wet kiss on her mouth. She accepted his tongue with ease; she looked directly into Asrul's eyes as she sucked on Tan Moe's tongue. She looked very different now, the kind of girl Asrul would have loved to kick down, make bleed, punish. He felt a mounting rage rising up inside him.

'What plan?' he barked, shaking, trying to contain his anger, the belts getting loose around his wrists, but still protected by the darkness. He had to play this to his own advantage, or that bat would come down again, fracturing his skull and bones.

'Haven't you had a chance to speak with my good pal Yew

down at the club?'

'What?'

'Yew ... the bartender you went for, my friend ...'

'That guy ...' The conversation the bartender had had with them at the restroom immediately came back to his mind: Tan Moe, this name was not new. Yew had mentioned it, in relation to the missing money.

'Yes, Asrul. He must have explained everything to you already, hasn't he?'

'Not before he got shot by the Nigerians,' Asrul spat out, giggling with an unknown pleasure. Tan Moe took the hit lightly. His face didn't change much; it seemed to Asrul like he had thrown a small stone into a lake and was seeing its surface open into a small series of circles for a moment, before becoming quiet again. Asrul noticed the outlines of a circular, black tattoo coming out of Tan Moe's shirt collar, the ink etched over his heart.

'Well, this is good news! So now, we have less work to do, Siti. Thanks for informing us, Asrul. When I decided to keep that shipment and the money, Yew covered me for a couple weeks. But he could not take it anymore; he was always such a nervous man. I wouldn't have had a problem sharing the money with him, but he was getting so tensed ... And I didn't want him getting more involved in this, you understand? So, I just disappeared,' he explained, keeping a low, quiet tone, like a classroom teacher.

'Do you know what it means to try to fuck with Sio Sam Ong, Asrul?'

'No...'

'Well, you die. Mister Chang is a serious businessman and

a fucking savage killer, Asrul. You don't want to end up getting caught under his paws, if you know what I mean. He has sharp claws. And fangs. And he has eyes, everywhere ... That's why we had to resort to using you, Asrul!' Tan Moe looked at Siti complacently.

'I observed you and your friend the day you came to see the apartment, and something rang a bell, Asrul,' Siti said, her eyes looking smarter than they usually did. 'It was so strange, two skinheads like you wanting to move into a place for immigrants. So, I started keeping an eye on you and your friend. One afternoon, I saw your friend Malik in town, having tea with an Iranian fixer me and Tan Moe knew ... it was easy to make the connection: you both wanted to work for them. This was confirmed by our Iranian friend.'

'You see, Yew and I have been working for Sio Sam Ong for about three years now,' Tan Moe entered the conversation. 'The pay is good, but the risk is too high for what they offer. It's hard to make it up the ranks too. So I simply decided to keep some of the money and get the hell out of Penang, along with this amazing lady!'

Siti blushed a little. 'You're too good, Moe,' she chirped and kissed him again.

'Fortunately for us, your boss takes orders from my boss. It would have looked perfectly credible that the two new fish in the net would try to sneak out some cash and jump the gun, if you know what I mean ...' he continued caressing the stick. 'You and your friend,' he said, 'were perfect for us to pin the blame on. And now that Yew is gone, I have one less problem to worry about!'

'So, how are you going to get this to work? Make them believe all of this? I'm still here, and alive ...' Asrul asked in a low voice. The belts were now rolled around his fingers, the thumbs sticking out, ready to rush out of the leather's grip. But he wanted to know more, to hear it all, before he could fight back.

'Very simple, my smart friend. You don't jump to conclusions easily, do you?' Tan Moe's laughed, and Asrul pressed his fingers into the leather, feeling it against his palms in the same way that he would have loved to feel Tan Moe's neck.

'It should be quite clear to you by now that this cell is a set up. Why would I want to take you to this house in the jungle otherwise, dear Asrul? It's obvious, isn't it? To tell them later on that this was the place where *you* kept me tied up to a wall and starving like a scum, beating me up and feeding me dog food for two months. This would just sound so right. They'll be told that *you* did to me what I'm doing to you now, Asrul. And you know why? Once they know that you're dead and you have taken the money to hell with you, I will finally be able to breathe, and disappear as quickly as I can. Besides, this will teach you a lesson: you fucked my girlfriend, man. How would you feel if you were in my shoes, dear Asrul?'

'It certainly didn't feel too good for me, Mister Quick,' Siti moved forward and looked at him with an uncompassionate, spiteful glance. 'They say Malays are strong lovers and have big cocks. But you, Asrul, you are the exception!' She laughed at him.

He knew he needed to keep his cool for the moment; he was almost out of the buckles and ready to strike. The two giggled together. To Asrul, who was silently building up all his power, which he had never dared to unleash before, they looked like two crows with broken wings, sitting on a flimsy branch and about to fall off at any moment into a gorge.

'When they see your body here, and all this set up, and me fucked up for good, they'll believe my story and leave me alone. You'll be dead, and the money will be gone to hell along with you. They'll then catch hold of your friend and make him talk. And trust me, he'll have to say something if he wants to keep at least one finger. Whatever he does say, we'll already be far away, and safe. Do you get it now, dumbass? You're my rag doll. My puppet.'

Asrul looked at Tan Moe as if he was a mere lump of meat: he focused on the neck, saw himself biting deep into it, making blood squirt out high, drenching the walls, eating his face up like a frenzied, rabid dog. Less than an inch was all he had to cover, and to have Tan Moe's attention distracted for only a moment was all he needed. And it felt, in that room's mouldy air, like that moment was about to come soon.

'It won't take too long,' Tan Moe continued, moving about in the small space. 'Just give us a couple days; we need to make sure that things out there are ripe enough for them to receive the news of your death, and of my return ... I'm sure they'll be very surprised to hear that a shmuck like you has been able to pull such a stunt. Oh man, I'm about to make you famous, can you believe it? Everyone will remember you as the knucklehead who almost ripped 40,000 ringgit off Sio Sam Ong's mitts! You'll become an urban legend, Asrul!' Tan Moe looked completely captivated by his own words.

'Fantastic,' Asrul said, mocking Tan Moe's excited voice. 'If I could move my hands, I would be clapping for you now! Do you really think they'll buy your shit story?'

Tan Moe looked at him for a while, without talking, tilting his neck upwards and trying to transmit fear through his prolonged stare. He stretched his left arm out before Siti as she tried to speak up, and then opened his mouth without emitting any sound, his lips frozen in a mute 'O' until his throat gurgled.

'This is my risk. I have to take it. They'll most likely believe me, someone who has served them so loyally for three long years, rather than a piece of brown shit like you. I'm one of them, not like you.' Tan Moe sounded like he was trying to convince everybody in that room about the logic and consistency of his plan.

Asrul didn't say another word. He needed to let Tan Moe feel like he had won. Asrul had to agree with him on one point though: his plan would serve as a pretty good way to misdirect the criminal organisation into looking for the money elsewhere, even distract them into investigating Asrul's life and family, leaving Tan Moe enough time to disappear.

'Baby, I'm going upstairs to wait for you. I don't want to see when you do it. You know that I hate blood,' Siti said to Tan Moe, smiling softly.

'It's OK, hun, you don't have to be around for this. This is man's work,' he put an arm around her shoulder and kissed her forehead lightly before sending her off towards the stairs. She started climbing up, and Asrul knew this was the moment he had been waiting for. Tan Moe was still watching Siti going up the staircase, hypnotised by the bulging movement of her buttocks, when he slipped out of the leather's bite and stretched his shoulders silently in the near darkness, crouching and waiting to jump, like the tiger he knew he could be, like the tiger he *had* now to be.

The blade of light coming down the stairs disappeared as Siti reached the landing. Tan Moe's turned back to his victim with the same complacent smile drawn across the face. But when he saw that the space where Asrul had been was now empty, his expression turned into a growl. Before he could scream, Asrul jumped out of the corner he had slid into and landed on Tan Moe's back with all his weight and force, crushing him down. In the fall, Tan Moe's lost the stick – it was thrust away into the darkness and slammed against the wall, while Tan Moe's face hit the ground under Asrul's weight. Asrul knew he had an advantage he couldn't lose now. He reached for the first thing he could find and as his fingers dipped into something cold and soft, he clenched his fist around the rim of the bowl he had found. He swung it in the air and back down against tan Moe's temple, as hard as he could, two, three, four times. Asrul had never really been in a fistfight before; he had never even imagined he could hit a man like this, but here he was now, doing just that.

All the fear and despair and hatred that had accumulated within him while he had been trapped against the wall flowed down like streams of water might from the cracks of a broken dam. He kept on hitting him, harder and harder, and he couldn't stop. It was like Asrul had left his body, had gotten out of that angry shell and was watching the scene unfold from the outside, unable to stop the fury that had been unleashed from his own body. At each stroke, Tan Moe's shoulder rocked under him like a horse running wild. The aluminium bowl had cut a nasty gash at the side of his head, and blood was streaming out, a red snake made alive and scary by the darkness. Asrul kept hitting the guy at his temple as hard as he could, with the bowl clenched in his right hand, while punching his neck and upper back with his left fist. He was a butcher equipped with a primitive meat cleaver made out of an aluminium bowl. The man jerked for a few more times like a dying mare, the hits discharging into raw, spastic strokes through his legs, until he slowly stopped the motion. The puppet's strings had been cut; blood was spouting from the side of his head and pouring out in a darkening pool.

22

It had finally happened. He had blood on his hands. At last, he was the man he was afraid he would become.

Asrul stood up. He moved a few clumsy steps backwards, examining the tiny room's surroundings. The body was there, lying in front of him, as if it had been thrown down from above, jerking in a spasmodic shape, its mouth corrugated into a sort of distant smile.

Asrul threw his hands to the air and then let them drop on top of his shaved skull. The palms savoured the light scratch of thousands of ultra-short hairs, a tactile hedgehog. Looking up at the sky above, he thought of God.

'Why did you make me do this? We had a pact. Now it is all lost, all gone,' he cried within himself.

Asrul fell down to his knees and looked back at the corpse lying in front of him, unable to judge whether or not he really had committed a horrible crime. It felt like he had picked the wrong song off the record; it couldn't have played out like this, he told himself. Or perhaps there was some horrible mistake in the lyrics?

The reality struck him hard in the face: Asrul had finally

killed. After endless failed attempts to fit the real, evil, Nazi skinhead role, he had made it. There was no reason to cry or be afraid. This was a real turning point in his life.

'Perfect, Asrul!' cheered a familiar voice from behind him.

'Now, you've made it. Don't worry too much; this just means that there's one less parasite in this world, my brother. You did great! It'll now be easier to do it again, later!'

Malik? What was Malik doing here? Asrul turned around and saw his friend's familiar shape at the top of the stairs. He was pushing Siti ahead of him, as she screamed and tried to get out of his hold. He held her arms by her wrists and pushed them against her back, blocking her movements.

'Stay quiet, bitch!' Malik thrust one hand into the back of his jeans and pulled out a gun. He pointed it at Siti's temple. The girl immediately calmed down against the lurid cold, toothless mouth of the barrel. 'I told you, didn't I, Asrul, that immigrant scum is dangerous? I always knew it, Adik. They would just kill for a visa, to be able to stay here and suck at Malaysia's prosperous tits. Look at her, she's just plain disgusting.'

Asrul didn't answer. He was still shocked about what he had just done. Malik reached the bottom of the stairs, pushing Siti in front of him, still keeping her nailed under the kiss of the gun.

'Moreover, she's a Muslim ...' He turned to Siti. 'How could you do something like this to your own kind?'

Siti was crying. Asrul noticed that her face was swollen under the left eye: a dark blue ring was expanding quickly around her eye socket.

'Did you punch her?'

'Of course, Asrul. She tried to shoot me as I got in ... I had to change her mind about doing such things, Adik. Are you OK? You look like shit man ...'

Malik pushed through the room's entrance and saw Tan Moe lying on the floor. The blood had finally stopped its flow from his wounds, the gash at the side of his head looked dry now.

'Get me your belt, c'mon.' Asrul untied it quickly from his pants and handed it to Malik. Malik kicked the back of Siti's knees, sending her down with a thump. Then, he bound her hands to her ankles and pushed her face down into the dark floor.

'This should keep her quiet while we talk, Asrul.'

She lay beside Tan Moe's stiff body. As her eyes fixed into the gash on his head, her face shook into waves of flesh and she started to cry. Malik stepped towards her and gave her a quick kick in the ribs.

'Why are you here, Abang?' Asrul regained enough sanity to be able to mutter this, almost stammering.

'Because in this story, you are the fool, Asrul, and I am not. I have been following you since last night. After those immigrants tried to nail you and after all that had happened with Porthaksh, I knew we both couldn't trust anyone else, Adik.'

'Did you hear what Tan Moe said to me?'

'Yes, I was behind the wall, on the other side. A pretty slick fucker he was, I must admit. He stole the money, and now he wants to make us look responsible. A damn cocky snake, much like this bitch you were both fucking.'

'Thanks for saving me again ...'

'Thanks? I didn't save you – you saved yourself, man. Finally, you have become the man I need you to be. How does it feel, eh? Isn't it great?'

'Well, I don't know, actually …'

Siti was moving under them on the floor, trying to slide sideways and reach for the door, crawling in the shadow and dust like a tapeworm that had just emerged from a dead anus. Malik grabbed her by the leg and pulled her back to where she had been without saying a word.

'Please, please let me go …' She was crying tears that had turned black, polluted with eyeliner.

'What do we want to do with this slut?'

'I'm sure she knows where the money is. And we need some time to think, Asrul. Whatever we do, there is a bunch of money involved, and if we are going to leave Penang for good, we will need money to start up somewhere new. Of course, on the other hand, we could just hand it all back to Porthaksh and ask for a reward in return, and save our asses anyhow. The fucker likes us, I'm sure. But, let me tell you, I ain't very comfortable with that Persian anymore …'

'You're right. This Chinese bastard had set up things in a clever way. Fucking me up and then leaving with the money for good …'

'Well, you saw this bitch, right? Irrational. They're all crazed. They don't have anything to lose, Asrul. Let's tie her up against the wall.'

'What?'

'Should we just leave her here and go then? And lose the money? And let her go to the police to tell them a bunch of lies?

I only have a couple friends in one police station, Adik. I can't control all the fucking cops in this world, man.'

Malik bent over and grabbed Siti by the ankles. As he dragged her across the wooden floor, she started sobbing again. Malik pulled her up and thrust her against the wall.

'Now, help me out as I untie her and put her in these belts. You were a lucky sod, Asrul – these two couldn't even manage to tie you up properly. But let me tell you, I was about to come in and shoot them both dead, if I had to. Thank god, you were faster.' He handed the gun to Asrul, holding it by the barrel. Asrul clutched it and immediately aimed at Siti's face, four inches away from her blackening, swollen eye. She cried and her mouth bent into a horrible downward curve.

'Don't do it! Don't shoot me, please ... I love you ... Please!'

On hearing her say these words, this time, Asrul did not feel any hot liquid pouring out of his belly button and into his bowels, down to his toes – he could only savour the metallic complacency of the gun pressed within his fist. This woman had abused him. She had wanted him to die and rot in hell.

'Love ...' He put the gun against her forehead and felt the metal cutting shivers into her. He saw that the seat of her jeans quickly turned into a darker blue, while spilling an acrid smelling liquid onto the floor.

'Oh shit, Asrul! This wrench has just pissed herself. Oh my, she peed herself like an old witch.' Malik broke into laughter.

She was sitting in a small pool of piss, which was drifting slowly out on the floor, following the wood's inclination. Asrul retraced one step, liberating her face from the barrel's pressure.

He didn't feel any mercy; he was getting a bit scared of this new self of his, and of the way things had gotten to be.

Malik secured her right arm into one of the belts and, stretching it tightly, he fixed the buckle into the closest hole. He did the same for the other arm. Siti stood shaking and crying; her face had turned so ugly, he thought.

'Alright, she is tied up for good!' Malik said with a sigh of relief.

'She will talk. Check if the Chinese has some cigarettes on him. They all usually smoke,' he motioned at Tan Moe's body. Asrul got close to the corpse and felt weird as he thrust his hands into its pockets and looked for the smokes.

'Don't touch anything else but his clothes; be careful.'

Asrul found a cigarette pack. He also found a lighter, neatly stashed inside the pocket.

'Give me.' Malik got the pack, put one cigarette in his mouth and lit it up, coughing lightly. 'Shit, cigarettes ... I hate them. But they do burn hot. Check this out, Adik.'

He knelt close to Siti, his face scrunched up as he tried to bear her urine's acrid smell.

'Babe, I will ask you once and not twice. Where is the money?'

She was muttering some sort of prayer in a low voice, staring into the darkness with empty eyes.

'Again: where is the money you two stole?'

'I didn't steal any money ... he did ...' she finally burst out. Malik brought the cigarette closer to her face.

'I don't know if you have any knowledge of other religions, dear Siti, but at this very moment, you must know that you stand like Jesus. And you do know what happened to him, right?'

He grabbed her ankle and brought the cigarette's tip to it. The fire sizzled against the skin with a hissing sound. Siti's face contorted, her eyes squeezed in, and her mouth cracked open in a high-pitched scream.

'They put him on the cross to die for everybody's sins, Siti. Are you ready for that?' Malik pushed another fire circle into the upper arch of her foot, just below the toes. Asrul was holding her other leg down by pressing a foot into her knee. After all, she deserved all this, he reasoned. She had cheated him. Had stolen his love. Had tried to kill him. An inhuman creeping sensation of satisfaction was crawling down his spine, slow as a black, alien crab.

'You see, Siti, you can either talk now and tell us where you guys have hidden the money, or decide to keep on paying for all your sins. And for his sins as well,' he pointed at the dead figure lying only a few steps away from them.

'I don't know where the money is, I swear. Tan Moe, he knows where it is.'

'But, he's dead!' Malik spat back, his face only two inches away from hers. She kept crying, drinking her tears and melted mascara, her face vertically scarred by black watercolour.

'Believe me, girl, I can go on like this forever,' he took some drags from the cigarette to keep it alive, ready to punch in another burn. 'Just tell me where the money is, and we'll let you go. I promise.'

23

Malik parked the car in front of the Happy Mart and rested his arms over the steering wheel.

'Do you really think she doesn't know anything?' Asrul asked. He looked dirty and beat up and didn't want to get out of the car.

'Well, I gave her so many burns that she won't be walking for a week, at least. But she didn't say a word. I guess she might really not know shit. That Tan Moe was smart, not telling his bitch where the money was. He was definitely not dumb like you, dear Asrul,' Malik broke into a quick laughter.

'Give her a few hours. We'll return before nightfall. Did you make sure she'll not choke to death on the rag you stuck into her mouth?'

'Sure. So, what do we do with the money, when we find it, Abang?'

'Well, I guess we could put it to good use. You see, I have this contact in England, a white power organisation. We could work for them, at gigs. Plus, can you imagine how much dirty work can be scored in London, Asrul?'

'Really? Why is that?'

'That city is full of immigrant scum, Asrul, from every place in the world you can think of,' Malik continued, his arms extended over the steering wheel, his voice rising. 'And now that you have proved yourself to be so bad ass,' Malik turned to Asrul, visibly excited, his eyes blazing, 'the path is all clear, and cleaned out of any obstacles, Adik.'

Asrul sank back in his seat, feeling like his strength was pouring out of his body and into the street through the crack between the side door and the bottom of the car.

'I don't know anymore, Abang … shit, I killed someone …'

'That was legitimate defence, Adik. He wanted to kill you. He chained you up. The girl's still there, Asrul. I understand it may sound like a fucked up story, and well, it is, but you have me to back you up for it. I'm your witness.'

'I just wish we had never left Alor Star,' Asrul said, looking outside of the window. He saw an old man curled up on the floor, watching people as they walked in and out of the shop, begging for some spare change.

'Don't say that. Today, you became a real man, Asrul. I'm proud of you. You could defend yourself, you didn't need me there to help you, Adik. You were great.'

Asrul's cell phone rang. He looked at the display and realised it was Porthaksh.

'Should I answer?'

'Yes, Asrul. Tell them what happened. It's best if they see this for themselves.'

'Hello? Asrul, are you there?' It was the dry, chopping accent of Ming Fei's voice that was filling up his ear.

'Hey, where have you been? You vanished, ma'am ...'

'No, actually you did. Where have you been all day? Didn't you check your phone? We tried to call you a hundred times, but it wouldn't get through!'

'Sorry, I had a situation here. I think you should ...'

'No, Asrul. We think *you* should come over here. Now.'

'I'm sorry, Ming Fei, but I'm not moving my ass. Tell the Persian or whoever else you want to – even your Chinese mafia friends if you'd like – to come and see me, where I am.'

'Asrul, I don't think ...'

'Listen, Miss China, you can come and see what's happening here for yourself, or you can just piss off. I said I had a situation here, didn't I?' Malik looked surprised at his friend's words.

A few moments of silence were broken by the muted, undecipherable chattering of people, caused by the holding of the receiver against someone's chest.

'OK, where are you?'

'Balik Pulau. Just come to the main intersection; there's a shopping area there, with a Happy Mart. We'll be waiting for you over there?'

'Who else is coming?'

'My honourable colleague, ma'am. No worries. See you very soon, I hope.'

He hung up and put the cell phone back in his trousers. He felt tired. The tension released slowly around his neck; the catch in his nape untightened, and his muscles let go into the seat.

'Very well acted, Asrul. Shit, I think I might have to kill a man today as well, so I can become like you, Adik!'

'Don't fuck with me, stupid,' Asrul started laughing, but he wanted to cry.

* * *

The car arrived almost thirty minutes later. It entered the parking area voluptuously, its striking black-shaded windows impenetrable from the outside. It stopped next to their car, but left a couple of empty spots between the two vehicles. A back door opened and a high-heeled foot touched the ground: Ming Fei. She was wearing black shoes, a white top and a grey chequered skirt, her face again mirrored behind her shades. She gave a nonchalant look around her, closed the door behind here and walked across the space swiftly.

'Hey, Ming Fei,' Asrul said without surprise.

'What happened here, Asrul,' Ming Fei dived directly into the core of her quest.

'Who beat you up?' she continued, lowering her shades and looking over their frame.

'I might have to ask you the same question: do they beat up Chinese people if they don't go around fishing for money?'

Malik laughed at her from the driver seat; Ming Fei stood motionless in the sun, her mouth reduced to a bloodless line of bitten lips.

'You know Asrul, and you, Malik, you both are really not in a position to act too smart. Why did you want us to come here? I hope this is serious.' She continued, 'They wouldn't be very happy, otherwise.'

'OK, listen. We know who has the money you are looking for, but we don't know where it is.'

They both saw her expression change for a millisecond before becoming again the same pale, hard face of hers. Her skirt fluttered in the wind, and she pushed back a curl of hair that had come out of her sock bun and fallen over her right ear.

'Fine, I will tell them. Now, you drive and we will follow you. Where?'

'It's a house, not so far away. First drive, then walk.'

'OK,' she said and turned around, took a few long steps. She reached the car and disappeared inside it.

* * *

Malik pulled over under the branches of a small palm tree. The other car followed suit, stopping a few metres behind theirs. The sun was strong, but was preparing to disappear and leave space for the quiet darkness of another night. They got out of the car and locked its doors. The black car opened and released Ming Fei, who quickly joined them under the palm tree.

'If you don't mind, it'll be just me coming along, Asrul.'

'What about them?'

'It's just the driver in there, Asrul. They're not here with me, of course.' She took off her shades and she gave him the look she usually gave him, the same inquisitive, specimen-raping gaze that made it seem like she enjoyed dipping her fingers into open wounds and then watching the blood drip from her fingertips. 'You will never learn,' she concluded, putting her shades back on.

'It's not safe to be together around here. Let's move. Show me what you've got.'

'Fine. This way, ma'am ...' Malik motioned towards the winding path with a sweeping movement of his left arm, giving her a stitched smile at the same time. Ming Fei began walking across the rubble, carefully putting one foot in front of the other, like a slow horse treading on high heels. Asrul realised he still had some sort of weird respect for this woman, who had used and sucked him dry, as if he were a clam that had been slow-cooked in the whirlpool of her post-defecation carnal desires. He moved forward, giving her a bit of a distance. When they turned down the slope and saw the house appear before them, emerging abruptly from the surrounding vegetation, Ming Fei stopped and looked around with cautious eyes.

'Is this the place?'

'Yes.'

'So this is where they are hiding?'

'Apparently ... And this is where Tan Moe wanted to tell you all that *we* were hiding him,' said Malik.

'Did you tell anyone else about this place, Asrul?'

'No. The girl brought me here, and luckily Malik followed us. I don't think anyone else knows about this house.'

Ming Fei extracted a cigarette from a small metal box that she had pulled out of her handbag, lit it up and sucked a long drag from it, then planted her heels firmly into the red soil. Asrul could see the house's appearance change as he saw it through the line of smoke rising up from the burning cigarette's tip. It seemed like a witch had touched it with her nasty wand and had given it a life of its own – the house looked like it was moving, slipping away slowly, trying not to be seen by them while it played this game of jungle hide-and-seek, its tiles slightly twitching, as if it were about to run out of breath.

Looking back before him, Asrul realised that Ming Fei was observing something; he tried to catch a glimpse of it by stealing a piece of her view from behind her.

'So, if you didn't tell anyone about this place, why is the door open?'

'What?'

Asrul finally noticed it: a tiny blade of darkness was cornering the threshold, mutating slowly in size as the breeze played a tug of war with the wooden panel.

'Shit, did you close the door, Malik?'

'Yes, I did. I still have the key.'

'OK, relax, boys,' Ming Fei said, throwing the cigarette to the ground and grinding it with the tip of her shoe. 'If the door is open, it probably means they have left.'

'Fuck!'

'Tell me exactly what happened in there, Asrul.'

'Well ... I had to defend myself, Ming Fei ... Tan Moe is dead ...'

She received this piece of information like a stab to her gut, her irises exploding wide.

'What did you do?' she finally exhaled, and then inhaled heat and red dust.

'I had to. They tied me up. He was beating me up with a stick. I was damn lucky as he didn't tie me up too well. I managed to slip off one of the buckles he had used to imprison me with ... Then, I attacked him and, well, it just happened, Ming Fei ...'

'OK, and then?'

'Then, Malik came down with Siti. She was my girlfriend. Well, actually, they had just used her to set me up. She was *his* girl. They had wanted to frame me, wanted to tell Sio Sam Ong that I was the one stealing the money, so that they could distract them, lower their attention long enough to flee.'

Ming Fei grinned. 'Well, a carefully thought-out and fucked-up plan, I must say. But you have stopped it, dear Asrul. Very well done. Mister Chang will be pleased to hear this news, I guess ...' She crossed her arms and did not speak for a long moment. The air buzzed in the late day's haze, a beehive of particles and dust and falling sunrays.

'What about the girl and the money?'

'Well,' Malik interrupted her, 'just go in and see for yourself. I tied her up with my own hands. I tortured her, burnt her feet off ... but she wouldn't speak. We just left her there for a couple of hours, and I doubt she could have escaped. As shocked as she was, and with all those burns ... I tied her up *well*, ma'am,' he said, pumping his chest out.

'Fine, one dead man and a tortured and shocked woman tied up in the basement. And now, an open door. Excuse my presumption, but I do not think we need a rocket scientist to tell us it's best to pull out our guns,' she confronted him with an embittered voice, facing him strongly.

'Don't tell me *you* don't want to go in and see? That you don't want to report this to the big guys?'

Asrul was afraid that Malik was being a little too edgy.

'Screw you, Malik, of course I do. Asrul and I, we're going in; you can have a look around the house first. This way, I also don't have to look at your fucking face for a while. Well, if she has escaped and considering that you made her unable to walk, she won't be too far I guess ... Go, now!'

'At your service, ma'am!' Malik mocked a military salute and fended off the air with a hard snap of his left forearm, then he stormed off towards the jungle that surrounded the house's backyard.

Ming Fei turned to Asrul and looked at him as if she wanted to bite into him, break open his shell with her front teeth.

'Are you coming in or what?'

She pulled up the left flap of her skirt and pulled out a handgun from the black garter belt wrapped around her snowy white thigh.

'Let's roll, baby,' she stormed off, leaving Asrul behind, watching her become smaller as she approached the front yard. She zoomed to the side of the staircase holding the gun close to her chest, and peeked through the dark threshold that lay behind the flapping panel.

24

THE AIR INSIDE the house smelled different from when he had first come in; it was like something was missing now, or had been removed along with its scent. The corridor branched off into the dark.

'Be careful,' Asrul whispered into Ming Fei's ear from behind, 'this is where Tan Moe hit me in the head. If someone's still around here, this is a good place to hide.'

Ming Fei lifted up her gun and proceeded softly, placing one foot slowly after the other and trying not to make the wood creak. They slowly reached the end of the corridor and then faced the door leading down to the room where Asrul's lycanthropy had taken its death toll.

'It's clear …' Ming Fei turned slowly to the left, pointing the gun at the door panel. 'Open it, will you, please?' she said to the door in a sarcastic voice.

In that precise moment, Asrul realised that he did not really know much about this woman. She had plucked his life by its leg as if it were a sacrificial chick and had spitefully thrown it into a blender, had switched on the power and enjoyed watching his balance get crushed between the blade and the plastic container. She had showed him her power, and she had taken him, and he was still trapped under her spell. He couldn't claim that he had fucked her: *she* had fucked him. She had mounted him as if he had been a mere lump of flesh equipped with a penis. That was all she had needed to get her rocks off. He opened the door, staying behind the panel, and watched the steps appear slowly in the blade of light projected from the corridor. There was nothing and nobody waiting for them on the other side.

Ming Fei lowered the gun.

'It's empty. How are the rooms set up downstairs?'

'As far as I know, there is only one room, and at the back of the wall there is a car. I didn't get a chance to see the other rooms down there.'

'You can go in first. I'll cover you.'

Asrul went down carefully, trying to look over the handrail and into the room, but it was still too dark to see anything but confused shadows. When they reached the bottom, Ming Fei thrust her empty hand into her handbag and pulled out a torch light.

'Would you mind using this, dear?'

The place seemed extremely and strangely silent. Asrul realised that Siti, although biting into a rag, should have broken the deadpan soundscape with her presence. Humans have that particular way of filling up space after all, just by being there, and breathing. That was not happening now.

He snapped up the torch light's switch, and a circle of light hit the wooden wall, making shadows bulge all around it. He moved it, and thus became the controller of reality in this surreal situation – a shoe appeared in the blaze, and slowly Asrul uncovered Tan Moe, his dead position still unchanged. He could feel Ming Fei getting stiffer behind him. The light then flashed against the floor beside him: he noticed that the thirsty wooden planks of the pavement had already drunk in the blood. The metallic bowl was turned on its side, and pieces of minced food were splattered over his hair and mixed up with his blood, making up a new recipe for dark, soggy rice. He played the beam of the torch over to the other side of the room then instinctively jerked it up towards the ceiling. He didn't like what he had just seen.

Siti was still there, the way they had left her, tied up against the wall, arms spread out over her head. Asrul pointed the light on her face and shuddered against Ming Fei. Siti's eyes looked directly into theirs, the irises exploding. Her hair was all over the place, tangled into braids and glued together with blood. A long, deep dark line ran across her throat and around her neck; her neck and upper chest were drenched in a shower of her own blood.

'Shit!' Ming Fei exhaled loudly, getting closer to him.

He could see her feet step into the circle of light pounding against the floor, a whirlpool of dust levitating in its ray. He moved the light forward and saw Siti's foot – three of her toes were scattered on the floor just before her heel, leaving behind three small lumps of flesh and bone with pink acrylic heads. It looked like they had snapped right off the foot – with a pair of big scissors probably, Asrul guessed.

After a long moment, when they had both gotten back some balance into their heads, Ming Fei spoke. Her voice sounded less aggressive than usual, and he appreciated that.

'Asrul, is there anything else you need to tell me?'

'No. Look at this …'

'Are you guys trying to impress me with this crap in order to settle things and keep the money?'

'I knew you would ask me this question, Ming Fei. I've already told you the truth. We did work on her a bit, but we didn't go so far as to kill her. Even Tan Moe was just a lucky mistake.'

She looked at him for a while, then grabbed his arm and pulled him to the outside of the room.

'Awk! Sorry, but I can't stand the smell of all that blood. Asrul, I think I might want to believe you. I don't think you're the kind of guy who can do this. You seem to have, by pure chance, stumbled into this mess. I don't know what's better for everyone involved – you killing him, or you having your head offered to us as the damn traitor.'

Asrul didn't know either. Someone had just maimed and sliced open the throat of his Indonesian girlfriend. His stomach was crawling inside of him, spun about by a whirlpool of conflicting feelings, tearing him apart. Then, like thunder, the thought fell on him. 'The Nigerians …' he said in a low voice, looking into her eyes but without actually seeing her. The moment his words flew across the air and pierced Ming Fei's ears, two gunshots thundered outside.

* * *

Malik had circled the house from the left side. The sun was going down and its last rays had painted the whole scene in low sepia light and had cast fat shadows on the ground. It was that moment of the day when looking for someone was the hardest, especially around a thick forested area. The whole point of his expedition was, in his own opinion, completely useless. He was convinced that Siti couldn't have escaped. He pictured her still tied up to the wall, blades of fear electrifying every single inch of her skin. Malik knew Siti wouldn't be able to walk, as wounded as she was. He still had to go looking for her though. This was just another way to amuse that Communist whore, he thought as he crossed the backyard and took a path that led deep into the forest. The evening was still lit well, but the thick rows of branches were darkening his vision. He kept walking and observing the insides of the forest, looking for a shape, a sound, for any trace that might lead him to find her crawling about in the dense black soil. After a few minutes, the path ended and a slope marked the end of the flat expanse, giving way to a series of low hills. Malik didn't think she would have gone up there and decided to work his way round the back, trying to connect to the right side of the backyard, thus having explored all the space around the house. It was getting even darker now, the last light was still fighting its way to survive, against the natural coming of the night's hordes, the daily ritual of sun suffocation. Malik kept going. When he had reached three quarters of his way back to the house, he overheard something move in the foliage around him. Instinctively, he reached for his gun and began to walk slowly, scanning the scene. He didn't realise that he had gotten very close to the house's backyard area when he saw two pairs of eyes staring at him from behind a tree trunk.

'Don't shoot!' said a deep, foreign voice. A tall black man came out of the foliage and reached the path with a small jump, keeping his hands up in the air.

'Please, don't shoot. I wanna talk to you,' continued the man, motioning with his left hand until another African stepped out, shaking a few branches and pressing the foliage under his shoes. This man was holding a gun, but he lowered it slowly and put it away inside his vest, all the while looking into the eye of Malik's barrel.

'Who the hell are you, may I ask?'

'You know who we are. You fought some of us at the Chinese club, remember?'

'Of course I do. You guys are not easy to forget, for sure,' Malik grinned at them. 'What do you want from me?'

'Don't play dumb, skinhead. We're here for the same thing you are – our drug money. There's one simple problem though. You killed the man who had it, and now we would like to know where it is,' said the man in his low, potent voice without any sign of fear of hesitation. It seemed like this man did not care about the gun pointed at his chest.

'The girl knows, but she ain't talking,' Malik answered.

'If the girl did know, she tried very hard to keep her secret, right until the end' the man's mouth opened in a big smile revealing two rows of white, sparkling teeth. 'In any case, she can't speak anymore ...'

Malik understood. These people really meant business. They were desperate for that elusive money. To him, it was not so important, after all. He could have had a lot of money, if he just cared to ask …

'So, let me get this straight. The man is dead, you killed the girl and you don't know where the money is. And you think I know, right?'

'Yes,' the African said, the shine of his teeth disappearing into a circle of dark lips.

'How do you possibly think I might know?'

'Because you killed Tan Moe. There has to be a reason for that. You have to know something about it, and we've decided to ask you. Just give us the money, or tell us where it is, and that would be fine too. It'll all be over then. No more killings. We go our own ways … at least until the next time you try to screw us over.'

The three stood in silence, without moving a muscle. The breeze howled low songs through the forest's thick body. Malik thought that it sounded quite weird that these people were trying so desperately to get hold of the money, while the organisation led by the Iranians and the Chinese were trying to do the same. There was no connection between those people and the Nigerians after all; at least, that was what Porthaksh had told them.

'OK, mister,' Malik fended the silence, 'did you know that Sio Sam Ong is after the same thing? They are here, now, and they want to talk to the girl … It would be a problem for them to see that you guys had itchier feet …'

The two Nigerians gave each other surprised, confused glances.

'What do the Chinese have to do with this? That's our money.

Tan Moe dealt directly with me; I gave him the bags and all. Don't bullshit me, skinhead … What's this deal with Sio Sam Ong now?'

'This is all very interesting to hear, Mister Africa. Are you trying to tell me that you don't know about the connection?'

'What connection?'

'Tan Moe and Sio Sam Ong …'

The tall Nigerian jerked his neck to the side and opened up his arms at the same time, and then returned it to its initial position.

'What the hell are you trying to say here, skinhead? He was buying the shit from us. What's this Chinese mafia bullshit all about? Just tell me where *my* money is and fuck off from where you came from. Isn't that easy?'

Malik came to his own conclusions about the information the Nigerians had just given him, but before he could say anything, the trees moved around them, and then he was on the ground, bleeding.

* * *

Ming Fei's handbag buzzed, the ringtone sucking them back into reality. 'Hello?' Ming Fei answered the call and stood there impaled by the voice coming out of the earpiece. The conversation lasted for about fifteen seconds, which seemed like the long, atrocious hours spent peeling the skin off a dead man's chest. Asrul could see her expression mutating slowly at each stroke of the passing seconds she went from being emotionless to getting filled up with surprise to then becoming astonished in bewilderment.

As she moved the cell phone away from her face and set it

down, slowly, Asrul spoke up, shattering the wall of emotional frost that was building between them.

'What was that?'

'The driver ...' she muttered. 'He's gone. The police are here, they have surrounded the house.'

'What?'

That was all Asrul could say.

25

'Stay on the ground and put your hands down,' a cop screamed from behind a smoking gun barrel.

The squad came out of the trees and surrounded them. One of the skinheads was on the ground – the bullet had torn through his left arm and had nailed him to the ground; the wound was a dark hole, a saw-toothed carnal mouth sputtering the man's blood. The skinhead had been lucky though, Cheah realised, as the bullet had only pierced the flesh, without shattering bone. He was curled up on the ground now, pressing his right hand over the wound, watching the dark red tips of liquid tongues licking out of the spaces between his closed fingers.

One of the Nigerians, who had been standing with his hands held up until that very moment, jerked to the side and ran towards the forest. The bullet hit him in his left shoulder. He flew off the ground and crashed among the bushes and tree branches. His back moved up and down, frantically painting the air with hot breath.

The second African didn't make a move. His lips had sunk somewhere deep into his cheeks. The handcuffs closed around his wrists with a metallic bite. The man kept the silent mouth-less expression on his face while Mr. Cheah's men dragged him away.

'Where's your pal?' he asked, standing in front of the skinhead, the tips of his boots only inches away from the boy's suffering face. 'You have a lot of explaining to do, my friend. For now, I want you to tell me where he is.'

'In the house ... He's in there,' the skinhead said, pressing his wounded arm. 'Get me a first aid kit and a bandage. I want to make a phone call first or I'm not going to talk, I tell you.' He raised his gaze directly into Mr. Cheah's eyes. It was a spiteful, angry but clearly resigned look that stirred the officer's feelings, deep inside of him.

'We'll see what we can do about that ...' he turned around, and left him down in the dust.

* * *

Those Vietnamese girls had indeed raised an important issue: someone in the lower ranks was fucking it all up. Big time. And he couldn't let that happen. No way. He still had a code of honour and conduct, something that related to the high ideal he'd always had of the police corps. This code was the reason he had decided to join the force, and he was still resolute in following it.

When the girls had come in with that story, Mr. Cheah knew that he could not let this one pass unattended. There had always been rumours of similar things happening within the police corps, to varying degrees of misconduct. Sure, he had sometimes helped cover up stuff and prevent bad news from hitting the headlines.

But when those two women had walked into his office and asked him for justice, he couldn't let their plea slip past.

Their story sounded almost made up, but he still wanted to believe their claim – apart from the law-breaking officers, who were the two plain clothed men the girls had described?

The women reported to have been abused just about a week before the club's shootout. Although there seemed to exist no logical connection between these two seemingly unrelated events, something had sparked Mr. Cheah to believe there did exist a link.

He had gone through the evidence pictures taken at the scene of the club shootout: a young Chinese man had been shot dead on the floor, and there were no other signs of disorder except for the chaos left by a running, scared stampede of dancers who had aimed for the exit door. He had acquired the CCTV camera recordings from that evening. Unfortunately, the murder had happened in a remote corner, far away from the centre of the action. Strobe lights and a mass of people running for their lives had only further rendered the tapes a real disappointing piece of evidence. However, he had gone through the recordings taken by the hidden camera placed over the club's entrance and had browsed through them to spot any unconventional people. Among a large number of pretty girls in short dresses and boys looking for some dance kicks, two young Malay men, one noticeably taller and bigger than the other, both more casually dressed than the club's regular crowd, had caught his eye. The strange thing about them was that they both had shaven heads, looking like they had just stepped out of an army camp.

He had immediately dialled the number that Cam had given

him, a weird excitement beginning to warm up his stomach.

'Hello, Mr. Cheah here. I'm sorry to disturb you again, but could you reconfirm some details from your previous statement?'

'Perfect. I'm aware that you couldn't see things too clearly, but you can definitely confirm that the two other men involved had shaven heads, right? Great. Thanks for your assistance; I'll keep you informed on any further developments.'

He replaced the receiver on the hook and sat silently for a while. He then rewound the CCTV camera footage and stopped exactly at the part where the bouncer let in the two suspects. He paused and went through the still frames to find the best angle, then zoomed in as much as he could, taking care not to shatter the image quality into squarish pixelation. He then clicked on the printing option and waited until the machine had vomited onto his desk a reproduction of the two heads. He grabbed the sheet and brought it close to his eyes, peering into the pair of paper pupils before him.

Without hesitation, he had begun an internal investigation of all the officers who had been out on patrol on the night of the reported rape case. In a matter of days, he had identified a few potential suspects. The list had included a couple of officers who hadn't reported for that particular night's 2 a.m. control check. On reviewing their files, he had noticed that their position details were missing around that same time as well; this was too much of a coincidence to not ring a bell. The files had shown that they had resumed normal operations at about 2.45 a.m. and had returned all the calls they had received after that. That one hole though, Cheah was convinced it had to mean something.

It had not been difficult for him to fish out the truth from the patrol officers' throats. When he had pointed out about their missed responses while being on call that night, their faces had immediately flashed some nervousness. Then, when he had pulled out the pictures, he had noticed pearls of sweat rolling down one of the men's necks, and he had been sure that he had hit the nail right on the head. After that, he had set about getting the names out of those two officers; luckily, he was the kind of man who knew a thing or two about making birds of prey sing.

* * *

'Shit, they left me here ... I can't ... I mean, I can't just ...'Ming Fei looked like she was on the verge of a nervous breakdown. The remains of her proud, impenetrable mask were falling off her face like stucco off a decaying concrete wall.

'Didn't you say they were very powerful? Call them. You have a phone. Ask them to do something for us!'

She looked at him with a different kind of eyes, apologetic ones.

'It doesn't work like that ...' Asrul realised that she was looking for help and comfort, and a quick solution. They wouldn't be able to escape via the front door. They both knew that the police had already surrounded the house, and that they were armed.

'Shit! There are two dead people in here ...'

'I might have an idea to get us out of here,' Asrul said. 'I don't know how the cops got here. Someone might have talked, or they might have followed you. Anyway, the only way out of here is through the front door.'

'And then?'

'Malik is out there, and I can't leave him alone. In any case, with Tan Moe dead, this shit will never stop. I don't have the money, and I don't know where it is. Even assuming that I might be able to escape now, they will come after me again ... And again, until I give them what they want. Or until I'm dead. I think I should just go up to the police now, surrender myself to them ...'

'And risk the death penalty?'

'I don't know. Well, the front door is the only chance you have out of here. It's dark outside now. You could try to run into the forest. If you make it back to them, they will surely help you; they would want to know what happened. And you must tell them the truth – that we never tried to screw them over, that this asshole is dead and has taken his secret with him. There is no way to know where that money is now. Tell them to forget about it, that the cash is not worth killing more lives over.'

'I don't know ...'

It was probably not the right moment to do this, but Asrul took a step forward and put his arms around her. Ming Fei was a small woman: he felt her breath against his Adam's apple, her hair sock bun against his nostrils. It smelled fresh. The gun, still in her right hand, bulged against his upper thigh. He felt that hugging her was the right thing to do, even if her response felt cold, as if his touch had taken out the breath of life from her.

'Why are you doing this?' she finally muttered against his chest. Her breath was hot against him. He suddenly remembered that night in Taipei, how that same breath had violently entered his face's cavities; now, it was the feeble puff of a dying emotional steamer engine.

'I don't know myself. I wanted things to go differently, but it's apparent now that I'm incapable of making things happen the way I want them to.'

He kissed the top of her forehead and let her go. 'Good luck.'

He turned around and reached for the staircase. She was still standing there, sandwiched between the dead and the living, struggling to make a decision. 'C'mon, Ming Fei, we have to be very quick. They're getting closer.' When he was halfway up the stairs, he turned around to see if she was following him. Instead of her face, he found himself looking into the single, black eye of her gun. Ming Fei was half a metre behind it, her arm slightly bent upwards to aim better at Asrul's head.

'What's this?' he said without much surprise. Never trust a Communist bitch, Malik had told him. Why don't I ever listen to my friend, Asrul wondered.

'I can do it, yes …' she wasn't the firm woman she had been thus far. Panic had crumpled the sheets of composure she had been sleeping under since she had set foot on Malaysian soil. Asrul raised his hands slowly and stood stock-still on the stairs.

'I can kill you now. I can tell the cops that I'm a simple stupid tourist and that I met you at some bar and we had a fling, that I didn't know anything about your business here. I'll tell them that I hung out with you to see some places here, and bang! You led me to this place here, with all of these dead people, and that you wanted to kill me too … I finally had to shoot you with your own gun, to save myself. Yes, the Chinese embassy will help …'

Asrul didn't reply, confronted as he was by her shaking barrel. Her hand was trembling; he could see a pearl of sweat rolling back towards her elbow, leaving behind a wet trail.

'Ming Fei,' he finally said, 'do you think the police are that stupid? Besides, Malik is out there, now. He might have already talked. He might already have spat out your name, since he doesn't like you that much. They'll surely have their ways to know that your story is full of shit.'

'No, we have a connection at the police headquarters. He helps cover up shit for us. He'll help me out. Don't move.'

'I'm certainly not moving,' he answered without batting an eyelid.

She dug her left hand into the handbag slung across her shoulder and tried to pull something out. She moved her gaze on and off Asrul, panicking, when the thing did not come out of the bag as quickly as she wanted it to. 'Shit!'

She finally managed to pull it out, it was her cell phone. She clumsily scrolled through the numbers on her call-log screen and thumbed the screen to make the call. She drew the earpiece to her ear and stood there, the gun in her right hand, the cell phone in her left, big drops of her sweat falling to the ground, leaving big stains. Asrul could see that, in that moment, Ming Fei was entirely focussed on that earpiece; she wasn't in that room anymore, with him or with the two corpses that lay behind her.

'C'mon,' she screamed.

She stood like that, her soul pouring out of her left ear and into the earpiece. Nobody seemed to give a damn on the other side.

'Fuck!' Ming Fei screamed loudly in the mouthpiece. The gun was not pointing at Asrul anymore, and he didn't even realise this.

'Calm down,' he said, from the stairs. 'I told you, they don't care about us anymore. It's just a waste of time. Don't try to contact Porthaksh now. Just focus on saving your own ass. Follow me.'

'She ain't following no one nowhere,' a deep voice shot out from behind Asrul. 'Put that gun down lady, or I'm gonna shoot you right in the head.'

The man had an African accent. Asrul turned around and saw him came towards them, down the stairs, slowly and potently, as an erection might bulge out of an unzipped fly. The first thing Asrul saw about the man, even before he had seen the gun pointed directly at them, were the bright whites of the man's eyes. The gun was only half as menacing as the man's face: a long scar ran across his left cheek, stretching from his lips to the bone of his jaw.

'Put that gun down, I said. *Now*,' the man growled.

Asrul let the man walk past him, down the stairs, and to Ming Fei. The man stood a metre away from her, positioning himself between her and Asrul. She finally let the phone fall to the ground. It disappeared into the floor, thudding away somewhere against the creaky wooden panels. Slowly, Ming Fei lowered her right arm, liberating Asrul's head from the hold of her gun's barrel.

'Let me get this straight once and for all. And listen to me carefully as I hate to repeat myself. We're fucking short on time, OK?'

Both nodded, in silence. Ming Fei's right temple was covered in small drops of sweat. The dark shadow of the African's gun barrel was projected on it, starkly contrasting with her white skin.

'So, where's the fucking money?'

'We don't know,' Asrul said, grabbing the man's attention. His face turned up to him – the scar gave the impression that one side of his face was always curled up into a smile, even when his lips were closed shut.

'Oh, you don't know? So what the fuck is this?' he pointed at Tan Moe's dead head.

'He was holding me captive. I killed him so I could escape, that's all … He was the only one who knew where the money was!'

'And what about that useless Indonesian bitch? Tell me. Don't fuck with me or I shoot down your girl here …'

'Actually, that dead Indonesian was my girl. At least, I thought she was. And you can gun down this bitch anytime you want, man! All women are bitches anyway … That Indo bitch conned me. She had a deal with this dead bastard, but I don't think she knew where the money was.'

The man laughed. 'Of course she didn't know anything, man. When I snapped off her toes, you should have seen her cry. Girls like her are not made for such dirty jobs. This Chinese here, on the other hand, she looks like she is one tough ho.' He turned to look at Ming Fei, 'The kind of bitch that wants to shoot you dead even if you're trying to help her save her ass.'

Asrul noticed that the veins on the man's neck were pumping so much blood that his eyes were bulging out much further.

'Lady, I'd slap your tight ass right now if I didn't have to hold you under fire,' he cracked out laughing again, licking his upper lip with fast movements of his tongue.

'So where's my money anyway?' he continued, 'because let me tell ya, forty K is quite a lot for me. I don't know about you, but I need that shit. Hard work's gotta pay off. We have given almost half a kilogram to this dead asshole over here, and he said he would pay us later, with interest. He'd come to us to buy, and then he'd sell it all off at a bar he worked at. He didn't seem like a problem, because he usually paid us on time. But then, he fucked us. After four weeks, there was still no trace of the money. And then he just disappeared.'

'Wait a moment,' Ming Fei came back alive. 'You're saying that Tan Moe owed you money? That he was getting stuff from you as well?'

'As well? Who else was he getting it from? And who the fuck are you, Miss Secret Services?'

'He did the same thing to us, to my organisation. I work for Sio Sam Ong!'

'Ah, I see ...' the guy nodded. 'So, you suck cock for the Chinese ... Very bad. Very, very bad. Now I've more reasons to hate you!' he spat out, the veins of his neck bulging, moving like snakes under his skin. 'Your people ruin my own people's business.'

'Mister,' Ming Fei burst in once again, 'business is business, and let me tell you, you come from Africa, so you're not –' Her sentence was truncated by the ebony trajectory of the man's hand. It hit her right across the face, folding her down like a piece of low-quality Tesco furniture.

'Give me respect, or I'm gonna blow yo head off right now,

you bitch scum ...'

He was eating out his own breath. Ming Fei was curled up on the floor; she had lost her grip on the gun and held her fingers against the side of her face, speechless.

'Where's my money?' he asked again. 'If you're here, it means you must know where it is ...'

'I told you already – we don't know!' Asrul broke into the airwaves of hatred transmitting between the two. 'She's in the same situation you're in. Tan Moe jumped the gun on the both of you, understand? He has *your* money, and he has *her* money. But he's fucking dead, can't you see?'

The African retraced a bit in the dark and half his shape got enveloped by a dense blackness.

'I see ... And cops are all around us now ... I need my money, man. I need that fucking cash!'

He looked directly into Asrul and cut off his head with his potent, inquisitive stare.

'So if you don't know where is it, who knows? I'm not buying your fucked up story. It's too complicated.'

The man lowered his gaze to Ming Fei and got closer to her, and grabbed at her arm, and she fought back, screaming and trying to kick him in the crotch.

'Stand back, you slut. I need ya ... We gotta get outta here ...'

Today was a day of moments: they were coming and going quickly; catching them or not was becoming the difference between someone's life and death. Asrul decided it was time to grab his own moment. He flew down the stairs, spread eagled in the air, reaching for the man's neck. He hadn't really thought about what he might do when he landed. Unarmed as he was, he might just have to bite into the neck. Considering that he was stuck from both sides between the soft, smelly walls of a shit sandwich, he thought this was the best thing he could do. However, as he was flying towards the man, he saw his arm twist, and his gun's mouth screamed into Asrul's forehead; he twisted in the air. The detonation made him deaf.

The gun had exploded so close to his face that he didn't even know where the bullet had hit him; when he fell onto the floor, he still had no idea where all that pain was coming from. His chest or his shoulder or his leg? He didn't know. There was a hole somewhere, and he could feel hot blood streaming out of it; his muscles contracted, trying to keep in his life. Then he turned his face to the side: the blackening gash at the side of Tan Moe's head had become a gouged orbit, and was looking blindly into him, spreading its deathly stiffness across the wood planks, enveloping Asrul in its embrace of Death.

Sleep, Nazi boy, sleep now, Asrul told himself.

26

'Move, get around the house. Fast!'

Mr. Cheah had not been this excited in years: he had finally resigned his sitting-in-the-air-conditioned-office position and was back where all the action was. It hadn't been too difficult, in fact. While interrogating those two rogue officers, he had gotten a name and a bloody cell phone number from them, pulled it out of their throats as if with a pair of forceps. He had then monitored the phone's signal; he had known even then, had had a deep gut feeling that he was onto something big. And here he was. Bingo.

His men had been following Malik for days, from a distance, and when they had seen the two skinheads returning with that Chinese woman to the house, they had ordered a full squad to come around, armed to the teeth. Now, his specimen was lying on the floor with a bullet hole across his left upper arm, and a handkerchief wrapped around it in place of a real bandage, sipping his blood.

The policemen had placed themselves a circle, stretching around the building, holding their firearms tight. Mr. Cheah already pictured the front page of the next day's *Sin Chew Daily*, and perhaps even *The Star*: 'Police heroes bust criminals at Balik Pulau's Jungle house.' He could also picture the subheadings: 'The operation was a huge success: international drug link dismantled.' While his thoughts went racing in a spiral of whirlpooling white horses, Mr. Cheah saw the house's door open slowly. Two figures came out on the creaking porch, making their way across the darkness. The officers standing up front shone their torch-lights against them, the beams erasing the darkness from the blackboard of the night.

'Don't move! Stand still! Or I will blow her head off!'

A tall African man was holding a gun against the temple of the Chinese woman; she had entered the house with one of the skinheads just before Cheah and his men had attacked the other in the jungle. The African was holding her tight against his chest; his left forearm was clutched around her throat, while his right hand pressed the gun's barrel against the right side of her head. She looked much smaller than him, possibly because she was wearing no shoes.

'I said, back off and don't move! If you come around or shoot, she's dead. You don't want to get this international criminal killed so soon, do you? This shit's so much deeper than you cops think it is ... This woman has many things to tell you. She'll help you bust a big drug operation.'

The African moved a step down the stairs and then froze: it was clear that he was expecting a shower of bullets to propel both their skulls into the wooden door, exploding their heads open and splattering their brains all over the house's decrepit porch. When he realised he was still breathing, he pushed the Chinese woman down a few steps.

'C'mon, get down,' he screamed at her.

'Officers, do not shoot!' Mr. Cheah ordered, attempting to establish some control over the situation. 'We need her alive!'

His dream of lining up a few more golden medals on his office's shelf started to seem less plausible now, its edges becoming smoky, mixing into the air, moving out of his reach. But one thing was clear to Mr. Cheah: he and his men were onto something much bigger than what they had initially thought.

The African had reached the bottom of the staircase and now faced a dozen of policeman, all of them standing there frozen with their barrels pointed up to the sky, following Mr. Cheah's orders. They looked like a row of neatly dressed scarecrows dotting the jungle clearing, their uniforms blending neatly into the night's dark fabric, the moonlight illuminating the details of their badges with its albino light. The African began moving sideways, his barrel still pressed into the Chinese woman's temple; the woman was almost lifted off the ground as she was dragged, her toes leaving behind their intermittent trail in the gravel. She rocked up and down as she tried to keep up with the tall man's jerky movements, a difficult task for such a petite woman. Regardless, her face looked imperturbable, as if that line of bitten lips would never change, even when the expected cascade of bullets would start burning holes into her body.

'C'mon, I told ya, we'll make it! We're going to make it ...'

Back beyond the police line, the two other Nigerians were looking at him with castrated, silent expressions. Their three pairs of eyes briefly met and the contact seemed to propel the gun-wielding Nigerian further away, quickly, until the forest was right behind him.

'Do not follow me, or I shoot! I'll kill her!' he screamed at the top of his lungs, and the reverberations of his voice hit the officers in their faces.

Cheah's men did not move. Not yet. The Chinese woman suddenly screamed at the top of her lungs and kicked back against the ground, trying to pry herself from the man's grasp. She abandoned her efforts to escape when the African tightened his grip around her neck and pushed the barrel of his gun into the side of her head with an angry grin, denting her skin with its force, taking away all motion from her body. It looked like as if he had pushed a secret switch hidden just below the woman's fringe. Then, pushing back against a palm tree's branch, he disappeared into the foliage. The moonlight didn't glow on their twin shapes anymore; the Chinese woman's white feet disappeared into the woods quickly, as if the trees had fangs and had just decided to finish her off, were sucking her into the depths of their green stomach.

The policeman, uncertain about what they had to do now, waited for further orders. Mr. Cheah ran forward to them and patted four of his men on their backs.

'Go, try to get them! Do your best! Bring her back alive!' he said, and they began their marathon in the dark, as if Mr. Cheah had passed onto them an invisible staff by merely touching them.

Mr. Cheah was aware that the operation had been compromised, that victory might not come to him tonight. He knew he would have to do more work now in order to get all the pieces right. In any case, he decided not to feel so dejected: he turned around and looked at his catch for the night, the two Nigerians who stood behind the police line and the skinhead who lay on the ground, and he felt some sort of satisfaction radiating from his heart. He walked towards them, in anticipation of the thousands of lines of information he would personally enjoy scrapping off their scalps later, no matter at what cost.

The skinhead looked at him from the ground with a controlled expression in his eyes.

'May I have a phone, Encik? I need to make a call.'

'Whom do you need to call?'

'My lawyer. It's my right, isn't it? Or I'm not saying anything else to you. Get me a bloody phone.'

Mr. Cheah really wanted to stomp on his face, but he had to control his feelings. He thrust his hand into his pants pocket and extracted a mobile, unlocked it and handed it to the skinhead without saying a word.

'Do it quickly,' he spat as the boy caught it with his right hand while trembling over his other injured limb.

'Hello, Osman Law Firm. How can I help you?'

'Hi, please put me through Dato' Kefli Osman, thanks.'

'Well, I'm afraid he cannot speak to you now, sir. The office actually closed two hours ago.'

'OK, so what are you still doing over there then, eh? C'mon, don't waste my time. I know he's in there! It's Malik Kefli speaking, and I need you to put me through now!'

The voice grew silent for a few seconds, but he could still hear the sound of breathing at the other side of the earpiece.

'I didn't recognise you, Mister Malik Kefli, excuse me ... Hold the line, please.'

As he waited, Malik looked at his wound from behind the bloody handkerchief and tried to make some sense of what was happening to him. When the tone finally buzzed and another voice came palpably on the other end of the earpiece, he shuddered lightly.

'Hello?'

'Hey, Bapa, it's me ... Yes, I'm sorry I had to rush off so early in the morning yesterday. Listen, I have no time to explain now, but I'm stuck in a very urgent situation here. I don't really know where to start ...'

When he finally handed back the mobile to Mr. Cheah, he was feeling more relaxed.

'Are you done now?'

'Yes. I will tell you my side of the story after I meet up with my lawyer. He's coming here as soon as he can ...'

'Fair enough. What about your friend?'

'Who? Asrul? I have no clue, and I can't be responsible for him. Go and look for him yourself, why don't you? Don't ask me about him.'

Mr. Cheah had known that this skinhead would be a huge pain to deal with ever since he had printed out a copy of his ugly face back at his office and had hung it on the wall across his desk. He had been looking at that shaven head every day for a good couple of weeks now, and how badly he had wanted to smack it down, into the dust. Protocol comes first though, Cheah decided. As he turned around, so he didn't have to look at the skinhead's face anymore, he felt his fingertips getting numb, as they tried to absorb the force of a hit they had not been able to strike. At least not at this very moment, Cheah told himself.

* * *

Asrul opened his eyes as a light beam tried to pry apart his eyelids. He felt an intrusive blade of pain shudder inside each and every one of his bones, as if he had been severed in half, from the tip of his skull down to his feet, cracked open, and death itself had put a sheet of metal in the middle of his body. He decided not to move, so he could avoid feeling that metal thing corrugating inside of him, absorbing his blood like a sponge. He knew he had been shot somewhere but he still could not tell where: his body was a mess of bulging pain, from head to toe. The torchlight ran across his face and then further down, examining his body. It seemed as if someone was studying him, preparing to give him an autopsy; soon he would see hands reaching into his cavities, tearing out hot, steaming, slimy organs, one after the other, to locate the source of his pain.

'Look, this one is still alive.'

'Yes, but he looks pretty bad … He's been shot just under the right clavicle. See that? This boy needs to be rushed to the hospital immediately or we'll lose him …'

The voices came from far away, as if from some far-flung dimension. Asrul tried to see through the dim light, tried to discern the shape of these extraterrestrial creatures that hung over him, their long heads melting into the surrounding shadows. Maybe they had not come to cut him up, after all, he realised. He tried to smile, but he was not entirely sure what kind of expression he had curled his lips into. Fuck, it really hurt. He looked up at the sky and thought of God, and he prayed that, maybe now, they could be closer. Yes, things had gone awry, for him and for others, but he would love to have a chance to make things right again. He wished he had the strength left to raise himself to his knees and kneel down, to kiss the floor with the front of his forehead – like he used to do back then, a long time ago, in Alor star. Releasing some of that overwhelming pain down into the ground, that action alone would have helped rid his body of this deathly sensation. Unfortunately, the sheet of metal that now separated his two halves was too heavy to push away and flip over.

'The other two have long been dead. Call the forensics,' one of the alien voices said from the distance. Asrul could almost see his words get painted across the walls in highlighter yellow.

Call the forensics: he ordered his lips to laugh, his teeth to clatter, but he was still unsure about the results his mouth produced. As the aliens grabbed him by the limbs and put him on top of some sort of small spaceship, which made him levitate in the air, the lights became circles, and he was shaken up and down until the air of the night splashed once again onto his skin. Then, his soul switched off, and Asrul went as blank as a turned-off TV screen. Stand by, low energy consume mode. Beep.

SYDNEY, AUSTRALIA

27

THE SUN WAS SHINING high over Bondi Beach, and she loved to tuck her toes under the small, warm mounds of sand. She had been sitting on her towel for an hour now, gazing at the people passing by. The concrete road behind her was filled with youngsters rolling over their skates and with bikini-clad girls swarming about, well-aware that their looks was the honey that glued it all together.

She knew she was different here. She was an Asian, and she had learned that her kind were quite popular in this city. She had been here for about two months now – her working holiday visa allowed her to stay on for one long, amazing year. She had left Malaysia in quite a hurry. The flight had been pleasant enough, but, contrary to her expectations, she had travelled alone. And that had been very hard on her. She had felt like she had been cheated.

She reached for her sling bag and fished out her purse. The last time she had read this letter, she had cried; but today, the warm sun above her was giving her new hope. She was sure the words would not fill her with the same sensation of grief, as they had before. The letter was hidden inside her wallet, tucked away in a remote pocket, for she didn't want to remind herself of its presence in her life; she knew she would always remember though, that it was hidden down there, always ready to project its long, dark shadows over her sanity. She pulled it out and carefully unfolded it.

She had always liked his neat handwriting, his way of penning down his strokes in a clean style. These thoughts threatened to push her down the cliff of memories again, but she stopped herself. Today, she wouldn't take that fall. She wouldn't let her emotions splatter all over the sand around her. She drew her knees close to the chest and began reading, while the hot sun fondled her back with soft kisses of white heat.

Dear Mei,

If you are reading this, it means that I have missed the flight. I'm terribly sorry for all of this, but you have to forget me. Please, forget me and forget about everything we have thought about doing together in the future. This might sound hard, and I wish this will not bring tears to your beautiful eyes – but if I'm not with you right now, it means that something has possibly gone very wrong. I apologise. We knew from the beginning that things might end up this way, with us getting separated.

I hope you remember what I've told you, about what you must do now. I have put some of the money into your bank account, and the rest is in the safe. I don't want to write any more about this. You already know everything after all. Put the money to good use. Spend it to reach your own new happiness, wherever that may be. It can help you start off right in Australia;

who knows where it will take you from there. You'll know what to do with your life ... You're a smart girl, something I know very well. You're so smart that I would have never been able to plan and do all of this by myself ...

From where I am now, I picture you lying on Bondi Beach, the place you always talked to me about ... I can just imagine how beautiful you must look there, lying there, lazing about under the sun of Sydney, with no worries on your mind and with all the money you'll ever need ... Just unwind, relax, enjoy. You're about to start a new life. I wish I could be there with you, but not everything turns out right in this stupid life.

Before I go, I'd like to tell you two things: one, I've always loved you very much, and two, you were never meant to live in Malaysia. Always remember these two things.

With so much love that you would never really know much,
Eternally yours
Tan Moe

She felt a tear form at the side of her eye and squashed it under her finger before it turned into a small river. She had already cried and suffered too much for his loss. He was gone. Where, she didn't know, but she did know they would never meet again. She decided that it was time to stop thinking about what might have been. Something had gone wrong with their plan. Perhaps, it was that Indonesian girl, she wondered. It was she, Mei, who had suggested that Tan Moe use the Indonesian girl in their scheme. Maybe that miserable cunt had fucked up something, had got them caught ... Better stop thinking about it. It had been hard enough for her to part with her beloved Tan Moe, to let him get involved with that immigrant bitch, just to cover up their tracks. Well, in the end, she had got what she wanted, regardless of her loss.

'Hey, hello …'

The voice brought her back to Australia, dragging her down to earth from a cloud-filled sky. It was a cute guy, tanned and muscular, looking down at her from his standing position.

'Hi,' she answered, pulling down her sunglasses and trying to look at his face, her eyes fighting against the sun's rays.

'I've never seen you around here. Are you a tourist?'

'Well, yes and no … I have a working holiday visa, and I'm looking for work at the moment.'

'Oh, great. I might know someone who could help you. Are you Asian?'

'Yes. I'm Malaysian, actually …'

'Ah, Malaysia, truly Asia! You know, from the commercial? It's everywhere.'

'Yeah, it's awful,' she laughed and stood up, dusting her legs to get the sand off her black bikini. As she looked up, she found herself staring right into a pair of sexy pink nipples, the stranger's. She was a small girl and was glad to be treated to this view.

'I've been to Bali with my mates. To Malaysia, never. I don't have a clue how your country is, but Bali looked like a cool place, with plenty of booze and partying. Do you like beer? Wanna grab one?'

'Well …' she stopped for a moment, thoughtful. 'Why not?' She smiled at him.

Beer, drugs and fun. That was everything she had loved about Tan Moe. She collected her towel and bag and went off towards the waves, along with this handsome stranger, flashing him her best smile and pushing out her chest to make her mid-sized breasts stand out as much as they could. She might as well try to have a little bit of fun. The money matters had been taken care of, after all.

Master Chef's Acknowledgements

Like every masterfully cooked delicacy, even this humble rice dish of mixed elements and origins has relied on a plethora of different, helpful people to take on its present, savory taste. First of all, thanks to Adrian Lewis, Dzulhasymi Hakim, Leon Qbp Low and Cole Yew for having welcomed and introduced me to Penang's – and Malaysia's – underground music scene. If it weren't for them, I would have never found the first and most important ingredient for my fried brown rice. Thanks to Monsoon Books and Phil Tatham, my publisher, who was bold enough to pick up my unrefined melting-pot of dangerous flavors, and decided to give it a try on a wider market. We will kick Kentucky Fried Chicken's ass, trust me. A very warm thank you goes to all of the 'immigrant scum' of various origins (Italians included) that took time to mingle and share their stories, time and local delicacies with this curious *orang putih* who, unlike most Malaysians, dared to befriend them. I wish that my recipe will help bring your voice and concerns to more influent ears. Thanks and respect to Tom Vater for his razor-sharp, realistic suggestions on the writing career. This deadly recipe is also a product of your kind advice.

I also take my hat off to Jill Girardi, who edited and read through the first draft of the recipe, savored its rough taste, licked her fingers, and told me it was so good I had to aim for higher recognition and better distributors. As a consequence, a very much deserved 'Chef Diploma' is awarded to my editor Sujatha Sevellimedu, who improved immensely the taste and stickiness of my multi-coloured rice with her accurate suggestions and experienced taste buds. Thanks, my friend; if the Nazi-rice's aftertaste is so haunting now, it's also because of you.

A special thanks to my home country of Italy for being so ridiculous, wretched and wrecked that it pushed me out and lost me along the World's Highways. Thanks for not recognizing any of your own talent if it's not coming from the sons and daughters of an elite of posh assholes and their Mafia of the Arts. Thanks for forcing me to write in a foreign language. It actually paid off. Regardless of the shame, as any good Italian son, my cooking ability has been nurtured by Tundra, my mother, who's not in this list just because, stereotypically, she should. In fact, she has helped me push with adamant moral support through the thick and the thin of an unconventional life spent in the underworld of the Devil's music first, and on the Open Roads of the World, afterwards.

And thanks to Penang for being Penang, such a beautiful and mysterious place if you take the time to get under its apparently sleepy surface, and unearth its treasure trove of forgotten secrets. Stefano Landi, you know that very well, don't you? Last but not least, a great hug and much more to my partner Kit Yeng, who has helped shape the basic ingredients of this lethal recipe with her Malaysian-Chinese stubborn skepticism. She especially had the balls to leave boxed Malaysian life behind for a long year 2012, storming off with this crazy wannabe-chef on an overland Singapore-to-Milano hitchhiking adventure. It was then that the very first parts of the Nazi Goreng's recipe were gloriously etched on a phantom file, as I sat on top of a Chinese hostel's terrace, facing the vastness of the Tibetan plateau's foothills. But that is another incredible story; and as Conan the Barbarian's narrating voice put it, you will have to wait for my new book to hear it, suckers.

Until then, follow me at *www.monkeyrockworld.com*.